ROBERT ALLEN

BILLY

A BIOGRAPHY OF BILLY BINGHAM

VIKING

VIKING

Penguin Books Ltd, Harmondsworth, Middlesex, England
Viking Penguin Inc., 40 West 23rd Street, New York, New York 10010, U.S.A.
Penguin Books Australia Ltd, Ringwood, Victoria, Australia
Penguin Books Canada Limited, 2801 John Street, Markham, Ontario, Canada L3R 1B4
Penguin Books (N.Z.) Ltd, 182–190 Wairau Road, Auckland 10, New Zealand

First published 1986

Typeset in Monophoto Ehrhardt
Printed in Great Britain by
Richard Clay (The Chaucer Press) Ltd,
Bungay, Suffolk

British Library Cataloguing in Publication Data available

'We have no art, we only do our best.'

Cantonese saying

CONTENTS

ACKNOWLEDGEMENTS

Someone once said that a book is like an iceberg; seven-eighths of it is under the surface. In the case of *Billy* that is particularly true, and without the considerable help of countless people the completion of the book within the time limit would have been impossible.

Researchers are often the unsung heroes of such a project, so my special thanks go to Johnny Lavery – who undertook the research work in Ireland and a lot more besides – Bill MacKinnon (Britain and Greece) and Jimmy Duggan (Ireland and Britain). Also to John Meehan, Aidan Rogan, Donal Brady and Pauline O'Hara for their last-minute forays into libraries and newspaper offices, and in Greece to Eleni Alexandrakis and Sotiris Goritsas.

The nature of the book meant that my home was turned into a minor writing factory for several months, where Sue Esterson and Jimmy Duggan read the first draft and made invaluable editing decisions, sometimes long into the wee hours.

Perhaps the people who really made the book possible are some of the footballers, managers and coaches who have known and worked with Billy Bingham, and the soccer writers who have followed his career so diligently over the years: Antony Antoniades, Koulis Apostolides, David Barber, Danny Blanchflower, Eric Bowyer, Malcolm Brodie (of the *Belfast Telegraph*), Steve Burtenshaw, Robert Daniels (former chairman of Plymouth Argyle), Martin Dobson, Peter Doherty, George Dedes, Pat Dunne, Takis Econoumopolis, Jim Emery, Bryan Hamilton, Len Hiller, Colin Hunt and David Jones (of the *Liverpool Daily Post and Echo*), Howard Kendall, Yianna Kontoyannis, Harley Lawer (of the *Plymouth Sunday Independent*), Emmanuele Mavrommatis, Fred Molyneux, Tim Morris (of the *Mansfield Chronicle Advertiser*), Joe Mercer, Ivan McAllister, Jimmy McIlroy, Alkis Panagoulias, Alex Parker, Bertie Peacock, Jim Platt, Billy Sinclair, Billy Stickland, Alex Toner (of the *Daily Mirror*) and Allen Wade. Also thanks to Tom Cannon, Bertie Entwhistle (Linfield club secretary), Ted Giblin, Jim Hunter (Elmgrove school), Bill Simmons (Sunderland club historian), Harry Wallace (former Linfield secretary), and Geoff Wilde (Southport club historian).

Thanks also to E. W. B. Astle, Anthony, Frank and Therese Lavery, Joe Mitchell (erstwhile editor of *Press Release*, Student's Union, Queen's University, Belfast), Aileen McDonald, Eugene McKenna, Mike Peterson, Keith Shanley (of Cantec, Ireland) and Ralf Sotscheck.

And finally thanks especially to Tony Lacey, Judith Flanders, and Janice Brent at Viking, Robert Armstrong and Phil Shaw (of the *Guardian*) and Fintan O'Toole of Magill, where the article which inspired the book was published.

FOREWORD

Billy Bingham is beyond dispute the most successful football manager ever to come out of Ireland, north or south of the border. No other Irishman has ever guided his countrymen to the finals of two World Cup competitions – indeed, only one manager in Britain has done so: Sir Alf Ramsey, who took the easy route to Mexico in 1970 without kicking a ball in anger, because England were already holders of the Jules Rimet trophy. Such is the breathtaking measure of Bingham's achievement.

Yet owing to the perverse nature of professional football, Bingham has never been short of detractors, even in his native city. Some claim that the man from east Belfast has never succeeded as a club manager, that he has an unhealthy obsession with hard cash, that he is reviled by several top players who have worked under him. Wee Billy tends to be presented as either a folk hero or a flawed character who makes his own luck.

It is true that on superficial acquaintance Bingham can often appear enigmatic, a magician who pulls off astonishing results with a patchwork quilt of a team, using brilliantly improvised methods. In spite of his relaxed, pipe-puffing style and his beaming smile, the Northern Ireland manager can be hard and abrasive, not above praising one journalist's work at the expense of another within earshot of both. Somewhere in his complex nature there is a touch of the street-fighter.

Certainly Bingham is secretive, never naming his team until hours before the kick-off and sometimes hinting at an 'attacking' formation which retreats to the trenches within five minutes. But this is all grist to the mill in the international arena and one's reservations pale into insignificance when set against the bare statistics of his stewardship – only thirteen defeats in a total of fifty matches played since 1980 when he began his second spell as Northern Ireland manager. When noting this fact, it is also worth remembering that Bingham draws his squad from a population only half the size of Birmingham's.

What is the basis of such a consistent level of performance among some of the most talented nations in Europe? Perhaps one should refer back to those persistent murmurs about Bingham's habit of naming his price. For the truth is that Wee Billy, like the great majority of Ulstermen, has an exact sense of his own worth and of the true value of his players. Bingham entertains no illusions about the limitations of journeymen from the lower divisions, but he is also aware that even rare talents can be pushed to exploit extra potential which they have never before realized.

Two notable examples of players whose careers blossomed under Bingham's motivation are Gerry Armstrong and John McClelland, both hardly household names before the 1982 World Cup finals. Yet Armstrong won an award as the outstanding British player in Spain, and later took up a lucrative contract in the Spanish League, while McClelland became captain of Glasgow Rangers before pursuing his career in the English first division. Bingham's faith in the ability of these two late developers was richly rewarded.

From the perspective of an itinerant journalist Bingham is a stimulating companion, especially on bleak, mid-winter trips to East European cities like Bucharest where the most exciting post-prandial diversion can be watching the wallpaper. At times Wee Billy may mischievously refer to himself as 'Anglo-Irish', perhaps to tease those of a Celtic sensibility. However, he remains as authentic as an Ulster soda farl despite having spent most of his fifty-four years in England.

Bingham's employer, the Irish Football Association, is rooted in the world of semi-professional football, but the national team manager shows an acute awareness of the valid claims for wider recognition made by some Irish League players. Despite making his home in Southport, where he can quickly check his hard core of full-time professionals, Bingham often acts on the regular reports he receives on the form of those talented part-timers who play for clubs like Linfield and Glentoran. Four Irish League players made the trip to Spain in 1982 and the same number is expected to be in the squad for Mexico.

Naturally, such responsiveness to local aspirations guarantees Bingham and his squad of 'Anglos' a passionate welcome home every time they play at Windsor Park in Belfast. The intimidating roar from the Spion Kop, not to mention the chilling wind and rain that sweep down from the Black Mountain, are sufficient to unsettle all but the most resolute visitors. Significantly, no European nation has triumphed in Belfast since October 1977, when Holland – World Cup finalists in 1978 – beat the Irish 1–0.

Without doubt Bingham's greatest asset is his skill in extracting the maximum effort and organization from players who often cannot get into their first team at club level. Northern Ireland score very few goals – forty-three in fifty games – but they give even fewer away: a lesson that West Germany learned the hard way in twice losing 1–0 during the 1982–84 European Championships. Bingham is a master in the art of the probable; that is to say, he never takes major risks with individual players and he never embarks on team strategies that may slip beyond his control.

Characteristically, Bingham's preparations for Mexico have been minutely detailed, down to the 10,000 bottles of water that will be flown in from the United States to shield the players from the possibility of a local virus. Nevertheless, Northern Ireland, who have never before played in Central or South America, face a searching challenge which is bound to test the manager's patience and ingenuity. Those who believe in omens will recall that the Irish defeated two of the tournament favourites, Uruguay and Mexico, when they visited Belfast in the mid-sixties. This biography, by a fellow Belfastman, will suggest reasons why Wee Billy has a better-than-even chance of succeeding away from home in 1986.

Robert Armstrong

INTRODUCTION

Belfast is the capital of the six Irish counties which have been known as Northern Ireland since 1922. A relatively young place, Belfast is a small town, aspiring to be a big city. If it ever achieves that distinction, it will be due to its one precious natural resource: its people and their desire to succeed. In spite of all the odds, the six counties of Ulster have produced a collection of sporting talent that transcends political adversity and geographical isolation and puts to shame nations ten times its size. The diverse skills of people like Dennis Taylor, Alex Higgins, Rinty Monaghan, George Best, Joey Dunlop, John Watson and Mary Peters, originating from the same piece of land no more than 200 miles wide, is more than coincidence. William Laurie Bingham's story, give or take a few names and faces, could just as easily be theirs.

A biography will always run the risk of appearing voyeuristic; I hope that *Billy* avoids that danger by presenting not just an individual but a type. Bingham's considerable success is the result of a simple, single-minded determination to succeed: no more, no less. There is no reason why Barry McGuigan or the Northern Ireland football team should be victorious, other than their straightforward desire to win. Billy Bingham is living proof of the power of positive thinking, the common denominator behind almost every northern Irish sporting achievement. He is not simply a very competent football manager; he is the hope, in Northern Ireland, for every person who desires to achieve something. Bingham's greatest asset is an unshakeable belief in himself and not for a moment have I attempted to undermine that. *Billy* is merely a celebration of that peculiar Irish quality – the will to win in spite of everything.

Dublin, April 1986

CHAPTER ONE

THE SPANISH TRAIL

BINGHAM'S *DÉJÀ VU*

Every player except the centre-forward must defend his own goal, and every player except the goalkeeper must assault his opponents' goal.

J. L. Carr, *How Steeple Sinderby Wanderers Won the FA Cup*

For most of this century, trains leaving Belfast from the old Great Northern Railway station shuddered past a large ramshackle football stadium which lay in the lap of the mountains to the west. The sight of the seemingly fragile, corrugated-iron stands probably meant little to most people but many would have at least known that the stadium was Windsor Park, home of Linfield Football Club. They would have known this because of the associations Linfield has for the severed community of Northern Ireland; to the Loyalists Linfield is to Ireland what Glasgow Rangers is to Scotland – more than just a soccer team; to the Nationalists Linfield is one of the many symbols of Ulster Unionism. The fact that the ground is also the venue for Northern Ireland's international games has only been credited with the significance it deserves in recent years.

Today, trains from the central station, now sited beside the river Lagan, still pass the eastern side of the ground. Parallel to the railway line, further to the west, traffic speeds in and out of Belfast on the M1. The view has changed. Aesthetically, Windsor Park is more pleasing; the success of Northern Ireland under Billy Bingham has allowed the Irish Football Association to spend £2 million, bringing the ground up to proper international soccer stadium standards, with a 6,800 all-seater cantilevered stand. Since the Bradford City fire in 1985, which prompted an inquiry into the condition of football grounds in Great Britain and Northern Ireland, the old corrugated-iron south stand has been deemed unsafe and has been closed. It is not unlikely that by the end of this century Windsor Park will be an enclosed, all-seater stadium. Such grandiose schemes have only been made possible by the achievements of one man, a man whose own dreams and ambitions have surpassed those of his employers – the IFA – and their often negative and insular view of world soccer. But then William Laurie Bingham has never really been working for the IFA; he has been working for the soccer-mad population of this tiny, northeastern section of Ireland, and for their future.

The IFA's cautious approach has been determined by their financial insecurity and is complemented by Bingham's insistence that there is a thin line between success and failure. Sammy McIlroy, captain of the Northern Ireland team for most of the 1986 World Cup qualifying games, is not known to be a super-stitious person, yet he believes that luck is a significant factor in modern soccer. Bingham knows about success and failure. He also knows about luck; how it can be kind and how it can be cruel.

Many critics of Northern Ireland have said, over the years, that the team has created its own bad luck, by losing to the minnows of the European soccer world. That is true. Bingham was put under tremendous pressure for all of the recent World Cup qualifying games after his team failed against Finland in the opening group-three game. Jim Platt, Northern Ireland's deputy goalkeeper, is sardonic about Northern Ireland's success: 'We always do it the hard way, we qualified the hard way, and we did it the hard way in Spain when we drew with Honduras and had to beat Spain to qualify. It was a hell of a result and it wouldn't surprise me one iota if we had to go into our last match in Mexico, against Brazil, needing a draw to qualify. It's crazy but that's the way we do things.'

Yet, according to Finland's Ari Valvee, who scored the winning goal in Pori in May 1984, beating the Irish was comparable to Northern Ireland's own double success over the European champions, West Germany, in the 1984 European Championship qualifying games. 'It was marvellous to defeat a team like Northern Ireland,' said Valvee, who, with Finnish soccer reporters, placed the result alongside Finland's previous most significant success – a 2–1 win over Hungary in 1978.

The critics point particularly to Northern Ireland's failure to beat Turkey in the 1984 European Championship qualifying games, when a win would have set up a thrilling encounter with West Germany, with the finals in France as the prize. On that occasion Turkey proved that no international team, no matter how small their reputation, is easy to beat. In the end, the Irish were frustrated after being caught by Selcuk's seventeenth-minute goal. Martin O'Neill and Ian Stewart hit the woodwork and chance after chance was squandered. Pat Jennings, the Irish goalkeeper, for once didn't have much to do except pick the ball out of the back of the net. It was cruel and, despite Northern Ireland's win over West Germany the following month, it ended Bingham's hopes of a trip to France – by the tiny margin of goal difference.

Yet for all this, Bingham's record since he returned for his second spell in charge of Northern Ireland in February 1980 compares favourably with the success of his neighbours – the Republic of Ireland, Scotland, Wales and England – British champions in 1980 and 1984; quarter-finalists in the 1982 World Cup in Spain; and qualifiers for the 1986 World Cup in Mexico.

In fifty-one games Bingham's teams have lost thirteen times. Over the same period, England – who are regarded as one of the world's strongest soccer nations – lost seventeen of their seventy-two games.† Billy Bingham does not have the wealth of talent England manager Bobby Robson has to call on. The historical reality is also that Northern Ireland have beaten England only twice in thirty years, and have not beaten them in Belfast since 1927. Yet after Robson's team had pummelled Turkey and Finland with thirteen goals during the opening stages of the 1986 World Cup qualifying rounds, they came to Belfast and received a lesson in

† To 23 April England's success rate is approximately 50 per cent.

tactical soccer, even if luck was against them that evening. After
Mark Hateley had given England an undeserved and fortuitous
victory one Irish soccer writer told his readers that Northern
Ireland had lost, 'primarily because, for all their admirable fight
and team organization, they are really second-class citizens at
international level'. Bingham has been extremely lucky during his
tenure as Northern Ireland manager. But he sometimes needs that
luck.

If luck deserted them against Turkey in 1983 and England in
1985 they were more fortunate in the 1982 World Cup qualifying
games when two of those soccer minnows upset the smaller nation
on the Iberian peninsula and consequently stamped and sealed
Northern Ireland's passport to Spain.

When the draw for the 1982 games had been made, Northern
Ireland was grouped with Scotland, Portugal, Sweden and Israel.
Danny Blanchflower had just resigned as Northern Ireland manager and Bingham had been offered a two-year contract as his
successor. His first game was the opening World Cup qualifier
against Israel in Tel Aviv. Bingham was confident 'that with a
positive approach, a settled side and proper organization' his team
would qualify for the 1982 finals, 'particularly,' he said, 'as two
go through from our group.'

Bingham's ultimate vocation in life is manager of all Northern
Ireland's teams, from schoolboy to senior level. When he took up
his appointment he told the local press that he couldn't wait to get
back. 'I've been thirty-five years with the Irish FA, from
schoolboy level,' he enthused like a young lad who had just won
his first cap, though he couldn't hide his bitterness when he said,
'I'll be dealing with better class players and hoping for a better
end result than you get in club football.'

Bingham had been the major contender for the job when
Blanchflower hinted that he might quit before his contract ended.
Immediately this was known, a lobby led by Linfield manager,
Roy Coyle, several of the Irish squad and the local press began
pressing for the winger, who had himself won fifty-six caps for

Northern Ireland. They made vociferous noises in the direction of Windsor Avenue, where Harry Cavan, the IFA president, was wary of giving the job to a man who had achieved very little success as a club manager. But, in fact, there were few who believed that a better man was to be found for the job. 'I don't think the time is ripe for one of the younger school to take over,' said Coyle, referring to Iam McFaul, Martin Harvey and Bryan Hamilton – the other contenders for the post.

Coyle rejected Blanchflower's suggestion that the job should go to a younger man. 'It's nonsense to say that he's too old at forty-eight. Billy has always kept young tactically, through involvement at club level and in the FA's frequent coaching schools. He has everything going for him. He is a noted disciplinarian, a fully qualified FA coach as well as an experienced manager, and he commands respect,' said Coyle.

Bingham had less than two months to prepare for the Israel game, but within a fortnight of his appointment he had compiled a dossier on most of the players available to him from British clubs. He called twenty-two players together for training sessions in Coventry and Leicester, and watched games at youth and inter-league levels. Players in the Irish league were scrutinized and checks were also made on several players in the United States and Europe.

When he named his team for the game in Tel Aviv he made four changes in the team which had beaten the Republic of Ireland under Blanchflower the previous November. The most significant was the inclusion of John O'Neill, a twenty-one-year-old who had joined Leicester as a teenager, in the centre-back position previously occupied by Ipswich's Allan Hunter.

Bingham regarded O'Neill very highly and Hunter, who had collected fifty-three caps and served Northern Ireland for over ten years, discovered that his international career was over. Bingham also dropped David McCreery, Derek Spence and Vic Moreland, and brought in Tommy Cassidy, Tom Finney and Terry Cochrane. The permutations in midfield and attack concerned Bingham and the dropped players, he felt, were not 'showing any scoring ability'. McCreery, Cassidy, Finney and Cochrane, Bingham would select again in the future, but Moreland (who had won only six caps – all under Blanchflower) never played for Northern Ireland again and Spence only came on for a handful of appearances as substitute over the following two years.

The Israel game ended in a scoreless draw, and despite his obvious concern and anxiety over his squad's lack of scoring potential Bingham was optimistic for the future. 'We must build on teamwork,' he said after the game, 'something which is essential if you have limited players of international calibre. You cannot do that overnight but there is plenty of promise in this team.' Bingham's cautiousness was not without reason. Israel might easily have won the game and their British coach, Jack Mansell, was in no doubt that the power failure, which doused the floodlights for approximately fifteen minutes, broke his team's rhythm just when they were threatening to score. The break came at the right psychological moment for Northern Ireland and when the teams resumed, Israel had lost their momentum. What little they had left posed few problems for Pat Jennings. Bingham's first point, in his second period as Northern Ireland manager, would be invaluable. Mansell's aftermatch comments would also prove to be very accurate. 'We were the better team, playing good fighting football, and we are not to be written off in this group.'

The British championship was next and Bingham surprised many people when he shrugged off the loss of Pat Jennings and Sammy Nelson, who couldn't be released by their club, Arsenal, because of their involvement in the European Cup-Winners' Cup. He gave Mal Donaghy, an eager young defender with Bingham's old club, Luton, his first cap, and resurrected goalkeeper Jim Platt's career.

Bingham selected the same team for each of the three home internationals and then shocked England, Scotland, Wales and everybody else who was watching, by guiding Northern Ireland to their first outright championship since 1914.

The most impressive feature of the team was the back four: Jimmy Nicholl, Chris Nicholl, John O'Neill and Mal Donaghy.

Few supporters may have noticed it at the time, but a familiar pattern was being established, with Cassidy and McIlroy forming triangles with their respective colleagues on the left and right of midfield. The roaming figure of Gerry Armstrong was the pivot of the attack and Bingham had his wingers supporting the midfield and defence, and his forwards falling back as extra midfield players every time the opposition had the ball.

Despite the 1–0 victories over Scotland (in Belfast) and Wales (in Cardiff) and the 1–1 draw with England at Wembley, Bingham was still not totally happy with his midfield players. 'I feel they are not positive enough in the box,' he said. 'They are not scoring sufficient goals.'

Before Bingham's next World Cup game, against Sweden, in Belfast, on 15 October, he had the luxury of a tour in Australia to blood more players. He wanted versatile players, and with John O'Neill and Mal Donaghy he had the beginnings of a new, strong and mobile defence. During the Scotland game he had brought on another young defender, John McClelland of Mansfield, and when Bingham sat down to select his team for the opening game against Australia on 11 June, McClelland started his first full game for Northern Ireland.

In a relatively short time Bingham had completely altered Northern Ireland's status in world soccer. He had taken Northern Ireland into the unknown – eight games without defeat – in his first five months as manager, even though one of those successes (against Western Australia during the summer tour) was not recognized as a full international. You had to go back to the reign of Peter Doherty to find a similar sequence, when Northern Ireland went through the qualifying stages to the 1958 World Cup in Sweden. The fact that three of Bingham's successes were against Australia did not diminish the achievement, and it gave him the foundation he needed to blaze the Spanish trail.

The difference in managerial qualities between Blanchflower and Bingham was now very apparent. Bingham's team had conceded four goals in eight games; Blanchflower's team, during his last year as manager, conceded seventeen goals in eight games, including two ignominious defeats by England, who rattled nine goals past Jennings in the 1980 European Championship qualifying games.

'The basic difference was that Danny wanted them to go out and do something they couldn't do,' said the *Guardian*'s Northern Ireland soccer writer, Robert Armstrong. 'He wanted them to attack and score goals, but given the players at his disposal, Northern Ireland are not able to do that at international level. If they commit themselves over-aggressively they get caught and lose the game, often quite heavily. Billy never asks players to do what they can't do, whereas Danny used to ask them to do things that were well beyond them. He tried to build them up with talk and rhetoric. Billy ignores their weaknesses and practises on the strengths and assets of particular players in particular situations. His view is that by the time he gets them he has got what he has got and that is what he has to work with.' It is a simple philosophy which Bingham learned the hard way.

When Sweden arrived in Belfast in October 1980 Northern Ireland were undefeated in nine games. Bingham's second World Cup qualifying game would be played almost on the anniversary of Northern Ireland's 5–1 defeat by England, the result which prompted Blanchflower's resignation.

On this occasion Bingham's emotions would be taken to the two extremes; of sadness and joy. On the previous weekend Bingham's mother died in hospital and on the morning of the game she was cremated at Roselawn cemetery in Belfast. The players were aware of Bingham's grief, but on the afternoon (the game was played in daylight because Windsor Park's floodlights were not up to standard) their thoughts were on maintaining their unbeaten record and their places in the team.

Those who watched the game remember a new spirit and aggressiveness among the players. John McClelland kept his place at the centre of the defence at the expense of the injured John O'Neill, who missed his first international under Bingham. Donaghy was preferred to Nelson and the midfield had the familiar ring of Tommy Cassidy, Martin O'Neill and Sammy McIlroy.

Robert Armstrong remembers that they went at Sweden 'like a bloody storm', and when it calmed at the interval, Northern Ireland were three up, with goals from Noel Brotherston, McIlroy and Jimmy Nicholl – his first for Northern Ireland. Jimmy Dubois, of the *Belfast Newsletter*, wrote that 'this was teamwork at its best and Bingham is to be congratulated for welding together a basically young team which is obviously beginning to believe in itself.'

Swedish manager Lars Arnesson reluctantly sent his beleaguered team out for the second half and with several swift counter-attacks they changed the balance of play, but the score remained the same. Bingham was ecstatic and described the performance as the best since he had taken over in February. 'Both collectively and individually there is a good organization in the side, which has a wonderful spirit,' he told reporters after the game. 'We buried Sweden in the first half and there was no comeback for them from three goals behind. With a little bit of luck we could have had more goals, but I'm well satisfied with the result and I firmly believe we can qualify for the final stages in Spain.' Northern Ireland had three points from two games. If they came back with anything better than a defeat from their next game against Portugal in Lisbon, Spain would be a reality.

Bingham was now assured of the loyalty he demanded from his players, despite the healthy competition for places, particularly in the defence. He knew the strengths and weaknesses of all the players available to him. The regular back four of Jimmy Nicholl, John O'Neill, Chris Nicholl and Sammy Nelson suddenly discovered their positions were under threat from Donaghy and McClelland. Right-back Jimmy Nicholl was the only player of the six who would be guaranteed his place. The positions were often determined by availability and injuries, and in midfield Martin O'Neill and Sammy McIlroy could expect Bingham to place their names on the team-sheet as soon as he knew they were fit and free from club commitments. The other midfield position would depend on the opposition, and alternate between David McCreery and Tommy Cassidy. 'If the opposition was quality,' said Robert

Armstrong, 'Bingham would use McCreery, because he would see
him as a more defensive midfield player. Cassidy had a bit more
quality than McCreery in terms of creating something.' In those
early days Bingham would occasionally substitute McCreery for
Cassidy when he wanted to strengthen the midfield at times of
pressure from the opposition.

The first stage of Bingham's journey to the citadels of the
World Cup was like Alice's chase after the white rabbit and her
descent into Wonderland. Every moment was an exciting discovery
and every step was a wondrous story. Then like Alice, Bingham
suddenly found his world shrinking and his destiny in the control
of others, but the characters in his story were not rabbits, cater-
pillars and hares; they were international football players from
Portugal, Sweden and Israel.

Portugal beat Northern Ireland a month after the Swedish
success in Belfast. Four months later Scotland's John Wark
cancelled out Billy Hamilton's opening goal at Hampden Park,
Glasgow. Bingham's team went home with one point instead of
two.

So Northern Ireland had four points from four games at the
halfway stage of the qualifying games, and if they were to reach
Bingham's target of nine or ten points to qualify they had to win
their next game – against Portugal at Windsor Park.

The positive spirit which had existed during the previous home
game, against Sweden, was not missing, but there was an incredible
amount of tension, both on and off the field. On the terraces,
behind the Spion Kop goal, Bingham's World Cup dream was
threatened by the stupidity of some supporters when they began
throwing bottles at the Portuguese goalkeeper. Bingham, already
frustrated at Portugal's defensive tactics, was alerted to the incident by the referee. Then another bottle came over and again
the referee warned Bingham that the game would be stopped.
Almost immediately the game was resumed, winger Terry
Cochrane chased a loose ball and crossed it to Gerry Armstrong
who headed into the net.

Bingham, clad in the traditional Northern Ireland team

tracksuit, jumped in jubilation from his position a few metres back from the touchline. When the euphoria began to subside the Irish manager strode like a green knight towards the Spion Kop end. With the eyes of every person in Windsor Park on him he showed the crowd behind the goal the offending bottle and then in a dramatic gesture he threw it to the ground. It was pure theatre but necessary. His team held on to win and there were no more incidents.

The next twist came after Scotland had beaten Northern Ireland in the crumbling British championship. England and Wales had refused to travel to Belfast and two valuable games were lost to Bingham. Two weeks later he took his squad to Stockholm for Northern Ireland's last away-game of the World Cup qualifying round.

Bingham needed at least a point to maintain his target for Spain and at half-time, following a dull first half, he told his players that he could not see them losing unless they conceded a penalty. Four minutes into the second half Sweden's outside left, Jan Svensson, raced past Jimmy Nicholl into the penalty area. Nicholl lunged, Svensson went down, and the referee whistled for a penalty.

But the drama wasn't over. Nicholl, demoralized by the decision, was substituted as the game became increasingly physical. Bingham later said that he had taken Nicholl off because he was afraid that 'he would be ordered off. He completely lost his temper and my decision was for his own good.' Bingham had just lost Terry Cochrane, who had been sent off moments earlier following a touchline clash with Sweden's Hass Borg – the scorer of the penalty – and the Irish boss was terrified that he would be down to nine players.

After the game Bingham defended Cochrane and said that his player had been obstructed and then fell in a tangle with Borg which 'was not malicious or dirty'. For Bingham the incident was just part of a game that had been a disaster for the Irish. 'We had a plum to pick and we have come away with nothing,' said Bingham. 'It was the worst possible result and makes things very difficult.' The uphill struggle Bingham had talked of was about to test his players in much the same manner as the sand dunes tested his players at Southport and Everton. They didn't like it but they came through.

Five months later Bingham heard a result which would reinforce his belief that no team can take another for granted in international soccer. On 14 October, the same day Northern Ireland played Scotland in their penultimate World Cup qualifying game, Sweden beat Portugal 2–1 in Lisbon. Scotland needed a point from the Irish game to qualify and Bingham told reporters that a defeat for Northern Ireland would 'be the end of the road'. That, he said, 'was motivation enough for my players. I'm having to calm them down rather than psych them up, they are so high. It will be a very hard and competitive match.' It was, but the Scots got the point they needed. The Swedish result, however, meant that Bingham was back where he started. It seemed that he needed both points from Israel. But then Jack Mansell's prediction came true and changed everything.

While Bingham awaited the Israelis, they still had to entertain Portugal in Tel Aviv on 28 October. And entertain they did! Three weeks later, when Israel came to Windsor Park, Northern Ireland needed only one point to qualify – Israel had shocked the soccer world by beating Portugal 4–1. Jack Mansell's team had done what they promised to do. Any thoughts Mansell had of doing Sweden a favour – an Irish defeat would have put Sweden through – were about to be dispelled as his team trotted onto the Windsor Park pitch to the deafening thunder of 40,000 patriotic Irish fans.

The Israel result was the inevitable conclusion to Bingham's second year as manager. He hadn't lost at Windsor Park and he wasn't going to set a precedent with the World Cup finals at stake. As the team left the dressing-room and walked down the long corridor towards the exit which brought them out parallel with the Spion Kop, Bingham whispered to Gerry Armstrong, 'Give me a goal tonight, Gerry.' The man from west Belfast obliged and Northern Ireland went on to the World Cup finals for the first time since 1958. Bingham had emulated Doherty and that meant a lot to him.

After the game Bingham told reporters that he felt Northern Ireland deserved to reach Spain. 'It is super for our little province and the players are ecstatic. They have made a new bit of history and we are going to enjoy our World Cup.'

It is now history that Northern Ireland reached the quarter-finals in Spain; what is not so evident is why a second-class soccer nation came so close to being one of the top four teams in the world, particularly when that team conceded twelve goals in four pre-tournament games, having conceded only nine in the previous sixteen games.

In his autobiography, Pat Jennings wrote that Bingham adopted the style that suited Northern Ireland best. 'Bingham is a sound tactician and knows our strength lies in good organization, with the emphasis on stopping the other side rather than trying to match them in all respects of the game. Billy favours playing from the back – and hitting on the break. He accepts Northern Ireland aren't likely to score many goals, so if we get one he wants to make it count.'

Northern Ireland had four games before Spain – against England, France, Scotland and Wales – and he had several problems. The first was motivation – his forte; the second was the bane of his job as manager of Northern Ireland – getting players from their clubs, fit and able. The players were very high, having reached Spain, and several soccer writers noticed that they weren't motivated for the friendlies. It took all Bingham's qualities to raise them for their only home game during that period, against Scotland, and the result was sufficient reward for his efforts. In his report of the game Robert Armstrong wrote that the team 'showed extraordinary motivation in the second half, proving yet again that a lively Windsor Park crowd is worth a goal in itself'. That in itself was not significant. What really made the difference and showed Bingham's true inspirational abilities was his inclusion of two Irish league players, Jim Cleary of Glentoran and Felix Healy of Coleraine. His makeshift team had problems which the press were not slow to notice. Armstrong wrote: 'Bingham's players relied heavily on a hurtling style of counter-attack, which placed a heavy burden on their strikers, Armstrong and Hamilton, who too often received the ball before adequate support had arrived.'

Bingham's other major problem was injuries. As the winter of 1981 became the January of 1982 Bingham learned that his long-serving goalkeeper, Pat Jennings, had injured his groin in a third-round FA Cup tie between Spurs and Arsenal, of all teams. It was five weeks before Jennings was declared fit, and although Bingham chose him for the England game many observers felt that the ageing goalkeeper had reached the end of the road after England had won 4–0. Jennings thought his 'injury problems were behind him' but a week after the England game his groin injury flared up again and Jim Platt was called into the team for the games against France and Scotland. Jennings had recovered sufficiently for Bingham to consider him for Northern Ireland's last game before the finals – against Wales, in Wrexham, on 27 May. Bingham still had a problem. Jennings had broken down twice in four months and had been out of Arsenal's first team for most of that year, while Bingham's second choice goalkeeper, Jim Platt, had finished the season as Northeast player of the year for his performances with Middlesborough. In his customary manner Bingham didn't name his selection until the afternoon of the Wales game; Jennings would play the first forty-five minutes and Platt would replace him at half-time.

The composition of the domestic soccer season did not allow Bingham to bring his players together until two weeks before the opening game in Spain. He took his squad of twenty-two players to Brighton and put them through an intensive training schedule under the English south-coast sun, which prepared them perfectly for Spain – they were suntanned and, more importantly, they were fit. His task had been to rejuvenate the weary limbs of those players who had come through a hard season with their clubs and bring them to a physical peak which would make them the fittest players in Spain. Most of the players had become accustomed to his training, yet several said that the Brighton session had been the hardest. Bingham took them on cross-country runs to build up their stamina and drove them to lap after lap around the track. Bingham didn't have the luxury of two or three months' preparation and he was determined to use wisely what little time he had. He was also determined to get the best out of his players.

Throughout his career in football Billy Bingham has acquired a supreme degree of professionalism that is rare in sport. From an early age he realized that he was a player of limited ability, but with an almost fanatical desire for fitness and a dedication to give nothing less than 100 per cent he became one of the most popular unsung soccer heroes of the '50s. He is fondly remembered by the supporters of Glentoran, Sunderland, Luton, Everton and Port Vale as a fun-loving player who always entertained and never held anything back. As a manager Bingham expects the same from his players. 'Billy's attitude,' said Robert Armstrong, 'is to get the maximum capacity out of his players, and he tells them that it's not necessarily the best players who win matches but those who want to win them.'

Bingham expects his players to adopt the attitude that they are professional footballers making a living out of the game. His success comes from his ability to motivate players of limited talent and impress on them the importance of determination and dedication, and he makes it an integral part of his management to know his players individually. When Northern Ireland play in foreign countries he inspects the hotels that the IFA have selected before the team arrives. He also has a chat with the hotel chef to make sure that the menu is suitable to Irish palates. 'Billy likes to show he's the boss in every respect,' wrote Jennings, 'even when it comes to ordering meals for the players. He feels that he knows what is best for them to eat and the lads accept his menu in the same way they accept his tactics.'

When the players assembled at Brighton, Bingham told them that no player was sure of a place in the team and that he wanted them to impress him during the sessions. Several players believed that their positions were sacred, yet nobody dared to tempt Bingham. Only Jennings was genuinely worried that Bingham would decide not to risk him.

In his autobiography Jennings said he 'wasn't confident' he would be the first choice. 'Since Platt had been playing regularly for Middlesborough while I'd been on the injured list, I could hardly have complained if he had got the nod,' he wrote.

As Northern Ireland's opening game with Yugoslavia in Zaragoza on 17 June came closer, the press speculated about how Bingham would motivate his players, what tactics he would use, and what his final choice would be. In his analytical preview of Northern Ireland's hopes in Spain, Irish soccer writer Paddy Agnew wrote that their 'proud record of having conceded but three goals in eight qualifying games' reflected well on the organizational abilities of Jennings and on the fact that 'Jimmy Nicholl, John O'Neill and Chris Nicholl had played together as a unit for seven of the eight qualifying games'. Agnew was not alone in believing that Bingham would use winger Noel Brotherston to 'great effect' and that he wouldn't make any dramatic changes.

In his overall preview Agnew stated that 'Northern Ireland's soccer tends to be basic, if not crude'. He wrote that 'tireless hounding and chasing from the midfield' had two objectives – to unsettle the opposition and win the ball. 'When the ball is won Northern Ireland have little shame in immediately knocking it up to the front. Deprived of outstanding talents who can create and construct, Bingham has little realistic alternative but to play a simple chase and run game. His defenders tend to be cautious about moving up to join the attack and, like the midfield men, prefer to hit the long ball, aimed at the front pairing.'

Agnew was not the only soccer writer to be proved wrong when Bingham finally announced his team for the Yugoslavia game which gave Northern Ireland a point and very nearly two from their first game in the 1982 World Cup. The first surprise was the selection of John McClelland instead of John O'Neill, but the real shock came when Bingham preferred Manchester United's

Norman Whiteside in place of Brotherston. Whiteside had just turned seventeen less than a week before the finals began, and his experience of senior football was limited. At United he had played only one full game when Ron Atkinson selected him at the end of the '81/82 season. And in goal Bingham, understandably, preferred Jennings' experience.

Bingham told reporters that he was 'pleased with the result against one of the premier countries in Europe' and then emphasized that Yugoslavia were unable to cope with the British style of soccer and fitness. The inclusion of McClelland alongside Chris Nicholl in the centre of the Irish defence was masterly, but on the warmest day of the finals it was Bingham's rigorous training which had his players finishing strongly as the Yugoslavs wilted in the heat.

Honduras, who had surprised Spain in the opening game by holding them to a 1–1 draw, were next, and Bingham had enough information from that game to negate the Central Americans' style. To minimize the Honduran threat from midfield, Bingham asked David McCreery to close Gilberto down at every opportunity and Billy Hamilton and Norman Whiteside were told to run at the Honduran central defenders – Costly and Villegas. Both tactics worked to great effect but Northern Ireland were unable to add to Gerry Armstrong's early goal and Honduras equalized in the second half. It seemed that Northern Ireland had lost their chance. To qualify for the second stage they had to beat the host nation, Spain, in Valencia.

Bingham wouldn't concede that his team were on their way home. 'It will take a lot of effort to beat Spain, but the will and the skill are there,' he said. Spain had built their World Cup games on a system of counter-attack which allowed the opposition space in midfield when they gained possession. Bingham realized this would leave the Spanish open to aggressive strikes. Gerry Armstrong, who had been playing on the right and dropping back to collect the ball, had been making thrusting runs in the previous two games. The Spaniards, without realizing it, allowed him to play the way he wanted, and with Whiteside supporting Billy

Hamilton from the left, Northern Ireland had a formidable attacking force.

With their fanatical, flag-waving supporters urging them on, Spain quickly took the initiative, but Bingham had stressed to his players that they must not lose an early goal. Gradually, after the opening ten minutes, when McClelland and Chris Nicholl seemed vulnerable in the face of the Spanish raids, the Irish defence settled as the game began to develop into a nasty, physical struggle for possession. Half-time arrived and Bingham ushered his players into their dressing-room confident that they could beat Spain.

The crescendo of noise which greeted the players on their return was gradually subsiding when Hamilton outpaced a Spanish defender and swung a low cross into the penalty area. The Spanish goalkeeper, Arconada, seemed unsure whether or not to commit himself, and then watched, agonized, as he pushed the ball into the path of Gerry Armstrong, who gleefully hammered it into the net. The Spanish, in the grand Luis Casanova Stadium, were stunned into silence.

Fifteen mintes later, as Spain hurled themselves into the Northern Ireland half, Mal Donaghy – the epitome of quiet efficiency – pushed the Spanish full-back, Camacho, up against the advertising boards surrounding the pitch and was sent off. A minute earlier Sammy McIlroy had been substituted by Tommy Cassidy after sustaining a leg injury as boots flew indiscriminately into tackles. Northern Ireland had thirty long minutes left to hold on to their lead. Bingham could do nothing but watch from the touchline; he knew that if all his rigorous training, psychological motivation and shrewd tactics were going to work it would be now. In that last half-hour those players became heroes as they dredged their reserves of energy to find the inspiration they needed to win the game. When the whistle finally shrilled in the din around the stadium, Bingham raced to embrace his goal-scorer, Gerry Armstrong. Bingham had not only become the first Irishman to be involved in two World Cups, he had equalled the success of the 1958 side and reached the quarter-finals. His feeling of *déjà vu* was all the more real because Northern Ireland's opponents in the second-stage group would be France and Austria. France were the team which had unceremoniously ended Doherty's World Cup dream twenty-four years earlier.

Bingham's emotions were shared by every member of the Irish squad, the officials and the journalists. 'This is unbelievable. Have you ever seen a feat like that?' With tears slowly running down his face he spoke of the team's success. Billy Bingham had at last achieved the success he so badly wanted. Robert Armstrong later wrote that Bingham's personality, 'which combines charm and determination in a fine balance', was the key to Northern Ireland's success. 'There is little doubt that Northern Ireland's domination of Portugal, Sweden, Spain and Yugoslavia on their way to the threshold of the World Cup semi-finals owed everything to his shrewd organization and tactics.'

Northern Ireland had started the World Cup as the bookies' outsider, at around 150–1. Nobody expected them to dismiss Austria and France in the same manner as they had beaten Spain, but then neither did Bingham. 'France are the favourites to win our group and that is a realistic view. Nobody expected us to finish on top of Spain and nobody thinks we'll finish in front of France, so the pressure is on them not us,' said Bingham.

Before Bingham could think about France, his team had to play Austria. He had boasted that Northern Ireland were the fittest team in the World Cup and that was about to be put to the test under the hot Madrid sun. Following their success over Spain, the Irish were being fêted by the host nation and it was not surprising that Whiteside, Hamilton and Armstrong picked up the label of the 'Three Musketeers'. The Austrian game was to be their command performance, and after Armstrong had powered his way past several defenders to supply Hamilton with Northern Ireland's opening goal, a place in the semi-final didn't seem that far away. Unfortunately the Irish were unable to add to their lead, despite their dominance in the first half, and when the teams resumed after the interval Austria gradually wore down Northern Ireland's tired defence and scored twice. Bingham's warriors hadn't come that far to give up without a battle and with sixteen minutes left, Hamilton equalized. After the game Bingham said that the final whistle had come too soon. 'If it had gone on another five minutes I believe the Austrians would have cracked,' he said. 'Conversely, had our second goal come a little earlier I believe we would have won it. It lifted our boys at a time when legs were beginning to drag.' Yet Bingham admitted that his players were 'low in stamina after the interval', and Austria had taken full advantage.

In the curious manner of history, Bingham was about to be taken back twenty-four years to the same stage of the World Cup when France had knocked a depleted Northern Irish team out of the 1958 finals with four goals. Georg Schmidt, the Austrian manager, said he would not dismiss Northern Ireland's chances 'of going to the semi-finals, for their spirit and teamwork will give France a lot of problems'.

Bingham had played Jim Platt in the Austrian game, because Jennings suffered a recurrence of his groin injury, and he was unsure about the veteran goalkeeper for the French game, which Northern Ireland had to win to reach the semi-finals. Bingham was eventually persuaded by the Northern Ireland trainer, Jim McGregor, and Jennings was selected.

The French had resurrected themselves after their opening 3–1 defeat by England, and with players of the skill of Platini, Rocheteau, Giresse, Genghini, Tigana and Soler they were capable of winning the World Cup. Realistically, Northern Ireland could only hope to frustrate the French and possibly snatch victory in the typical Bingham style of breaking positively from a strictly defensive formation. Jimmy Nicholl, Mal Donaghy, John O'Neill, John McClelland and David McCreery certainly represented Bingham's strongest defence, and with Martin O'Neill and Sammy McIlroy in midfield, Northern Ireland were capable of counter-attacking in style. But the dream was over, and the French played the sort of quality football that is impossibly difficult to suppress. The only surprise was the 4–1 scoreline in favour of the French, which flattered them, and sent Northern Ireland home with memories of what might have been.

Bingham has been criticized for his defensive tactics as a club manager, yet when France went into the lead in the thirty-third minute, Bingham had no other option but to attack. 'If we could have held out until fifteen minutes into the second half, I thought we might disrupt them, but they scored a brilliant goal before the interval so I had to throw more people forward. When you do this you play into their hands, because they are a tremendous counter-attack team; still, my lads pushed forward and did not lay down.'

The press had no heart to criticize Bingham for his selection of Jennings and Donaghy and it is only in hindsight that their poor performances are noted. Bingham knew that his team had given 'everything'. There was nothing else to be said. 'It was no disgrace to lose to France. Only the Brazilians could have lived with them on this form. The championship has been a marvellous boost, not merely to the team but to all the people of Northern Ireland and I am proud to have been part of it,' said Bingham.

But the story had not ended in Spain. It had only begun, and Bingham had at last found his vocation. Spain has now become a memory, and Bingham is taking Northern Ireland to their third appearance in the World Cup finals. The reason is not because he is a great manager, it is because of his almost Calvinistic desire to be perfect in a less than perfect sport, and to that end he has never stopped improving himself. Bingham began the process the day he laced up his first pair of boots and his success owes as much to his working-class Presbyterian background as it does to any natural ability he possessed as a player or now demonstrates as a manager.

CHAPTER TWO

BALLYMACARRET

BILLY'S BOOTS

The crowd surged around the dining hall,
McCaffrey tallest of us all,
Pushed and shoved his rough way through,
    To get his plate of Irish stew.
This was the big counter-attack, the servers
    had no time to check,
As one by one the boys were served,
Some got more than they deserved,
But others further down the queue got less
    of that thick Irish stew.
That was the first day we were here,
    but now meal times are not so queer.
One by one each boy in place bows his head
    and says his grace.
So those boys further down the queue
    now get their plate of Irish stew.

W. L. Bingham, age 11

In east Belfast, under the shadow of the monolithic Harland and Wolff cranes, stands the Oval, the home of Glentoran Football Club. Forty years ago it was in ruins, devastated by German bombers whose night raids had saturated the nearby shipyards and the Short Brothers and Harland aircraft complex with large tonnage bombs. Dwarfed by the shipyard gantries to the west, to the east of the Oval lay a maze of tiny streets, of small two-up and two-down terraced houses, which stretched to the river Lagan; the natural boundary which cut Ballymacarret village off from the rest of the city.

The Second World War was over, and Irish league soccer was

returning to normal. It was also about to enter an era which would produce the most talented team ever to wear the green shirts of Northern Ireland. In those post-war years Glentoran would nurture the nucleus of that team and, by coincidence, three of its players would emerge from those tiny streets, beyond which the Castlereagh hills reached out to the mountains of Mourne in County Down.

Glentoran were the 'week cock and hens', the pride of County Down. In the mid-fifties Billy Bingham and the Blanchflower brothers, Danny and Jackie, would also be the pride of the county. Their paths to professional soccer would be very different, their fates varied and, in Jackie Blanchflower's case, tragic. In east Belfast, in the '60s, Danny Blanchflower would be a legend who had played for the great Spurs double winning team, and every soccer-mad child would worship and revere his genius. His brother Jackie – the no less skilful member of the Manchester United team which was virtually wiped out in the Munich air disaster of February 1958 – would be less well known. He would never play football again after the tragedy. Billy Bingham would be remembered as the ever-present, speedy winger in Peter Doherty's international team which peaked in the mid-fifties and went on to the quarter-finals of the World Cup in Sweden in 1958.

The Binghams and the Blanchflowers lived in the Dunraven area of Bloomfield, in the leafy outer suburbs of east Belfast. Today the area that is known as Bloomfield is caught between Orangefield, a sprawling estate of semi-detached red-brick houses, and the terraced houses which jut out from the Beersbridge and Newtonards Roads like the teeth of a comb. In the mid-thirties the topography of east Belfast was very different. Bloomfield was a concoction of misplaced Edwardian architecture which tamely met the Conswater River to the south-west and the sandhills and fields of Clarawood and Knock in the south-east. The streets of Bloomfield were lined with deciduous trees, which knew nothing of the stale air and stench of the industries from which the people of the area made their living.

The ropeworks factory, which employed many of the people

from those streets, is now a depressing reminder of the dreary industry which thrived on the banks of the Conswater, a wandering tributary from the mouth of the Lagan. In Bloomfield, the only glimpse of that world was the railway that cut Ballymacarret off from the shipyards and then proceeded parallel with the Bloomfield Road towards the seaside resorts of Millise and Donaghadee. The steam trains which chugged through carried the dreams of happier days for the children of the district.

William Laurie Bingham was born on 5 August 1931, about twenty-five minutes' walk from Bloomfield, in Moore Street, near the Woodstock and Albertbridge Roads which merged to meet the Lagan. He might have been born in the mountains, because his two childhood homes were worlds apart. His father, also named William Bingham, worked in the shipyard as a driller and his mother was a spinner, when she could get the work; employment in Belfast in the early '30s was as much of a luxury to some people as it is today. The boat to Britain was the release many sought to bring back the shillings to feed their families and William Bingham found work in Glasgow.

The Binghams were thrifty Presbyterians who valued the few possessions they had, yet they were acutely embarrassed by their poverty when they moved to the richer surroundings of Dunraven, in Bloomfield itself, a couple of years before the Second World War began. 'We lived in fairly poor circumstances, but around the age of six I remember getting a house in Bloomfield that seemed like paradise by comparison,' recalls Bingham.

The move had an indelible effect on young Billy. 'I remember sitting on a cart pulled by a pony, at night-time, late, and the lamp was swinging. I can see the lamp still, swinging. We had to move late at night you see, so that nobody would know how little we had. We did not have many possessions, just bits and pieces my parents had gathered together.'

This enforced frugality did not generate a cold atmosphere in the Bingham household, which had grown to four with the addition of a younger sister. 'There was always love and warmth in the home,' remembers Bingham. A childhood acquaintance remembers that Billy, who was known to school friends as Laurie, was 'incessantly kicking a ball around the district'. He may not have had any choice. Bingham has said that he felt a loss as a child because his parents had to work long hours. For a young boy developing an interest in outdoor sport, particularly soccer, the move to Bloomfield was like a never-ending paradise.

In Europe any notion of paradise was shattered by the satanic rumbling of tanks, the stomp of marching soldiers and whining fighter planes. Belfast, an industrial heartland, was a target, and Bingham's after-school hours of football around the lamp posts and air raid shelters were about to end.

Billy was nine when the German Luftwaffe launched their heaviest blitzkrieg on Belfast in April and May 1941. Like thousands of other children, he was evacuated to the country as the Luftwaffe droned incessantly over Belfast, bombing the schools and houses in their flight-path. On the night of Sunday, 4 May 1941, east Belfast was consumed by an inferno which had spread from the shipyard and harbour area after the fall of nearly 100,000 incendiary bombs. Ravenscroft school, attended by the Blanchflowers, was destroyed and some streets were entirely gutted by the fires.

As the war raged on, young Billy played football around the streets of Dunraven and in the fields around Orangefield. Jackie Blanchflower's mother played football herself and encouraged the boys to organize a team. The whole district seemed to be soccer-crazy, despite the war. Billy's mother added her own encouragement when she gave her son half a crown (twelve and a half new pence) to buy a pair of second-hand boots. It was a gesture Billy appreciated and remembered. 'When you don't get much you appreciate what you have. I am sure that this experience was a tremendous motivation for me to make sure that I would not fall into the same trap myself.'

Bingham attended Elmgrove Elementary School on the Beersbridge Road. The destruction of Ravenscroft school nearby meant that Elmgrove had to house pupils from both schools after the blitz. To relieve the burden on Elmgrove and other schools in similar situations the Belfast educational authorities organized summer schools in the country. For Billy this was the move which would shape his life.

John Arnold, a senior teacher at Elmgrove, was given the task of providing entertainment for the boys at these camps and he didn't need much persuasion to organize a football tournament. Bingham remembered these games and the team which Elmgrove entered in organized schools' soccer matches as his early inspiration, yet the reality may have been different. Arnold had little or no interest in football. One of his colleagues at Elmgrove said that he doubted if 'John would have known whether a football was blown up or stuffed'. Arnold, he said, was very 'interested in helping working-class kids to get on. He was a good teacher but he wasn't a football man.' Bingham's idealistic reminiscences of those days ignores the ambitious drive which carried him from the various junior teams to the Elmgrove team, schoolboy international fame and the Glentoran senior team in less than four years.

The Second World War continued to dominate the headlines as Elmgrove slipped, virtually unnoticed, into the semi-finals of the Ulster Schools Cup and a derby clash with their Ballymacarret neighbours, Templemore Avenue. Billy's success as a goal-grabbing centre-forward had propelled them into the last four and on St Patrick's Day, 1945, his tenacity and his goals took Elmgrove into the final. He was thirteen, captain of Elmgrove and no longer an anonymous schoolboy. On 2 April, the morning of the final against Larne Technical College, the *Northern Whig* daily newspaper made Elmgrove the favourites. 'They are real warriors and possess in Bingham a real sharp-shooting match winner,' wrote the reporter. In a tough and typical schoolboys' game Elmgrove came out on top in a seven-goal thriller. Surprisingly, Billy didn't score, but it didn't matter. When he was selected for the Northern Ireland schoolboy international team against Eire that year he hit two goals in Belfast and three in the return at Dalymount Park, Dublin. Although Elmgrove was unable to repeat its success, largely because the post-war soccer boom had intensified the competition, Billy had done enough to impress several Irish league clubs.

The school-leaving age in the mid-forties was fourteen but scholarships and passes allowed many children to further their education. In Belfast that meant either the Belfast Academical Institution ('Inst') or the Belfast Technical College ('Tech'), the latter being considered by many as the poor boys' grammar school. Billy went to the 'Tech'. There were thirty pupils in his class; twenty paid £2 per annum for books and tuition and ten, including Bingham, received scholarships which entitled them to free education.

Billy's teacher was an enthusiastic man called Edward William Brown Astle, but his interest in sport stopped firmly at the cricket crease. However, football was the most popular sport in the Tech and Mr E. W. B. Astle, an overworked and underpaid teacher (even in those days), combined it with a little bit of psychology to make his job easier. 'The football was a mild form of bribery,' remembers Astle. 'You just turned up and the kids would be on your side the next day in class. We'd train on Wednesday afternoon, but I used to pray for rain.' Astle recalls that the Tech team paraded in 'bright yellow jerseys', which were much too big for some of the boys, including young Billy, who was smaller and slimmer than most of his team-mates. Astle now believes that the kit 'must have been a job lot' because yellow was definitely not the fashion for football teams in those days. Astle knew Billy as 'Laurie' Bingham and his memory of him as 'a little ball of India rubber bouncing around' in a strip of canary yellow is not a derogatory reminiscence. 'Laurie was a very likeable, personable and extremely talented individual.'

Billy studied French, commerce, history, mechanics and physics at the Tech. He was bright, but his real interest remained football, and he was soon made captain of the under-fifteens. Billy was diverting his energy into the sport as if his life depended on it. 'I had a lot of drive and I used to give everything to every game. Then there was the consideration of a job and they tried to get me a position as a cost accountant, because I was quite good at maths, so I passed a test with a firm that made gravestones, but I left after only two days because I couldn't stand being indoors.'

East Belfast had a tradition of son following father into a trade, and that usually meant the shipyard, the aircraft factory or one of the engineering works. 'Like all the other fathers, my old man used to keep on about getting me put to a trade. He wanted me to be an electrical engineer, so I worked in the manufacturing shop in the shipyard and went to night school, but by then the football thing was beginning to show,' recalls Bingham.

In Bloomfield Billy had played football for St Donard's youth club team and he continued to play in the district with fellow Tech pupil Jackie Blanchflower. Football dominated his young life; it would only be a matter of time before he joined an Irish league club.

Organized soccer in Northern Ireland began an upsurge immediately after the war, as the senior clubs attempted to replenish their staffs. Billy's local club, Glentoran, had sent two of its former players, Johnny Geary and Tony Wilkins, out to find talent and their first objective was to round up enough players to form third and fourth elevens for the Oval club. They began by asking several young boys to join a team entered in one of the many summer competitions. It was June 1947.

Billy was asked along with several promising young players in the Bloomfield area and when Geary eventually took them into battle Bingham added another medal to his collection as the team carried off the S. J. Taylor Cup. They played only a handful of games, but Geary had seen enough to ask Bingham, Jimmy McIlroy, Artie Taylor and Billy Neill to sign as amateurs for Glentoran's new third team – the Co-op Rec, in the Northern Ireland Amateur League. Within two years all of them would be in the Glentoran first team. Bingham has said that several other Irish league clubs were after his signature but he gave none of them a second thought. As an east Belfast boy Glentoran was his only choice.

Johnny Geary was regarded as one of the most important football trainers in Northern Ireland. 'He had been an inside forward with the Glens,' remembers Danny Blanchflower, 'and he brought a number of talented players into the team at that time. He probably had quite an influence on players like Bingham and McIlroy because he was a gentleman of great pride and satisfaction who would do anything for you.' Bingham himself would later acknowledge the tremendous influence Geary and Wilkins had over his career.

During Billy's first season ('47/48) with Co-op Rec he moved from schoolboy to youth international football, where he gained nine caps. These games took Bingham and his contemporaries to England and the Glentoran manager, Frank Grice, decided to pre-empt English league clubs by offering his junior players professional terms. On Billy's seventeenth birthday he became a part-time professional, with a wage of £6 a week.

The new season was a revelation for Billy as he moved into the Glentoran second team, but it also gave his mentors a problem. At centre-forward Billy was a prolific goal-scorer against junior opposition, but could he do the same against experienced players? Or was he, at five feet six inches, and nine stone five pounds, too slight for the job?

Glentoran persisted with their ebullient striker as he rattled in the goals for Co-op Rec. On his increasingly frequent appearances in the Glentoran second team he did the same. He had taken his total of goals into double figures when Grice decided to try him in the first team.

It was 12 March 1949. Billy made his senior debut in a 1–1 draw with Ballymena United at the Antrim club's showgrounds, but not as a centre-forward; 'Frank Grice, the Glentoran manager, thought I was a bit light for a centre-forward, so he moved me to the right wing.' Despite his reservations about the move, Bingham later admitted that Grice's decision had been perfect.

A month later, with Glentoran in the final of the Irish Cup, Bingham made a decision which indicated where his priorities lay; he chose to go with the Northern Ireland youth squad to an international tournament in Holland. Coyly, he recalled: 'I decided to go there instead of playing in the cup final because I believed it was more important to travel.' The tournament was to produce the first of many thrilling games with England involving Bingham, as a player and manager. On this occasion he scored twice as Northern Ireland moved into the semi-finals, where they lost to their hosts.

Billy's days at the Oval were, in retrospect, quite uneventful. He rested in the eye of the football tornado he had created. Even then he knew how to survive a storm. There have been many anecdotes about Billy Bingham from people who have known him for part or all of his soccer career, yet none more accurately reveal his true character than the story he himself tells of his shipyard days. 'I used to get out of the shipyard and do early training before the others arrived. I reckoned I was getting better and I wanted to be fitter than the other guys.' Training began about five o'clock and Billy would sneak out early, climb over the Oval's perimeter wall, and put in an hour's extra training which doubled his quota. That he was prepared to risk his job, in his teenage years, for his soccer career was a testament to the extreme faith he had in his ability to become a professional footballer. Jimmy McIlroy who accompanied Bingham into the Glentoran team, wished he had half of Billy's confidence.

Nearly forty years on McIlroy believes that Bingham has changed very little from those days. 'Bingy to me has always been the same type of person. His two biggest assets were his tremendous enthusiasm and his confidence. He was very confident and very determined; he was a fighter.'

Billy became a regular in the Glentoran first team in the '49/50 season, but the change of position did not diminish his appetite for goals. When selected for the Irish League to play the Scottish League on 4 October 1950, Billy was among Glentoran's top scorers with five goals. If Bingham was finding Irish league football easy, the inter-league game would give him a shock. He came up against Sammy Cox of Rangers, an experienced full-back who shackled the young Irishman. Bingham still had a lot to learn.

Billy's confidence was high when the Irish League played the English League on 18 October. After the game, which the Irish lost 6–3, he was in the bath contemplating the rumours about his future when 'a tall, craggy, stranger held out his hand and said, "Congratulations, you've been transferred to Sunderland." I was too elated and bewildered either to protest that I couldn't be transferred to anyone without my own consent or to ask the stranger who he was that he knew more about my affairs than I did myself. Only later did I learn from one of my team-mates that it was Charlie Buchan, himself a Sunderland star of bygone days and a distinguished football writer.'

That evening Billy met the Sunderland manager, Bill Murray, and told him that he wanted to talk to his parents before signing anything. His father's joy was met by his mother's reticence but they agreed that they wouldn't stop him. On 22 October the *Northern Whig* reported that Billy Bingham had been transferred to Sunderland 'for a fee in the region of £8,000' and lamented, 'How will Glentoran fare without Bingham, their most consistent forward?'

CHAPTER THREE

THE BANK OF ENGLAND CLUB

BINGHAM THE PROFESSIONAL

Billy wasn't a great player but he always gave 100 per cent, and that's 500 per cent better than that lot out there today.

Bill Simmons, a Sunderland supporter since 1924

Billy Bingham arrived at Roker Park on Wednesday, 25 October 1950, with his parents. As a teenager about to be elevated to a status he had no conception of, he gingerly approached his new club with a naïveté which lasted only the short time it took him to realize exactly where he was and what role he was expected to play.

He continued his apprenticeship as an electrical engineer at Doxford's in the Sunderland shipyards and he probably felt reassured by that affirmation of his life in Belfast. Belfast and Sunderland had more than just football in common; they were burgeoning industrial centres, and Bingham was at home in the dirty little streets of both environments.

The only shock came when Bingham turned up for training the first morning and discovered the extent of Sunderland's playing-staff. With nearly fifty players for manager Bill Murray to choose from, Bingham inquired about the players in his position. 'Imagine, then, my astonishment and dismay when I learned that they already had two very good outside-rights.'

Bingham's ego was dented when he realized his first match for Sunderland was not to be against 'Arsenal, Manchester United or Wolves' but against Spennymoor in the North-Eastern league, where Sunderland reserves played their fixtures.

Bingham's role had been defined and he realized that he had been bought by Murray as cover for the regular outside-rights, the ageing Len Duns (who had played for Sunderland during their first FA Cup success in 1937) and Tommy Wright, a Scot who had only joined the club eighteen months earlier.

Bingham was not the only person who thought he should be awarded an immediate first-team place. After hearing good reports about him from Sunderland reserves' 5–0 win over Spennymoor, Argus – the football correspondent for the *Sunderland Echo* – told his readers that he was of the opinion that, 'Billy Bingham should come into the outside-right position to see if he can improve upon the play of Tommy Wright.'

Argus was obviously impressed by what he had heard of Bingham. After watching him during that first training session he wrote: 'Bingham is small but stocky, and looks to have a good pair of shoulders on him. One thing about him is that he has a goal-scoring record and if you accept the opinion of George Gray [Sunderland trainer] who saw him play in Ireland along with Jack Hall [Sunderland scout] he will make the grade and won't draw back.'

However, Bingham could not 'improve upon the play of Tommy Wright' because his football league registration had not been completed. On Tuesday, 14 November, Argus reported that the Irish League was not forthcoming with full details of the financial arrangements between Glentoran and Sunderland. It is not known whether Argus realized that the 'financial arrangements' were being looked at by the Irish League.

In the post-war years of the English League, with money in abundance, gates climbed to record levels – for the first time in the club's history, over one million spectators passed through the Roker Park turnstiles during the 1949/50 season. Players demanding signing-on fees above the statutory £10 became commonplace, and clubs like Sunderland, who demanded the best talents in the first division, were allegedly not loath to make under-the-table payments.

Bingham's own transfer to Sunderland went largely unnoticed because during the same week the club was negotiating for the signature of the Welsh international forward, Trevor Ford.

Sunderland manager Bill Murray had snatched Ford from under the noses of several wealthy and equally goal-hungry clubs by paying £30,000 – a record amount – to Aston Villa. At the time it was believed Murray had secured Ford's impressive goal-scoring talents because he had organized a part-time job outside football. Yet there were other rumours, and when the Football League and the Football Association set up a joint inquiry 'into the circumstances surrounding Ford's transfer from Aston Villa' the player was fined £100 in February 1951. The Players' Union immediately called for the £12 maximum wage to be abolished. It was not the last Sunderland or Bingham would hear about such scandals.

Ford, Murray hoped, was to be the final link in his team of stars. The Welsh international was expected to spearhead the Sunderland attack with Len Shackleton and Ivor Broadis. The soccer-mad faithful at Roker had already had their appetites whetted during Ford's home debut when he scored a devastating hat-trick and cracked one of the goalposts. They were again treated to this feast when, within a few weeks, international soccer returned to Roker Park for the first time since 1920 and Ford scored Wales' goals in the 4–2 defeat by England.

Yet the combination of Ford, Shackleton and Broadis still hadn't jelled after almost five weeks of the Welshman's signing. The supporters became impatient.

On 25 November 1950 the celebrated trio ran on to Roker Park grass together for the first time. It was obvious to all but the completely uninitiated that something wasn't right. Players often find it difficult to blend into a new team; Ford and Shackleton gave the impression that they were on different planets. Only a few years later did it become known there was a certain amount of animosity between the two off the field. If the Sunderland supporters were disappointed with the lack of understanding on the field between Ford and Shackleton they were even more disenchanted with Ivor Broadis, whose magical talents began to fail him on match days. With results going against them, the supporters began to turn on some of the players. Broadis was singled out on several occasions but he managed to endure till the following season. Then, in a post-match depression, with insults still ringing in his ears, he requested a transfer. Bingham particularly had come to like Broadis and to respect him as a footballer. 'He was an intelligent player with considerable talent and he was especially difficult to shift off the ball once he was in possession.'

Bingham also seemed to understand at least one of the reasons why Ford and Shackleton failed to hit it off on the field. Ford, Bingham believed, was never a good positional player, and despite being 'the most dynamic spearhead in the game at that time', he never seemed to know what Shackleton was going to do with the ball. Subsequently, Ford believed that Shackleton was ignoring him on the field. He made this known to the press and during a friendly with the Dutch B team, which Sunderland won 7–3, Shackleton retorted in bizarre fashion. After taking on the whole Dutch defence, leaving the goalkeeper chasing a shadow, Shackleton stopped in front of the empty net and rolled the ball to Ford, who was standing on the edge of the penalty-area. 'Here,' Shackleton shouted, 'don't say I never give you a pass.'

If Bingham was bemused or affected by the uneasy dressing-room atmosphere this created, he never showed it on the field, and from the day he became a First Division footballer he was a favourite with everyone at Sunderland – players, press and supporters.

It was after only five weeks of North-Eastern League football that Sunderland manager Bill Murray included Bingham in his first team for the 2 December fixture against Stoke City at Roker Park. Argus wrote: 'Billy has made a big impression upon reserve-team supporters and his debut in the senior side has been delayed only by the stringent conditions now imposed upon the transfer of Irish players to English clubs.'

It is doubtful whether Murray would have thrown Bingham into the Roker Park cauldron any sooner even if the Football League had allowed him to. Argus, like most of the Sunderland supporters, had an idealistic notion that fresh talent in the team would change the club's flagging fortunes, so when Murray dropped his regular outside-right, Tommy Wright, Bingham was welcomed with open arms. Yet almost a year later, with Bingham a familiar cog in the first-team machinery, Argus admitted that his selection had been premature.

The characteristics that would embellish Bingham's soccer career were evident from the beginning. 'Bingham certainly has grit,' wrote Argus, 'and he made good use of the ball on the odd occasion when it was served to him in an acceptable fashion. He seemed a little out of his depth, but he certainly showed fight. McCue, the Stoke full-back, tackles severely at all times, and he made no exception in Bingham's case. Many a player would not have gone back for more but Bingham stuck it out to such good effect that by the end of the game he had McCue on the run.'

This attitude endeared Bingham to the Sunderland supporters, who immediately realized that their new Irish winger was something special, though in a very different way from the naturals, like Shackleton and Broadis. 'Billy had good speed and ball control,' remembers Bill Simmons, Sunderland's official club historian and a supporter for the past sixty-two years. 'But most of all he was so determined to win the ball. Everyone seemed pleased with "Little Billy", as he came to be called by the lads.'

Ted Giblin, a Sunderland supporter in those days, also remembered Bingham as 'not being very skilful, but he was very popular because he was all heart and fire'. Giblin said he was more impressed with Bingham than he was with Wright. 'Bingham had more football sense – more vision. Wright used to just put his head down and run.'

Bingham's joy at being selected was short-lived. Murray included him the following week for the game against West Bromwich Albion at the Hawthorns when he tried a third forward line in as many weeks, and then dropped him back into the reserves. It was going to be a miserable Christmas. Bingham later wrote that being dropped was the biggest tragedy in his young life: his pride had been hurt and his ego had been dented. He somewhat modestly decided that the reason was because he was not a Duncan Edwards or Jimmy Greaves – 'a ready-made star'. Bingham thought that he was immature and so was his football. He realized that his strengths were his speed and courage which he said he needed, 'merely to offset the physical advantage' most of his opponents had over him. Argus agreed with some of Bingham's arguments. 'At the moment, his lack of height and weight is a bigger handicap than his obvious lack of experience, but he is the most enthusiastic player I have seen for some time and he obviously enjoys playing,' wrote a reporter.

Murray, however, was still undecided about his forward line and on 26 December, Bingham found himself travelling with the first team to Old Trafford. Tommy Wright was moved to the inside-right position and Broadis was also back in the team and relishing the experience. He scored a hat-trick as Sunderland won 5–3, with a devastating display of attacking football. Bingham also had cause to celebrate, after scoring his first goal in senior English football. Argus wrote that the Sunderland forward line of Bill Watson, Ivor Broadis, Dick Davies, Tommy Wright and Billy Bingham had been a delight to watch. 'It takes a good side to beat Manchester United at Manchester,' he reported in the *Football Pink* that evening.

Most Sunderland supporters were astounded by the amount of effort Bingham put into his game. They marvelled at his seemingly endless stamina and his vivacious approach to the sport. What many of them didn't know was that Bingham was finding First Division football very strenuous and that he was training and practising outside the club's mandatory training schedules. Twice a week Bingham endured a weight-training programme which he had designed to improve his strength, stamina and fitness.

Today circuit-training is an integral part of any soccer team's physical-training programme. In the immediate post-war years, according to Bingham, training never allowed players' muscles to become properly developed, because the important element of resistance was missing. 'I had been taught that using weights provided the resistance against which the muscles had to work if they were to become fully developed,' said Bingham.

Simmons realized that Bingham was doing some extra physical training because 'after each game he looked stronger when in possession of the ball'. Yet Murray obviously felt Bingham wasn't quite ready for First Division football and he wasn't selected again until mid-January, when he played against Bolton Wanderers at Roker Park. Three days later Argus, as undecided as Murray about Sunderland's best forward line, argued that their best attack was Wright, Ford, Davis, Shackleton and Bingham. Murray didn't seem to agree. Bingham's name wasn't to appear on the team-sheet again until 7 March, when Sunderland faced Huddersfield at Leeds Road. In his weekly analysis, an optimistic Argus wrote: 'Bingham kept up his record of never having had a bad game in the senior side'. Murray got the message because he kept him in the side for a further two games before he brought Wright back for the local derby against Newcastle United.

It is often said that some footballers put their heads where others wouldn't put their feet. To back up that argument, today's soccer fans would probably refer to the antics of Manchester United's Bryan Robson and Kevin Moran. Yet they talk about their exploits as if they were a phenomenon new to the game. Argus would have corrected them, although when he witnessed Bingham's performance during Sunderland's game against Burnley at Turf Moor in March 1951, even he was a little incredulous in his report later in the day. Sunderland were a goal up and the Burnley defence was under siege. Trevor Ford headed the ball onto Bingham, who in turn headed it into the goal. A Burnley defender, racing back, managed to kick the ball away but the referee immediately awarded a goal. Then he changed his mind after consulting the linesman. In the meantime Bingham was being carried off the field for treatment. Beating the Burnley goalkeeper, Strong, to the ball had meant taking blows from both the goalkeeper's fists on the mouth, and a knee in the solar plexus. 'It took five minutes to bring the tough little Irishman round but he came back with a plastered upper-lip as soon as he could walk,' wrote Argus.

Whatever could be said about Bingham's courage, the outside-right position was still a straight contest between himself and Wright, with the Irishman the junior partner in the arrangement. After four months at Roker Park, Bingham had played seven games for the senior team and Sunderland, for all its multi-talents, was languishing in mid-table, like a bulbous whale, its life blood oozing away. Murray's attempts to staunch the wounds appeared to resuscitate the team until Wright badly injured his knee against Arsenal. With five weeks of the season remaining Bingham became the automatic choice for the outside-right position.

Suddenly Bingham was truly out of the wilderness of the North-Eastern League, yet he couldn't have imagined that the season still had some surprises in store for him. He had made thirteen appearances and scored four goals in his first season in English football. Sunderland eventually finished twelfth and, apart from a friendly with the touring Yugoslav club, Red Star Belgrade, Bingham thought his season was over. The friendly was scheduled for 16 May as part of the Festival of Britain celebrations. Bingham's own festival celebrations began four days earlier, when he returned to Belfast at the behest of the Northern Ireland selectors, who had chosen him for the outside-right position against France.

Sunderland was to the '50s what Manchester United is to the '80s; a rich and prosperous club, with a squad of soccer talent who were household names to a large and vociferous group of supporters – yet their following was frustrated at the inability of the team to bring success to Roker Park. Bingham always advocated that harsh and uncomplimentary vocal criticism on match days erodes and demoralizes a team's confidence, whether it be directed at the players or the management.

Yet the Sunderland supporters singled out Bill Murray's team one by one and hurled abuse from the terraces. A few, including Bingham, escaped this victimization, but none of the players could avoid the atmosphere which pervaded the dressing-room afterwards. Eventually, the unmerciful abuse hit a psychological nerve and a player snapped. Some supporters cannot believe that Ivor Broadis, who later became a successful English international, left the club because of this terrace-power, yet Bingham recounted the aftermath to the barracking which prompted Broadis' transfer request. 'When the game finished Ivor walked off with his head down, almost in tears. Once in the dressing-room, he ripped off his boots, flung them into a corner and said bitterly: "That's the last ball I ever kick for Sunderland."'

This left a profound impression on Bingham. Many years later, when he was manager of Mansfield Town, he picked up this 'terrace-power' theme in his weekly column for the *Chronicle Advertiser*. Plymouth Argyle had been beaten 4–1 at Home Park by Mansfield only a few weeks into the season. It was Mansfield's first league win of the new season and it took a considerable amount of pressure off Bingham himself. His sympathies, however, were with the Plymouth manager, whom Bingham praised for giving 'several promising young players a chance to make their mark. But,' Bingham emphasized, 'the attitude of a section of the club's supporters is not helping matters.'

Bingham said that he appreciated that managers, directors and players expected abuse from the terraces, but the effect was detrimental to the club and a 'hindrance' to players, who certainly wouldn't 'improve their performances or regain their confidence' under such pressure.

'All clubs, no matter what their status, just as all players, no matter what their quality, run into bad patches, when little appears to go right. It is encouragement which is then required, not discouragement, for with firm and loyal support at those times, the lack of form, collectively and individually, would be rectified much more quickly – a fact which many fans fail to realize.'

Back in the '50s, the Sunderland board of directors was trying to appease its own critical followers by giving its manager, Bill Murray, an open chequebook to buy players. Another mediocre season followed in 1951/52 although Bingham enjoyed himself. Tommy Wright's injury kept him out for the full season and Bingham revelled in his role as Sunderland's regular outside-right. As his soccer horizon widened with visits to the grand stadiums of Villa Park, Highbury, Stamford Bridge and Goodison

Park, the encouragement Argus had given him in his early days had dried up. In November 1951 Murray decided to drop Bingham back into the reserves and Argus agreed. 'The resting of Bingham is a good idea,' he wrote. 'He is not fully developed and but for the injury to Wright he would have been only given the occasional run in the senior team.' The supporters, however, enjoyed Bingham's dashing runs and his heroic displays of courage and in nightly letters to the *Sunderland Echo* demanded he be kept in the side. 'Billy was always a favourite with the fans,' said Billy Simmons. 'Although some players had upset the supporters, they never gave Billy any stick and I'm sure if we had had "player of the season" in those days he would have been a winner almost every time.'

While Argus acknowledged that Bingham had become a 'more successful winger' in his first twelve months with the club, he took a pedantic, tough line over the Irishman's style. 'Bingham continually fails to get his body over the ball while centring, with the result that his kicking lacks length,' Argus wrote on one occasion, while using every opportunity he could to boost Wright's claim for his place back on the right wing.

When Wright – against all the odds – recovered from his knee injury, the Sunderland manager put the Scot back on the team-sheet. Instead of dropping Bingham from the right-wing, as Argus and many supporters expected him to do, Murray persevered with the Irishman and put Wright in midfield. Argus praised the decision, but Murray was still unsure and he dropped Bingham back into the reserves the following week. Murray was unhappy with his team, yet the supporters believed he had got the permutation right. At the halfway mark of the '52/53 season, Sunderland were sitting proudly on the pinnacle of the English Football League. Then the cracks started to show. Scunthorpe, then in the old division three (north), came to Roker for the third round of the FA Cup, and with a spirited performance took Sunderland back to their Old Show Ground. Although Sunderland won the replay – Trevor Ford hitting the winning goal after receiving a blow on the ankle which necessitated moving him to the left-wing – the initial draw was the turning point of the season and instead of finishing up with a league-championship medal, Bingham was left to ponder over his nineteen league appearances, following his impressive run of thirty-six appearances in 1951/52.

The Sunderland board were also pondering over the season and how they could improve on it. With Broadis gone and Ford and Shackleton at each other's throats, they made the decision which gave them the indelible title of 'The Bank of England Club'. Like a kid let loose in a toyshop with an unlimited supply of cash Murray raided the squads of the top clubs and, in deals totalling £70,000, ran happily back to Roker Park with three top internationals: Ray Daniel, a Welsh centre-half from Arsenal; Billy Elliott, an outside-right with England, from Burnley; and Jimmy Cowan, the Scottish goalkeeper from Morton. Murray concluded all these deals in one week in June 1953, creating a sensation in the soccer world, in much the same way as if one club today bought Ian Rush of Liverpool, Bryan Robson of Manchester United and Peter Shilton of Southampton over a period of seven days. Sunderland now had eight international players and when the 1953/54 season began against Charlton, on their old Valley ground in south-east London, Sunderland's travelling support had every reason to believe that their new team would begin in style. Instead it was Charlton who turned on the style, winning 5–3. The mood had been set. Billy Simmons said the team 'never got over that defeat' and that the results after that 'would just not come'. The Sunderland supporters were treated to one brief glimpse of what the team could achieve when Arsenal went to Roker Park on 12 September 1953. They left in shame after their heaviest post-war defeat as Ford hit a hat-trick in Sunderland's 7–1 victory. But the following Saturday Sunderland were back to their true selves again, losing 4–1 to Portsmouth at Fratton Park.

Murray was given yet more money to spend, and, in transfers which took Sunderland's total spending for the season to £110,000, he bought Ken Chisholm from Cardiff, Ted Purdon from Birmingham, Joe McDonald from Falkirk and Willie Fraser from Airdrie to Roker Park. Meanwhile, Bingham and

Wright continued their private contest for the outside-right position.

Throughout the '53/54 season the Sunderland supporters continued to pledge their allegiance to Bingham in their nightly letters to the *Echo*. Bingham was still very much part of Murray's plans and although the Irishman was given only nineteen league games that season, the Sunderland manager had great confidence in him. But Bingham was far from Murray's worried mind. His star-studded team had been knocked out of the FA Cup in the third round by Doncaster Rovers, and had narrowly avoided relegation for the first time in the club's history, eventually finishing in eighteenth place. There was no doubt that only the frenzied signings during that winter had kept the club in division one.

Bingham's own analysis of this period is revealing. The Sunderland board, he said, were not to know that players of the calibre of Ford and Shackleton would not reach an understanding and that Billy Elliott, a prolific goal-scorer with Burnley, would lose the knack of hitting the back of the net. But they should have known that by buying Ray Daniel they were drafting an adventurous centre-half into a set-up already founded on attacking wing-halves.

Bingham felt that the national press had been 'unfairly hostile' to Sunderland, ridiculing the team when it was doing badly and resenting its success when it was winning.

It was winning for most of the following two seasons, but the near-miss for the championship in the '54/55 season and the FA Cup runs in 1955 were scant reward for Murray's efforts. He probably never came to appreciate the retrospective compliment that his mid-fifties team was the greatest side never to win the First Division championship.

In successive seasons Sunderland attempted to emulate their neighbour, Newcastle, by forging an exciting and pulsating run to Wembley. Newcastle had won the FA Cup in 1951 and 1952 in impressive style, beating Blackpool and Arsenal respectively. In 1955 the north-east of England was buzzing with the anticipation that there would be a Sunderland–Newcastle final for the first time. Both sides had reached the semi-finals and had avoided each other in the draw. Newcastle faced York and Sunderland were to travel to Birmingham to meet Manchester City at Villa Park.

On the morning of the game Birmingham was deluged by rain, which caused flooding, and more significantly, left the Villa Park pitch waterlogged. The ground staff pumped water off the pitch until minutes before the kick-off, and to the dismay of both teams the game went ahead. Sunderland dominated the first half, but failed to take advantage of their chances. Bingham wasn't expected to perform well in the mud and the pools of water, and they expected even less from Billy Elliott on the other wing. The conditions became worse and gradually City wore down Sunderland's attack. Inevitably, City finally turned one of their many break-aways into a goal, when Bill Spurdle evaded Shackleton's weary challenge and crossed to Roy Clarke, who put the ball in the back of the net. The first ever north-east final was not to be. The Sunderland team was: Willie Fraser; Jack Hedley; Joe McDonald; Stan Anderson; Ray Daniel; George Aiken; Billy Bingham; Charlie Fleming; Ted Purdon; Len Shackleton and Billy Elliott. Sunderland supporters still argue that Murray made a tactical error by excluding Ken Chisholm from the forward line that day and that his height and strength in those conditions would have made the difference. Bingham also believed that Chisholm 'would have been an asset' in the mud. Argus made it known that in his opinion Murray had made a mistake. Despite the inquests, the Wembley dream was over for Sunderland, whose players and supporters believed they would have beaten Newcastle in the final – after all, the supporters argued, they had done the double over Newcastle in the league. Instead the Tynesiders won the Cup for the third time in five years with an emphatic 3–1 victory over City.

The Cup run also appeared to have sapped the team's strength and diverted them from the title challenge. When Sunderland had earlier met Wolves in the sixth round of the FA Cup in March, the two teams shared the top two positions in division one. Bingham, who played what many people believed was his best season for the club, blamed their failure to win the championship on too many drawn games that should have been won. The little Irishman made forty-two appearances in the League and Cup in the '54/55 season and scored nine goals. He would never better that total for Sunderland again. The following year Sunderland reached the semi-final of the Cup again only to lose comprehensively to Birmingham, 3–0. In the League, after a good start, they finished ninth. The storm clouds which had gathered over Villa Park that Saturday in April 1955 were nothing compared to what would happen later.

The 1956/57 season began disastrously for Sunderland, and a series of defeats placed them in the relegation zone. Bingham had been at the club for seven years when he was dropped from Sunderland's team to play Tottenham Hotspur on 1 October 1956. He asked Murray for a transfer. However, Murray was worried that Sunderland's sixty-six-year tenure of the first division was in jeopardy and he dismissed Bingham's impetuous request. Selling his experienced players was the last thing on his mind. The following month he added to the squad, bringing Don Revie from Manchester City, at the cost of £20,000, after lengthy and protracted negotiations with the Lancashire club, who had asked for Bingham as part of the deal. Murray resisted this request, although Bingham was asked by the Sunderland chairman, Bill Ditchburn, if he wanted to go. Bingham said no!

As a player, and subsequently as a manager, Billy Bingham has been directly involved with most of the significant events which have shaped British football since the Second World War. Such are the twists of fate, that probably the most significant of those – in terms of the financial rewards players receive from football – completely changed the direction of Bingham's career. It could also be argued that had it not happened Bingham would not be where he is today.

It all began during the opening days of the new year when two letters, signed by a Mr Smith, arrived at the offices of the Football League, containing serious allegations against Sunderland Football Club. On Sunday, 7 January 1957, Fleet Street ran the story.

Three weeks later a joint Football Association and Football League commission was set up to investigate Sunderland's affairs.

In March, at two venues in Sheffield and York, the commission interviewed manager Bill Murray, club secretary George Crow, chairman Bill Ditchburn, and seven directors. Charges that they had broken the laws of the Football League by making illegal payments to players of approximately £5,000 over five years were made against Ditchburn and one of the directors, Bill Martin. On 10 April the FA made its judgement.

They announced that Sunderland were to be fined £5,000 (the heaviest fine ever imposed by the FA); Ditchburn and Martin were to be permanently banned from football and the players involved had to answer the charges against them. The football world was shocked at the harshness of the FA's decision and over the following three months, all the Sunderland players who had received sums of money, either as extra signing-on fees or as bonuses for the Cup runs, forfeited their qualification for benefit for periods ranging from six months to two years. In Bingham's case this amounted to £75. The commission acknowledged that Murray was a servant of the club and was simply doing as he was told, yet they fined him £200. Understandably, Bill Murray resigned when this was made public and Sunderland began the '57/58 season with a new manager, Alan Brown from Burnley.

Sunderland had been made scapegoats by the football authorities in an attempt to stop the illegal payments which most of the top clubs were making to their players. It was to have the opposite effect. Within five years the maximum signing-on fee and the maximum wage were abolished. Jack Ditchburn, on behalf of his father, and Bill Martin took the FA to court. 'By the time the case was finally heard in the High Court in April 1962,' wrote Simon Inglis,* 'the FA and league had already recognized their mistakes and paid damages out of court to the five players [who had been fined for receiving illegal signing-on money], in return for a

* For a fuller account of the affair see *Soccer In the Dock* by Simon Inglis, (Collins Willow).

pledge that the charges of conspiracy against each member of the commission be dropped. This was agreed. The benefit money was also refunded.' For manager Bill Murray it was too late. His £200 was returned to his widow.

Murray's resignation in the summer of 1957 not only finished him with football, it literally broke his heart. His successor, Alan Brown, also broke a few hearts at Sunderland as he brought an almost ritualistic approach to training at Roker Park and then gradually phased out the 'Bank of England' squad, replacing them with new and significantly younger players.

Brown was a fitness fanatic with a scientific approach to the game, but it was obvious to Bingham and most of the Sunderland players that he did not believe his present squad could adapt easily to his methods. It could be said that Brown was Bingham's nemesis, despite the Irishman's undoubtedly liking Brown's technique. Unfortunately for Bingham, it wasn't mutual, and when the new Sunderland boss bought Irish international inside-forward Ambrose Fogarty from Bingham's old club Glentoran the writing was on the wall. At the end of that year Brown decided to use Fogarty on the right-wing, but to do that he had to drop Bingham.

The Belfast man took this challenge a little more philosophically than he had done when Murray dropped him, perhaps because he felt he could still do a job for Sunderland. Some time later, after a post-training row with Brown, Bingham realized that that might be harder than he imagined. He did not want to leave Sunderland, yet it seemed that the club no longer wanted him, and when Luton Town made a bid for him in July 1958 he decided to go. The manner of his leaving, however, was appropriately bizarre and was probably the catalyst which prompted Bingham to think more carefully about his future in the game.

Bingham believed he had reached the peak of his career in 1958 when George Crow phoned him that summer with the information that Luton had made an offer and asked him if he wanted to go and talk with them. Bingham was undecided, yet, when he tried to talk to Brown, he discovered that the manager was on holiday. Still unsure, Bingham told Crow that he would go down anyway.

On 26 July 1958 Eric Pugh, sports editor of the *Luton Telegraph*, wrote: 'The biggest inward transfer in which Luton have been involved went through with a minimum of fuss and bother on Thursday when Irish international Billy Bingham agreed to become a Luton player.' Bingham, wrote Pugh, had been at the top of the Luton list in their quest for a 'top-class winger'. The transfer negotiations had taken four and a half hours, and Bingham later said that he believed he came as near to putting through his own transfer as any player can. Bingham also believed that Sunderland had been wrong to release him. Fate would determine that the timing of his departure was right, but it is only in hindsight that Bingham could appreciate that.

Billy Bingham in his early playing days at Sunderland (*Sunderland Echo*).

Bingham arriving at Roker Park with Sunderland trainer George Gray on 25 October 1950 (*Sunderland Echo*).

Bingham giving 100 per cent on the right wing for Sunderland (*Sunderland Echo*).

Bingham practises what he preaches. On the wallbars at Sunderland, with Tommy Wright and Dick Davis (*Sunderland Echo*).

The Northern Ireland team that played England at Windsor Park on 4 October 1952:
Standing (left to right): Cunningham, Uprichard, McCourt, Dickson, D'Arcy;
Seated (left to right): Blanchflower, McIlroy, McMorran, McMichael, Bingham, Tully.

Bingham in action against France, 11 November 1952. Played at Colombes Stadium, Paris, the game ended in a 3–1 victory for France. Bingham had made his international début the previous season against France in Belfast.

CHAPTER FOUR

THE DOHERTY INFLUENCE

BILLY'S CAPS

He was a player I cared a lot about because he was playing for me, fighting for me and he was listening to what I was saying when some of the others might have been falling asleep.

Peter Doherty, Northern Ireland manager 1951–62

On Wednesday, 7 November 1962, right-half Jimmy McIlroy came out onto the Windsor Park pitch before Northern Ireland's game against Scotland to thunderous applause. The occasion itself was not particularly pleasing because the Scots went on to win 5–1. For McIlroy though, and more significantly, for Glentoran Football Club it was a momentous event. McIlroy had gained his fiftieth cap, joining Billy Bingham and Danny Blanchflower on the half-century mark, and as they were former Glentoran players the club was celebrating the achievement, which was unparalleled in its history. Sadly, however, it also signalled the end of the Doherty era in Northern Ireland international soccer.

Peter Doherty became Northern Ireland's first manager when he joined the international selectors in 1951. A brilliant wing-half, Doherty, according to Danny Blanchflower, scared the people who ran the Irish Football Association, because 'he was too clever'. Fortunately, not everyone regarded that as a threat and when Harry Cavan, an IFA official with progressive ideas, advocated that Doherty be given responsibility for the selection of the Northern Ireland team, the suggestion was not scorned. 'Before Doherty came in as manager,' said Blanchflower, 'we used to lose by eight and nine goals because the selectors would change five or six players every game. Now we didn't have that many players, but they dug them up from somewhere and they were never given a second chance. Doherty, as a player, understood that it took a while to settle players in, and so he persuaded the committee to give the younger players a chance.'

Those younger players included Bingham and McIlroy, both of whom had impressed Doherty at Glentoran and later at Sunderland and Burnley respectively. Referring to Bingham, Doherty said: 'When you look at this type of player you say that one is going somewhere. Billy was the type of player who would stand out in any game because of the energy he had ... He had determination. It was written all over Billy when he was on the field. When a manager is looking at players, he knows the ones he can depend on, and the ones who are a bit touchy. Billy was my man.'

Billy was Doherty's man because he did what his manager told him. Bingham listened intently to the Doherty theory of football in the dressing-room and then religiously put it into practice on the field. 'Billy always had the potential of what I was looking for in a wing-forward and in those days you could look at a player and see his development in two or three years,' said Doherty.

Bingham's development over his early international years meant that Doherty also had a winger who would double as an extra fullback. Doherty never allowed any passengers in his team, particularly his wing-forwards. 'I wanted the wingers to become part of the team,' he said. 'In other words, if a member of the opposition takes a throw-in and throws it to one of his players and that player passes it back to him, I used to cut that out. I would have Billy standing on the free man. I wanted everybody to be marked and marked tightly because if they are tight they can't go through you.'

Bingham has said that Doherty had the 'greatest influence' over his career. 'He kept picking me for thirteen years. He had credibility with the players and I was quite impressionable as a youngster. He was a very inspiring talker, inspiring leader, and I knew he liked me and I responded to him,' said Bingham.

'I would say possibly that is true,' reflects Doherty today. 'Billy was a lad who wanted to go places. In my opinion Billy Bingham is a dedicated professional and when you have a dedicated pro-

fessional you have a good player. He was a fitness fanatic and that
was one thing that stood out when he was on the field. He would
run for ever.'

Bingham made his debut for Northern Ireland in a 2–2 draw
with France in a Festival of Britain game on 12 May 1951. For
most players such an occasion would have been extremely intimidating yet Bingham turned it to his advantage, to such a degree
that the opposing full-back that day, Roger Marche, later described the Irishman as the best forward he had ever played
against, on the evidence of that game. The local papers also lauded
the nineteen-year-old's debut. 'This was Bingham's match,' said
the *Ireland Saturday Night*. 'No player has filled the Irish right-
wing position better this season or last,' said the *Belfast Newsletter*.
They were right, and for ten years Bingham would hold on to the
number seven shirt to establish a record-breaking sequence of
forty-three consecutive caps, a sequence only broken on 12 April
1961 because Everton would refuse to release the Irishman for a
game against Wales.

Bingham's international career is not remarkable because of
Doherty's faith in him, but because he was part of a team which
grew up together and became, according to Belfast sports writer
Malcolm Brodie, the most talented team ever to come out of the
north. 'We had a variety of talents,' said Danny Blanchflower,
'who weren't all world-class, but they came together. I think it
was as much fate as it was our own ability to do it. We had limited
numbers, but necessity is the mother of invention and if we had
had all big players we wouldn't have had all these qualities. I
think Peter Doherty was the start of all that.'

'All that' meant Northern Ireland's legendary triumph in their
first World Cup finals in Sweden in 1958 when Doherty's team
narrowly failed to reach the last four.

Somewhat modestly, Bingham has said that if he had been born
in a country with a wider choice of players he would have been
dropped early in his international career. That is probably true
because, on Bingham's own admission, he 'played badly enough
to deserve to be dropped' on many occasions. In his second

international, against Scotland in Windsor Park, in October 1951, the local soccer reporters wrote that Bingham 'had a patchy sort of day'. Perhaps there was a lack of confidence on Bingham's part because his opponent in the Scottish left-back position was Sammy Cox, the player who had given him a hard time a year earlier in the inter-league game, before his transfer to Sunderland. 'There was a backwardness in his play,' wrote one reporter. 'He wasn't just the same bundle-of-energy Billy.'

Peter Doherty was player-manager with Doncaster Rovers when he was appointed to the part-time Northern Ireland post. If Bingham had played poorly in those early internationals it would not be long before Doherty would instil confidence in the young winger's game. Bertie Peacock, another of Bingham's former Glentoran team-mates and the man who replaced Doherty as Northern Ireland manager in 1962, said that many of the players came under Doherty's spell. 'I think anybody could learn from him,' said Peacock. 'Peter Doherty was different from his time, different in style, and he was a strict disciplinarian. As a manager Billy now has many of Peter's habits. He keeps them together and goes with his players and he doesn't complain if he has a bad result.'

With a policy which encouraged Ireland's younger talents, Doherty gradually built a team which had the self-belief to beat teams that had previously hammered Ireland out of sight. 'One of Peter's first recommendations,' said Danny Blanchflower, 'was why should we be defending, when we are losing by eight or nine goals; why don't we attack and lose by eight or nine; so we became an attacking force and surprised many teams.'

Realistically, Doherty had no intention of allowing an Irish team under his tuition to lose by such high scores and in his first three years as manager he devised a tactical system, which Bingham has since used effectively for the modern team. Tactics at free-kicks, covers and throw-ins, were worked out to a fine art. However, Doherty's greatest asset was not simply tactics and set-pieces, it was his ability to motivate players to work for each other. 'What Peter wanted was loyalty to the cause. If you keep playing while you have the right to play then you're loyal,' said Danny Blanchflower.

There is no doubt that Northern Ireland under Bingham is not that different friom Northern Ireland under Doherty. Pre-match team talks, said Bingham, 'kindled a will to win in the team'. These talks were not without humour. With so many characters in the Ireland squad in the '50s Doherty didn't always get the response he wanted. Jimmy McIlroy remembers one pre-match talk when Doherty was attempting to stress the importance of tackling. 'He was really frothing at the mouth and getting us worked up about tackling, about getting stuck in, saying, "I want BITE in the tackle." Danny suddenly looked up and said, "Peter, they're bringing a new boot out next month which will suit you; they're having false teeth built into the toe-caps."'

That Blanchflower was able to mock Doherty's team talks was symptomatic of the spirit the manager had instilled in the team. Danny and Jackie Blanchflower, Bingham, McIlroy and Peacock were all players Doherty could trust to do the job that was required of them on the pitch. In Danny Blanchflower, Doherty had a captain who could make his tactics and particularly his set-pieces work. 'Peter used to say, "We've got to get it right on the field. If we make mistakes it doesn't matter. You have the authority on the field," so I started getting these set-pieces together. Jimmy McIlroy helped a good deal. He was inside-right and Billy was outside-right and I was behind them. That was the triangle that began to get everything going.

'I thought the mainstay of our team was the triangle. Peter gave me the authority which most managers wouldn't have, because they would have wanted to run it themselves. He had been an individualist himself so he realized that we would have to do it because he couldn't come out onto the pitch,' remembers Blanchflower.

Unlike the triangles Bingham now uses very effectively in the modern team, Doherty did not devise the tactic. 'They were like three brothers,' he said. 'They had a great something between them, that no one else seemed to have and they loved each other.

If one got fouled badly you could see the others looking for the bloke that did it. That was the great quality they had. I encouraged it but I didn't encourage them to kick, just to chase the other player and at the right time use his head.' This almost telepathic understanding was not missed by the soccer writers or by the supporters, who fondly remember the success of the triumvirate and their ability to torment opposing teams.

Between 1951 and 1958 Doherty's team became the tormentor rather than the tormented. Opposing teams were no longer allowed the luxury of eight- and nine-goal wins over Ireland. Doherty's first two seasons as Northern Ireland boss did not halt the run, which had seen the Irish fail to win a game since October 1947, but then came a 2–2 draw with England in Belfast in the 1952–53 season. Ireland were winning, with a few minutes remaining, and the Irish players regarded the final result as a victory. When the British championship began in 1954 it was obvious that Ireland were becoming a formidable force and over the following two years Doherty's team recorded two wins, three draws and four defeats. This compared with two draws and seven defeats over the previous nine games.

It was during this period that Bingham began scoring the goals which would take him to a grand total of ten in his international career – two less than the record held by Billy Gillespie and Joe Bambrick. One of Bingham's earliest goals for Ireland is remembered by McIlroy. 'We were playing Scotland and the ball went to the Scottish goalkeeper. He looked up to see who to give it to when Bingy suddenly realized that he was hidden behind the full-back. Bingy was aware that the keeper was looking that way so he actually made himself smaller and for that second or two the keeper thought that the full-back was in the clear and he rolled the ball to him; Bingy nipped around the back, got the ball and stuck it in the net.'

The World Cup qualifying draw for the 1958 World Cup had put Northern Ireland in the same group with Portugal and Italy. On 16 January 1957 Bingham volleyed Northern Ireland's first World Cup goal against Portugal in Lisbon. The game ended in a

1–1 draw yet a result such as that, even in the modern era would be regarded as a moral victory. In 1957 it was more than that; it was the beginning of a sequence of results which would take Doherty's team to the pinnacle of World Cup soccer, in Sweden in the summer of 1958, and two shared British championships in the '57/58 and '58/59 seasons.

Bingham particularly remembers two games from that period, against England at Wembley on 6 November 1957 and against Wales in Belfast on 22 April 1959. Doherty's team had been threatening to give someone a football lesson when the England game came around. However, few believed that an England team consisting of their greatest-ever footballers would be on the end of the 3–2 scoreline, which gave Ireland their first victory over England for thirty years. Doherty remembers that Ireland just 'clicked' against the likes of Duncan Edwards, Roger Byrne and Tommy Taylor of Matt Busby's great Manchester United team; Billy Wright of Wolverhampton; Don Howe of West Bromwich Albion and Johnny Haynes of Fulham. Ireland's team was: Gregg (Manchester United), Keith, McMichael (both Newcastle United), Danny Blanchflower (Tottenham Hotspur), Jackie Blanchflower (Manchester United), Peacock (Celtic), Bingham (Sunderland), McCrory (Southend United), Simpson (Rangers), McIlroy (Burnley), McParland (Aston Villa).

The England result was a tactical victory for Doherty, yet perhaps the best football was played against Wales almost two years later. In many ways the Wales result was more surprising than the England result because it came after that Ireland team had peaked. Their World Cup sojourn had ended with a 4–0 defeat in the quarter-finals, a result which had flattered the winners, France. But if Bingham learned much during his international days under Doherty he learned a great deal more about European football from Ireland's experience in Sweden.

Northern Ireland were drawn in the same group as Czecho-slovakia, West Germany and Argentina and the Irish FA had arranged for the seventeen-man squad to live in Tylosand, which Bingham described as 'on the Swedish Riviera. Our hotel overlooked a splendid beach and for training we had a secluded pitch in the middle of a wood.' Halmstad, the nearest major town, was the venue for Ireland's opening game against Czechoslovakia.

During his seven years as boss of the Irish team, Doherty had been able to field a settled team in defence, midfield and on the wings. His problem was that Northern Ireland did not have a natural striker. To alleviate this problem, Doherty decided to take the then unprecedented step of playing two forwards, which also allowed him to play the now more modern 4–4–2 formation.

That Northern Ireland reached the quarter-finals of the World Cup was due to the same determination and dedication Bingham now demands from his present squad of players. Tactically, Sweden was a disaster. Against Czechoslovakia, Doherty's double-spearhead of Derek Dougan and Wilbur Cush was ineffective because Dougan found it difficult to adjust to an unfamiliar position. Doherty's plan to play his wingers deep, with Bertie Peacock and Peter McParland in defensive roles, and McIlroy and Danny Blanchflower the midfield links would probably have worked had Dougan not fought against his manager's instructions. In the end Doherty allowed Dougan to roam free and Ireland narrowly scraped through with a one-goal victory. Bingham wasn't impressed. 'Dougan was always a law unto himself and hated being told what to do,' he said. The lesson stuck; Bingham is now loath to tolerate undisciplined players in the present Northern Ireland team. He also makes sure that his players are capable of carrying out his instructions. No player is asked to do something that is alien to him.

In the next game, three days later, at the same venue, Doherty's double-spearhead plan was exposed again when Argentina played a 4–2–4 formation and went on to win 3–1, despite losing an early goal to Ireland. The Irish had been told that the South Americans were likely to fall apart once in arrears, but no such thing happened. It was another lesson that Bingham would not forget.

Against West Germany, whom the Irish had to beat to qualify for the last eight, the tactics didn't matter. Every Irish player ran his heart out and Harry Gregg's magnificent performance in goal helped Ireland to a 2–2 draw. It didn't seem to be enough, but then the Irish heard that the Czechs had hammered the erratic South Americans 6–1 and earned a play-off – with Northern Ireland.

On 17 June 1958, Northern Ireland travelled to Malmo where they beat Czechoslovakia for the second time in the tournament. Malcolm Brodie wrote that the result, which took Northern Ireland into the last eight of the World Cup at their first attempt, was a 'wonderful achievement for a country so small and with such a limitation of players'. The *Belfast Telegraph* reporter also wrote that Ireland had eight players on the injured list but, despite that, everyone 'sang and joked' during the 110-mile journey from Malmo back to their headquarters outside Halmstad. However, not everyone was happy. 'It was unbelievable,' said Jimmy McIlroy. 'We had the play-off on the Tuesday night in Malmo and that was a long way from where we were staying, yet we had to journey down there to play an evening match; instead of stopping, we made the long journey back, three or four hours by coach, so we got back in the middle of the night – on Wednesday morning. After breakfast we set off to travel right across Sweden by coach, and we were virtually all day in the bus and then we had to play France the next day. The arrangements were diabolical and I think it was really hammered home to Billy then how important it is to make the proper arrangements. We had one or two players who weren't fit to play at all and there seemed to be three or four players who needed at least three days to get over their knocks and get back to full fitness.'

The team which Doherty selected for the French game had only two changes from the play-off side, but the 210-mile trip to Norrkoping, the venue for the quarter-final with France, had sapped the energies of his half-fit players. Doherty recalled Harry Gregg in goal, despite not being fully fit, and Tommy Casey, who had eight stitches in his right leg from an injury he had received in the German game, was put on the right-wing. Ireland, who had played five games in ten days, were up against a team who had rested the previous four days and were familiar with the venue.

Bingham would remember Sweden. Northern Ireland would not lose in Spain or Mexico because the arrangements were poor or the tactics were wrong.

CHAPTER FIVE

HEART AND FIRE

BINGHAM THE FOOTBALLER

When I first saw him play I thought he was just a runner, but he became a good player in the end.

Joe Mercer, former England manager

The three Hungarian football officials had waited patiently in the lounge of the fogbound London airport terminal building for seven hours when an official from the English Football Association informed them that their vigil was useless and arrangements were being made to send them home. It was just before two o'clock on Wednesday, 4 December 1957. In Windsor Park, Belfast, a crowd of 35,000 passed rumours around the ground that the referee had not arrived and that the World Cup game they had come to watch, between Ireland and Italy, was in jeopardy. Kick-off was minutes away when the public-address system crackled with the voice of the Irish FA secretary, Billy Drennan. There was a sombre hush as he explained that the referee and two linesmen had not arrived and announced that the two teams would play a friendly instead. Drennan's voice was immediately drowned as the crowd stamped their feet and jeered in disapproval and disappointment.

A few minutes later the teams ran out and the band struck up the British national anthem. Danny Blanchflower remembers that the crowd 'went mad when they heard it wasn't going to be a World Cup game and it was only going to be a friendly. They thought they had been cheated and when they played the national anthem they all kept silent, but when the Italian national anthem was played – the crowd had never heard it before – they were screaming and going mad about the match and the Italians thought it was their anthem the crowd was booing, so they got the needle and started clobbering us on the field. It was far from friendly.'

Ireland, wrote a local reporter, 'got going like demons, throwing their full weight at the Italian defence' and for thirty minutes they bombarded their illustrious European opponents, with Billy Bingham involved in most of the raids. Then, against the run of play, Italy scored. Three minutes later Bingham set up Wilbur Cush and Ireland were level. The reporter wrote: 'The green shirts owned the penalty area and had the Italian defence kicking anywhere and everywhere – including at the Irish players. It was tough stuff.'

Bingham, on the right-wing, was at the heart of everything that Ireland threw at the Italians. For the crowd, despite the bad start, it was thrilling entertainment; for the players there was never a dull moment.

Ireland had been lining up their forwards at the far post for corner kicks, and this unsettled the Italian defence. On one occasion the Italian centre-half, Ferrario, lost his patience and instead of going for the ball he jumped into the waiting Irish forwards. Tommy Mitchell, the replacement referee, gave Ireland a free-kick and the Italians lined up a defensive wall.

'They hadn't seen a wall until we had played there earlier that year,' said Blanchflower, 'but now they were putting one up themselves. We'd gone there in April and they were back in December with our own tactics as they had sent their scouts to watch us play England a few weeks before. They put the wall up but it was only a yard from the ball and the referee was going red in the face. The Italians took no notice of him so Bingy just went up and tried to push the wall back, but their centre-half – a big, strong, tough guy – caught Bingy by the collar and threw him onto the path which surrounded the pitch.'

Bingham, a little dazed, got up and eventually the kick was taken. It would be the only time the Italians got the better of him. Neither would they intimidate him in the replayed game the following January, when Ireland won to qualify for the World Cup finals in Sweden.

The Italian friendly was Bingham's twenty-sixth consecutive cap since May 1951. Peter Doherty's belief that a winger should not 'just sail the wing and play football' had made Bingham an automatic choice for the number seven shirt. Bingham had known since his early days at Sunderland that he was not in the class of Tommy Lawton, Stanley Matthews and Tom Finney, and that to succeed he had to work hard at both the practical and the theoretical side of the game. 'He was a thinker,' said former England manager Joe Mercer. 'He became a mature, quality player but he wasn't a natural kind of player.'

While Bingham did not possess those ball skills, he was an instinctive winger, orthodox in style, which meant he had the ability to beat full-backs with a combination of clever control and coordinated speed, and then deliver incisive and menacing crosses or direct shots. It also meant he could poach goals with his lightning pace, by turning up in the six-yard area, seemingly from nowhere.

Ron Henry, a defender with Tottenham Hotspur's double winning team of 1961, said that Bingham 'delighted in cutting inside the full-back and turning the defence. I only ever spotted one weakness and that was something he could do little about. He was not robust, so some defenders tried to intimidate him physically. It rarely worked though, he was a gutsy little player.' That quality, to get off his backside and fight back, endeared Bingham to the supporters of all the teams he played for in England. They also appreciated his willingness to come up laughing every time. Bingham, they realized, clearly enjoyed his football.

As a teenager Bingham had made his reputation as a brave forward who scored goals against all adversity. Throughout his formative footballing years, when he played in several positions at schoolboy and youth international level and at centre-forward for Co-op Rec, soccer reporters wrote of his 'dash and enthusiasm' and 'clever individual play'.

After a youth international between Ireland and England at Solitude, in Belfast, on 15 May 1948, a reporter, from the *Ireland Saturday Night*, described Bingham's performance as 'a delight to watch'. Bingham, he wrote, was 'snappy, tricky and tireless – the outstanding man of the day'. Others who watched the game remember that Bingham did not have it easy against the powerful and towering English backs and it was only perseverence and stubbornness which finally cracked his markers. The blond-haired, lithe figure of the Irish sixteen-year-old gave the English defenders no quarter, and when one of them failed to clear a punt into their half Bingham raced in to score with a rasping shot, which belied his strength. At half-time Ireland led the previously unbeaten English youths 1–0. The reporter wrote: 'The mercurial Bingham was posing problem after problem for Leake, the head taller and stones heavier English pivot.' The game ended in a 2–2 draw but Bingham had impressed a lot of influential soccer people. They would watch his development in the Glentoran senior team in the hope that he would mature into a player capable of withstanding the pressures and rigours of the modern game. They need not have worried; Bingham knew where he was going and knew what to do when he got there.

Bingham got there two and a half years later when he joined Sunderland and immediately discovered that he was not the complete footballer he thought he was. He had been taught the rudiments of the game by John Geary and Tony Wilkins at Glentoran, where he had been moved from his schoolboy position of centre-forward to right-wing because of his light build. When Bingham arrived at Roker Park and witnessed Sunderland's impressive array of football talent he realized that he only had the ability of an average player. He began to train furiously to make up for his shortcomings. In fact, Bingham's obsession with physical fitness went back to his Belfast days. During his college years he had met Buster McShane, a young lad smitten by the body-building bug. Bingham and McShane set up a small studio in Ballyhackamore, in the suburbs of east Belfast, and started a weight-training and body-building club. Bingham had been able to improve his physique using weights and when he moved to Sunderland he joined the local YMCA and continued his Belfast training programme. Bingham's team-mates at Glentoran had marvelled at his tenacious approach to fitness. 'He was a ball of fire, with loads of enthusiasm and because he was built lightly he was always improving himself,' remembers Bertie Peacock. Bingham knew that if he was to succeed in English football his natural speed and courage would not be enough.

When Billy Bingham's playing career ended in the spring of 1964, after he had broken his leg following a collision with a Brentford defender, he had recorded 419 league games and 103 goals for Sunderland, Luton Town, Everton and Port Vale between December 1950 and April 1964. He had been capped at schoolboy, youth and senior international level, played twice for the Irish League, and finished with the impressive total of fifty-six caps and ten goals; an incredible achievement for a player who had started with limited ability and became, according to soccer writer Brian Glanville, 'one of the most effective outside-rights to play in British football since the war'.

Very few soccer observers believed that Bingham was a world-class player and neither was he regarded as Ireland's greatest outside-right, 'not with the likes of George Best and Davy Cochrane around', said Malcolm Brodie, who reported on all Bingham's international games as a player. 'He was not a world-class winger, he was on the periphery, and to get where he got, he did it with sheer dedication and professionalism.'

It was that dedication and professionalism which Luton Town benefited from when Bingham signed for them in the summer of 1958, after he had fallen out of favour with the new Roker Park boss, Alan Brown. After almost eight full seasons with Sunderland and no success, Bingham went to Kenilworth Road and stayed for only two seasons, yet he left with a lot of happy memories and an FA Cup Runners-Up medal. There was no doubt in anyone's mind, including Bingham's, that his two years at Luton were his best.

In the introduction to Bingham's autobiography, *Soccer with the Stars*, Glanville wrote that Bingham at Luton was 'no longer a star among a team of stars, as he was at Sunderland and was to be at Everton, but a star refulgent among largely obscure players'.

Bingham, wrote Glanville, was expected to perform and 'his part in Luton's Cup run, when they surprised the football world by reaching the Cup final, was decisive'.

Joe Mercer described Bingham as a ''50s kind of player', implying that the Irishman's penchant for positive soccer reflected the manner in which the game was played then. However, Bingham was not content with the orthodox style. 'He was a very neat, precise winger with good control and the ability to drag defenders away into a corner and then suddenly cut away or, with a pass, take out the defender completely,' said Robert Armstrong. 'He was very modern in his style of play and won back balls. He would drop back and cut out passes from the wing half to the winger and he made it his business to do this and counter-attack.'

Bingham was a fast, progressive winger whom Luton hoped would enhance their standing as a first division club after many years in the lower divisions. Although Luton had finished eighth in the first division in 1957/58, the season prior to Bingham's arrival, they had no significant honours to boast of, except the 1936/37 Division Three (South) championship. On the Saturday after Bingham's signing the soccer writer of the *Luton Telegraph* wrote: 'In considering their wants, the Town have borne in mind the crying need for directness on the wings and Bingham is just the type to supply it on the right.'

Bingham made thirty-six league appearances for Luton Town in his first season and scored eight goals as the club attempted to improve on their position of the previous season. After two months of the new season Luton, with Syd Owen – a former England international – at the centre of the defence, Allan Brown, Gordon Turner and Bingham in attack, seemed capable of doing just that, as they topped the first division. Then Luton very decidedly lost their grip in the top rung of the Football League and their manager, Dally Duncan, during the first two weeks of October. Owen, by then one of the FA's bright young coaches, had announced his retirement for the end of the '58/59 season, and he was offered the job of caretaker manager. Luton's problems did not ease and by Christmas they were in mid-table with nineteen points from twenty games.

Bingham, however, was enjoying his football and despite some apprehension about his early performances from the supporters and the press, everyone expected great deeds from him. They got their first glimpse of what was to come when Bingham scored twice in Luton's 6–3 victory over Arsenal at Kenilworth Road, on 26 December 1958. Less than a fortnight later he hit another two goals as Luton beat Leeds United 5–1 in the third round of the FA Cup. Bingham and Luton had stated their intentions for the remainder of the season but it wasn't until they came back from Filbert Street, where the little Irishman had moved to centre-forward and scored the equalizer which brought Leicester City back to Kenilworth Road, that anyone thought a Cup run was a credible possibility. Bingham was in top form and his non-stop running, precision crosses, bubbly presence and goals were taking Luton to Wembley.

In the replay Leicester were dismissed in contemptuous fashion, as were Ipswich Town in the fifth round at Portman Road, where Bingham scored again. Luton were in the quarter-finals and Bingham had scored in each round! Blackpool at Bloomfield Road were in Luton's path to the semi-finals for the first time in their history and when Bingham scored in the second half it looked as though both the Irishman and his club were writing themselves into the record books. Then Blackpool equalized when the Luton left-back, Ken Hawkes, mis-hit a back-pass and let Ray Charnley through to score. Luton took their opponents back to Kenilworth Road and in a game which Bingham described as one of the hardest matches of their season, Allan Brown scored the goal which took them into a semi-final encounter with third division Norwich.

Norwich City were also in the semi-finals for the first time in their history; this and their lowly status made them the romantics' choice for Wembley. On the Monday after the game the *Daily Telegraph* soccer reporter, Donald Saunders, suggested, after the teams had drawn 1–1 at White Hart Lane, that the Norwich manager had two problems. One, he wrote, was 'the menace of Billy Bingham', and the other was manager-elect, Syd Owen. 'There is little doubt', he wrote, 'that Bingham's Irish magic all but caused Norwich City's historic Cup run to splutter tamely to its end before half-time. During those first comparatively quiet forty-five minutes, Bingham seemed to be the most dangerous winger in British football. No one in that hardworking Norwich defence could control the fleet-footed, quick-thinking little Irishman as he danced down the wing and curled the ball menacingly into the penalty area with ever-increasing frequency. And worse still, from the Norwich point of view, was the effect Bingham's mastery had on the rest of the Luton forwards.' Saunders concluded with the advice to Norwich that 'they keep a wary eye' on Bingham in the replay.

Norwich probably took the reporter's advice. Unfortunately, an eye wasn't enough. On Thursday, 19 March 1959, Eric Pugh of the *Luton News* celebrated Bingham's performance in his report of the replay. His report read:

At precisely 4.12 p.m. yesterday another page in Luton Town's long history was made. It was at that moment that referee Bill Hickson sounded the final whistle on this pulsating, drama-packed FA Cup semi-final replay at St Andrews, and heralded Luton into the Wembley final for the first time.

And the man that made this possible was the Town's magnificent, tiny Irish international right-winger, Billy Bingham. It was wee Billy, in the fifty-fifth minute, who endorsed the Town's passport to Wembley with one of the best goals I have seen – the only one of the match. In attack Billy Bingham was again the man who took the eye. He gave Norwich skipper Ron Ashman the run-around throughout the match and often popped inside to take a crack at goal. It was Bingham's inclination to wander inside that brought that vital goal.

This is how it came. George Cummins moved into a Luton ball midway inside the Norwich half, and then slung a long pass out to Bob Morton, who had exchanged positions with Bingham. Bob, standing on the extreme right, saw his chance and wasted no time in pushing through an immaculate pass that caught the whole Norwich defence on the wrong foot. Bingham streaked between two Norwich defenders and cracked the ball on the volley into the roof of the Norwich net. Don't blame South African goalkeeper Sandy Kennon for missing this one. It was the sort of shot that would beat any goalkeeper.

Bingham scored six goals in Luton's eight-game march to the final and, more significantly, he scored in every round, to equal the record then held by Stanley Mortenson. Sadly, Bingham would not break it as Nottingham Forest carried off the F A Cup for the second time, winning 2–1, even after their right-winger, Roy Dwight, had been carried off with a broken leg.

Luton failed to match Forest and Bingham said that he felt more 'like a spectator than a player' as the Nottinghamshire team tore through Syd Owen's beleaguered defence with football which the newspapers described as 'dazzling, brilliant', assisted by the 'fast and controlled attacking skills from Stewart Imlach and Roy Dwight'. Forest had surged into a two-goal lead when Dwight was injured on the half-hour. Bingham, whose short corner led to Luton's only goal, believed his team should have been more positive. Not surprisingly, he was disappointed that he did not break the individual scoring record and that Luton had not played better on the day; an F A Cup-loser's medal was scant reward for almost ten years in the top division of the English Football League.

Bingham's goal-scoring record at Luton had improved from his days with Sunderland and his ratio of thirty goals in eighty-five League and Cup games for the Bedfordshire club made him a target for several managers when Luton were relegated at the end of the '59/60 season. He scored twice in five second division games when Luton visited Anfield on the evening of Wednesday, 7 September 1960. Among the spectators that night was Everton manager Johnny Carey, placidly puffing at his pipe in his seat in the stand. When Bingham took possession of the ball about thirty-five yards out from the Liverpool goal Carey was not alone in his wonderment when the Irishman drew back his right foot and rifled in a shot which hit the net as if it had come from a crossbow rather than the boot of a footballer. The Liverpool *Daily Post* reporter, Horace Yates, wrote that Liverpool 'goalkeeper Bert Slater has never been more comprehensively beaten and for a minute or more afterwards the crowd buzzed with this shot of a lifetime'. Bingham said later that he found the crowd's reaction to the goal very eerie. Carey didn't, and when a proposed move which would have taken Bingham to Arsenal in exchange for two players broke down, the Everton manager put his own proposal to Luton and Bingham. On 10 October 1960 – almost ten years to the day of Bingham's signing for Sunderland from Glentoran – Luton agreed to Everton's terms of John Bramwell, Alec Ashworth and £15,000 for Bingham. Five days later the Irishman made his debut on the right-wing for Everton against Fulham at Craven Cottage. To facilitate Bingham's arrival, Carey asked his regular right-winger, Micky Lill, to move to the other wing. Lill was joint top scorer for Everton and Yates wrote that 'Everton now possess the most goal-worthy pair of wingers they have had for many a long year.' Fulham certainly had no cause to disagree, for the Irishman had hit three goals against them in their two League games with Luton the previous season.

Bingham's style suited Everton and he blended quickly and easily into the team, establishing a good relationship with his right-midfield colleague, Bobby Collins. Everton were in contention for the title until Christmas that season, when Tottenham Hotspur came to Goodison Park and won 2–1. The London club went on to win the League and Cup double while Everton failed to win any of their festive season fixtures and then lost to the Second Division leaders, Sheffield United, in the third round of the FA Cup a few days into the new year. Yet there was a lot of talent in the Everton team and Bingham also built up a good understanding with the Scottish international full-back, Alex Parker. Bingham later said that Parker was the finest full-back he had ever played with.

The feeling, perhaps not surprisingly, was mutual. 'He's probably the best winger I've played with,' said Parker. 'I could read him and he could read me and that's why we played well together.' There was one occasion, Parker recalls, when he realized that Bingham was not a player who would tolerate selfishness. 'I'd pulled a hamstring against Tottenham and I was playing outside-right because we had already lost a player and I couldn't be taken off. The ball came across to me when I was on the wing and at about the six-yard box I had a go myself; I wanted to score against Bill Brown, but he saved it and Bingy was screaming at me, that I should have passed it back to him and he would have had an open goal. He had already scored and we were winning 3–0 but he was a straightforward player, he wasn't a messer.'

Strangely, the one time Bingham did mess was while he was with Everton and it put a massive blemish on his otherwise un-soiled playing career: he was sent off twice during the club's appearance in an international tournament in North America in the summer of 1961. The diminutive winger was sent off for the first time in his career in Montreal when he retaliated against a player who had attempted to head-butt him. A couple of weeks later, Everton moved south to New York for the second stage of the tournament. Once again Bingham was provoked when the left-back with Bangu, a Brazilian club, kicked him and then clung on to his shirt. That Belfast temper surfaced and Bingham was promptly ordered off. The irony is that Everton had played the same team in April that year and refused to release Bingham for Northern Ireland's game with Wales. It would have been his forty-fourth consecutive appearance.

Bingham had played under two managers at Sunderland in eight years, three at Luton Town in two and a half years and when Everton's new chairman, John Moores, unceremoniously sacked Johnny Carey in April 1961 and appointed Harry Catterick, there was a feeling among several players that if the results didn't come it wouldn't be just the manager who would suffer. When Bingham started his first full season with Everton, in August 1961, it was clear to many that Catterick would break up Carey's team. Happily the Belfastman's playing days in the first division would end with a league championship medal, despite making only twenty-three appearances in Everton's title-winning team of '62/63.

Catterick bought the Rangers' and Scotland winger, Alex Scott, for £40,000 in February 1963 and that ominous feeling Bingham felt about his place in the team at Sunderland when Alan Brown bought Ambrose Fogarty surfaced again. Catterick had considered doing what Carey had done when Bingham arrived; move his outside-right to the other wing but that did not appeal to the Irishman, who knew he could not settle in an unfamiliar position; reserve-team football did not appeal either. 'I would only be slightly affected financially if relegated to the second eleven but that type of football is not for me. I am looking at [Scott's signing] merely as a challenge and I am prepared to battle for my place,' said Bingham. He added that he would let events run their course. They did.

That natural progression took Bingham east, across the country, in June 1963 to the Potteries and down into the third division, to Port Vale, where he suffered a tragic end to his playing career – a broken leg after only fourteen minutes in a league game the following spring. It might have been different. In January 1964 he had turned down a £12,000 transfer back into the first division with Nottingham Forest. His refusal to break his contract with Port Vale was symptomatic of his professionalism and loyalty. Bingham had given the English Football League fourteen years of his life. He was thirty-two.

CHAPTER SIX

LILLESHALL

BINGHAM THE COACH

I don't think that negative football will ever be as interesting as positive football, but that's the way most teams are playing and it's the majority who rule. It's easier to defend than it is to attack.

Danny Blanchflower

Billy Bingham completed his teenage years as a bewildered young man under the guidance of a professional football club. It was summer 1951, a year after England had suffered a humiliating defeat by the United States in the Brazil World Cup finals, and a year before Lilleshall was established as a national sports centre, initially for athletics and football.

England's failure in the 1950 World Cup disconcerted many people outside the game; it did not shock Bingham and, more significantly, people like Stanley Rous, who led a small group of men inside the Football Association who were determined to revolutionize the way the game was being run. When the young Irishman arrived at Roker Park he was astounded by the traditions which dictated how impressionable, yet immature, young players learned the game. 'When I first came to England to play in the Football League I quickly made two discoveries that astonished me. One was that I had so many weaknesses and faults in my play and the other was that there was no one at Sunderland to point them out to me and see that I put them right,' said Bingham.

Fortunately, Bingham was not the only person in football who felt this way about the game. Higher up, in the offices of the FA, Stanley Rous was advocating a need for development in football coaching. Walter Winterbottom had been appointed the FA's director of coaching immediately after the war, and when the South African government made a gift of Lilleshall to Britain as a memorial to World War II, Rous was able to initiate a coaching scheme which would placate those players who thought the British game was stagnating. Those who didn't think there was anything wrong with the British game had their illusions shattered the following year when Hungary brought a brand of skilful soccer to Wembley that nobody had believed existed outside Britain and thrashed England 6–3. Six months later, when England went to Budapest, Hungary wrote the final epitaph when they won 7–1. British football would never be the same again.

Allen Wade, a former director of coaching, remembers that in the early '50s professional players were the prisoners of their own experiences. 'The training of professionals was ludicrous. I was trained as a marathon runner, not as a footballer,' he said. Bingham remembers his own training at Roker Park with equal disdain and he had to improve the physical side of his football outside the club. As for playing skill, Bingham said he learned that by 'painful experience'.

Lilleshall was one of several coaching centres established in the '50s for the improvement of the game. However, it differed from the others because it was a summer course for players who wanted to achieve the FA's coaching badge. Situated in the heart of rural England, approximately twenty miles from Wolverhampton, Lilleshall is a centuries-old home of the aristocracy. In 1952 the house and some 150 acres became the National Recreation Centre and in conjunction with the Sports Council (then the Central Council of Physical Recreation) the Football Association invited players from all over the world to enter the courses.

Bingham was with Luton Town when he sent off his ten shillings (50p) registration fee, and on 20 June 1959 he paid a further £6 10s. (£6.50) charge for the preliminary course. The course programme advised students that they 'should bring gym shoes for indoor work (studded shoes are not suitable), two soccer strips, a track suit or sweater, football boots, towels and soap, and notebook, as well as personal equipment for golf and tennis, if desired, for recreation'. The eight-page programme, which included the course outline, informed students that they should 'make a study of coaching textbooks and particularly the referees' chart. If possible, they should also arrange for some practice in coaching before attending the course.' Bingham joined over seventy other students, including football luminaries from other Football League clubs and from clubs in Turkey, Austria, India, Holland, Singapore and a reporter from the *Daily Mail*. Some of the names of those present are familiar today: John Bond, Noel Cantwell, Tommy Cavanagh, Bill McGarry and Frank O'Farrell. On the advanced course were Malcolm Allison, Tommy Docherty, Bob Paisley, Dave Sexton and Ken Jones of the *Daily Mirror*. Illustrious company indeed!

The following year Bingham returned to do the advanced course and at the age of twenty-eight he became a qualified coach. He later said that he had one regret, that he had not done the course eight years earlier.

Wade succeeded Winterbottom as director of coaching in 1966 when the senior coaches who had taught the post-Hungarian generation retired. Within a decade, the bright young players who had gone into the game with, as Wade put it, 'great expectations about what would be done for them and how much they would be taught' were no longer disillusioned. At Roker Park Bingham had learned that a club could not simply buy talent because, according to Wade, 'that talent was often more illusory than real'. As Bingham had come to Sunderland at the beginning of their 'Bank of England' spending-spree, he was able to witness this at first hand. When Alan Brown succeeded Bill Murray and brought with him an entirely new method of training, the Irishman knew he would have to attend Lilleshall if he was going to make more than a natural progression in his own game. Brown almost certainly instilled in Bingham the concept of scientific training.

'At places like Lilleshall,' said Wade, 'centres which catered for all sports – national coaches, physical educationalists and emerging sports scientists cross-pollinated their ideas and knowledge. It was an exciting innovative time in British sport.' It was also an innovative time in British soccer. 'In the late '50s coaches and would-be coaches flocked to Lilleshall and did so until the late '60s. For about ten or twelve years the desire to learn was a sort of crusade in England, helped, of course, by England winning the World Cup in 1966.'

Joe Mercer remembers those summer courses and the response many players showed to Walter Winterbottom, the director of coaching. 'Some of us resented Walter. You see, he never played at any level, but he was a talker and we wanted doers, not talkers and while I don't think he was a good England manager, he was a good coach and he laid the basics that won England the World Cup. He got people thinking about the game and Billy is a thinker and Walter was just right for him,' said Mercer.

Bingham came away from Lilleshall with more respect from his peers than he realized at the time. Further visits to the centre, for the refresher course and the managers' and trainers' course placed him among the best coaches in the country. When Wade succeeded Winterbottom he had to find new staff coaches. 'I had to search out their successors and these were Bob Robson, Don Howe, David Sexton, Graham Taylor and Howard Wilkinson and the such like, and, of course, Billy,' said Wade.

Wade wanted to offer Bingham a staff position as an FA coach. 'He did a demonstration for the course and for me and I reckon was more scared than he has ever been in his life before or since. Billy was a very good coach, who should have remained a coach, in the day-to-day sense, for a few years longer. He should have learned his trade as an apprentice manager-coach,' said Wade. 'Unfortunately the same comment applies to most managers, especially those who have been famous international players. In professional football, jobs wait for no one.'

Eighteen months after his playing career had ended, Bingham was manager of fourth division Southport, and part-time manager of Northern Ireland.

Southport is a sleepy seaside-town on the Lancashire coast, with a retiring and salubrious population more suited to knotted handkerchiefs on a sunny afternoon than the frenzied rigours of

Association football. In the early '60s Haig Avenue was an equally sleepy place, except on match days, when Southport Football Club entertained their neighbours from Accrington, Barrow, Rochdale, Stockport or Tranmere in the fourth division. The boom gates of the '50s – when over four million people poured through the turnstiles of fourth division clubs – were fading, and by 1964 those figures had dropped by one million. Between 1960 and 1964 Southport's gates at Haig Avenue averaged 3,820. Then Billy Bingham took his wife's advice and answered Southport's advertisement for a player-coach. The cheery young Irishman, who only a few years earlier had delighted crowds of 50,000 at Goodison Park, had recovered from his broken leg and was taking his first tentative steps into management. Like most of the Fourth Division clubs in Lancashire, tottering on the brink of League membership, Southport had little ambition other than to survive in senior football and remain one of that élite group of ninety-two League clubs. The directors and supporters had cast a cold eye on the events in the cotton-mill town of Accrington, a few miles north-east of Southport, and the sad loss of Accrington Stanley, who had been founder members of the Football League. Virtually overnight Bingham removed the deadly cloud of re-election which had hung over Haig Avenue for years.

Bingham persuaded the Southport board to give him the job of trainer–coach on 19 June 1965, and at the end of his second season at Haig Avenue the club followed Stockport County into the third division as runners-up in the fourth division in the 1966/67 season. Bingham's infectious enthusiasm for the game had changed the atmosphere sufficiently at Haig Avenue to get him the manager's job in December 1965. Southport moved into the third round of the FA Cup with victories over Halifax and Stockport County. The gates climbed to an average of 5,340 as the supporters cheered the team Bingham had taken to the fifth round of the FA Cup – with further victories over Ipswich and Cardiff – and to a safe position in the third division.

Bingham, however, had ambitions in soccer management that could not be realized at Haig Avenue, and after his appointment as part-time Northern Ireland manager in October 1967 it was obvious to everyone that someone would come calling for his talents sooner rather than later.

As Bingham prepared for his first game as an international manager – against British champions Scotland at Windsor Park on 21 October 1967 – the Merseyside and Lancashire press, sniffing a possible story, sought the Southport directors. Was it true that Bingham was on the move to a bigger club? Had he accepted any of the offers made in the past few weeks? The Southport chairman, John Church, tried to be philosophical. 'All this talk of a move has taken me by surprise,' he told sceptical reporters, emphasizing that Bingham had recently reassured him that if he did receive an offer to his liking he would give Southport three months' notice. Church then tried to placate the club's supporters, revealing that the club had offered Bingham a three-year contract with a salary comparable to that of first division managers. 'He is very happy with us and is thinking over our new offer to him. We don't want to lose him and of course money speaks in any language,' said Church.

That Southport were prepared to double Bingham's salary to keep him showed that they knew he would soon be leaving for the higher reaches of the Football League. In October, Church probably realized he was fighting a losing battle to keep Bingham at Haig Avenue and when he stated that 'only one of the top clubs could give Bingham a greater financial incentive than us' he was informing the Southport support of the inevitable.

Before he left for the Scotland game Bingham confirmed Southport's worst fears that he 'would consider an offer if it was the right one'. In the meantime, Bingham was less concerned with managerial positions than he was with his plans for the defeat of Scotland and world champions England in the European Nations Cup.

Bingham had taken over the Northern Ireland job from his old Glentoran team-mate Bertie Peacock and was hamstrung by the insufficient time he had to establish his own style of management before the Scotland game. He told reporters at the time that he wanted to 'get the players together a few times and build up team spirit and some kind of system'. The nucleus of the Northern Ireland squad played with First Division clubs and Bingham had been told he could hope for no more than 'two or three days before each international' to get them ready.

It wasn't what Bingham had hoped for and it certainly didn't fit in with his plans for improving Northern Ireland's results. On this occasion Bingham was prepared to wait and hope that 'things would improve' the following season. He was also prepared to accept some guidance from the selectors for the Scotland game although his nomination of Manchester City's Johnny Crossan was arguably Bingham's first mistake as Northern Ireland manager. Crossan had been out of favour after several mediocre performances, yet Bingham believed that the Derryman was the type of player he needed on his team for the build-up to the 1970 World Cup. Bingham's appointment, however, was welcomed by the players, the press and Northern Ireland's loyal following. The soccer critics expected Bingham to 'administer field discipline' – referring mostly to the wayward talents of George Best and Derek Dougan – and employ 'shrewd tactics' which, they hoped, would bring about 'the much needed revival in Irish fortunes'.

Looking back to that Saturday in October 1967 most people don't remember that it was Bingham's first game as Northern Ireland manager. They remember it because George Best demoralized Scotland with a brilliant display of exhilarating skill. What surprised everyone was Best's ability to leave the royal-blue jerseys of the Scottish players trailing in the mud. A few days before the game Bingham had said there would be 'no elaboration' because he expected the pitch would be very heavy after the torrential rain. Either Best wasn't listening or he didn't care that the press criticized him for 'not playing to the team plan and running across the pitch'. Bingham respected Best's superb talents and even if he did not want the little Irish genius running diagonally across the pitch, the other Irish forwards' inability to score goals from these runs told Bingham that he had problems. Dave Clements' sixty-eighth-minute winning goal was scant reward for Best's efforts and Bingham didn't need the press reports to tell him that Clements, Nicholson and Crossan were not forming the 'effective links' the Irish needed to win matches.

To the surprise of many people, after the Scottish success, Bingham returned to Southport and signed Church's three-year contract – taking his salary to £4,000 a year. This was a substantially higher amount than Southport could afford but the directors agreed that it was the only way they could show their appreciation of the success Bingham had brought to Haig Avenue and, more importantly, the only way they could keep him there.

Bingham never equalled or bettered the success he had at Haig Avenue with any of the English league clubs he subsequently joined. Neither did he again achieve the harmony between manager and chairman he had at Southport, but then the board of directors at Haig Avenue knew when they were onto a good thing. What he achieved at Southport was a reputation for being one of the hardest soccer coaches in the Football League, a reputation he established in the sand dunes of Southport's beaches.

When Bingham was appointed manager of Everton in 1973 a reporter, who had witnessed Southport's pre-season training sessions for several years, wrote of the day when he first encountered Bingham's training methods on the Southport sands. The article, written by Brian Caven in the *Liverpool Echo*, was titled 'Bingham's Hill'.

A haggard face materialized over the top of the small sand dune. Tired arms pulled an exhausted body after it and leaden legs propelled the sturdy frame in an erratic course towards me.

The young man collapsed at my feet, his huge mouth gulping huge, painful lungfuls of air into his sweat-stained chest. He tried several times to speak.

Only by leaning forward and listening intently could I make out the words. They were colourful, wholly expressive, and totally unprintable.

The Billy Bingham era had dawned at Haig Avenue.

Caven went on to write that if the players 'had been horses the RSPCA would have had a field-day', yet as everyone at Haig

Avenue had witnessed, it was this kind of training which built Southport's success in the F A Cup and brought them promotion to division three when, only a season before Bingham's arrival, they had to apply for re-election. The Billy Bingham era had indeed arrived at Haig Avenue.

One of Bingham's first signings for Southport was a twenty-one-year-old centre-back from Liverpool called Fred Molyneux. Born and bred in Merseyside, Molyneux was understudy to Ron Yeats at Liverpool. 'I wasn't going anywhere at Liverpool because nobody got injured,' said Molyneux and Bingham, who obviously realized that a football talent was being wasted, brought him to Southport. Bingham's next move was to bring his old team-mate, Alex Parker, from Everton and put him in the defence. Bingham had strengthened his defence with a blend of youth and experience and it cost Southport only £1,000 – the fee for Molyneux; Everton had given Parker a free transfer.

Everton rejected several younger players, and Bingham immediately brought them to Haig Avenue. Within a year he had a team – individually and collectively – better than anyone else in division four. Success for the club seemed inevitable. So did a move for Bingham. There was nothing the Southport board could do except wait – and hope that he would stay.

When Plymouth requested permission to speak to their manager it was obvious that Bingham would ask for, and get, a higher salary than he was being paid at Haig Avenue. Despite the Southport board's insistence that Bingham give three months' notice before taking the Plymouth job, it was unlikely that he would agree and ignore the challenge to keep Plymouth in division two.

On 14 February 1968, Bingham became the tenth Plymouth manager since the Second World War. Crookes, the chairman, told reporters that Bingham 'has a mind of his own'. Crookes, who would vacate his position the following season, was providing the predictable quotes when a club appoints a new manager. He couldn't have known that Bingham would not provide the predictable solutions to Plymouth's problems.

CHAPTER SEVEN

PREDICTABLE QUESTIONS, PREDICTABLE ANSWERS

BINGHAM THE MANAGER

Bingham has served his apprenticeship at Southport and has proved that the intelligence and knowledge of the game he showed as a player fit him adequately for a managerial role.
Horace Yates, *Liverpool Daily Post*, October 1967

Plymouth inquired about Bingham on the recommendation of Frank O'Farrell, then at Torquay and later to be manager of Manchester United. The Plymouth board had tried to tempt O'Farrell to join them and when he refused they asked him to suggest someone else. O'Farrell, believed that Bingham 'was doing a very good job at Southport with limited resources' and in casual conversation with O'Farrell, Bingham had mentioned that he didn't think he could progress any further with the Lancashire club.

Plymouth came for Bingham too late. They had persevered with Derek Ufton's despairing attempts to take the club out of the second division's relegation zone and when Bingham moved to Plymouth in mid-February 1968 he had sixteen games left to produce a miracle at Home Park.

If managing Southport was like riding the roller-coaster at Blackpool's fun-fair – safe in the knowledge that it would eventually stop and you could get off – managing Plymouth was like skiing down the slopes of a volcano which might suddenly erupt and spew molten lava over you. Bingham moved to Plymouth because the money was right and because the Plymouth Argyle board had convinced him that the club could be big. The soccer potential in the area was enormous. What Bingham didn't know

Bingham arrives at Plymouth in February 1968. On his right is Robert Daniel, who became chairman of the club in the following year. The other Plymouth directors in the front row are Stafford Williams (*far left*) and Brian Williams (*far right*). Harry Deans is immediately behind Bingham (*Sunday Independent*).

Bingham drinking a toast with chairman Clifford Crookes on the day of his appointment at Plymouth (*Sunday Independent*).

Clearly not all Bingham's training sessions were torturous. This sequence
shows him in jovial mood with members of the team (*Sunday Independent*).

Above: Blowing the whistle on Pat Dunne, the Republic of Ireland and former
Manchester United goalkeeper who was at Plymouth from 1967 till 1970.

Below left: Showing Norman Piper how to do it. Piper went on to play for
Portsmouth. In the background is Michael Everritt, who left Plymouth shortly
after Bingham joined.

A reflective Bingham fishing on the Hoe at Plymouth (*Sunday Independent*).

Plymouth Argyle's line-up for the 1969–70 season: *Back row (left to right):* Norman Piper, Mike Reeves, John Tedesco, David Burnside, Colin Sullivan; *Middle (left to right):* Bob Stuart (physio), John Hore, Pat Dunne, Andy Nelson, Martin Clamp, Eric Burgess, Frank Lord (coach); *Seated (left to right):* Mike Bickle, Stephen Davey, Billy Bingham, Bob Saxton, Richard Reynolds, Duncan Neale (*Sunday Independent*).

or didn't realize was that the board of directors knew very little about football and only one man – Robert Daniel, who became chairman the following season – had the ambition to bring football success to Home Park. The former Republic of Ireland and Manchester United goalkeeper, Pat Dunne, who joined Plymouth in February 1967, said the board appointed Bingham in a bid for success, but no one was 'terribly interested in how he would achieve it'. They were the sort of men, he said, who would sit up in the directors' box and 'enjoy the game'. Dunne imagined them thinking, 'if we win, great. If we lose, well let's hope it's not too often during the year. Billy's the man we've picked and he's going to do the trick.'

Plymouth were also on the verge of bankruptcy; they had a massive overdraft which had only been reduced by Ufton's shrewd transfer deals. Unfortunately, after selling good players to balance the books, Ufton was then forced to reverse that policy to try and keep the club in the second division. Whether Ufton panicked or was just unlucky, the players he brought to Home Park failed to bring about a revival and, according to Harley Lawer, a Plymouth soccer writer, many of them 'finished up playing long spells in the reserves'. Bingham inherited this squad and a club which would report a 'record loss of £45,000' to their shareholders in the autumn.

Plymouth had offered Bingham a salary of £5,000 a year and a bonus of £2,000 if he could keep the club in the second division. In a matter of months he had gone from being Southport's highest-paid manager ever to being Plymouth's highest-paid manager ever. At Haig Avenue they could just about afford him. At Plymouth the board bought Bingham with money they didn't have and that simple fact would eventually lead to the Irishman's downfall at Home Park. But that was still to come. It was now 18 February 1968, and Bingham was watching his new team in action for the first time, against Blackburn Rovers at Home Park. Two first-half goals were enough to give Plymouth their first win in three months but Bingham wasn't happy. 'I have played in relegation-fighting sides myself,' he told Harley Lawer, 'and know what it's like. You are frightened of making mistakes. Even when moves are on out of defence, you'd sooner give it to your goal-keeper. This is a lack of confidence. We broke out well to get two good goals. We contained them well enough in the second half, but we fell back too far and I wanted them to come out in more open combat.'

Three weeks later, after another victory, Middlesborough denied Bingham a hat-trick of wins. These vital points would have taken Plymouth out of the bottom two for the first time that season. The euphoria generated by Bingham's arrival and his infectious enthusiasm had worn off. Bingham, having believed he could get the 'best out of the players' he had, was forced to begin trading. After the Blackburn victory he asked the 'Pilgrims' supporters to give him a little time to 'see what we can and cannot do'. Time was not on his side.

At Southport, Bingham had inherited some very good players and with some shrewd talking and subtle dealing he was able to build a team with just the right blend of youth and experience. Most of that experience was in his back four, which, in Bingham's soccer philosophy was, and still is, the basis for success. When he arrived at Home Park Bingham ominously had a personality clash with full-back Mike Everitt, which was unfortunate for both, because Everitt was a solid and reliable defender. Several players knew that their days with Plymouth were numbered. Despite their experience Bingham felt that centre-half Andy Nelson and midfielder Jimmy Bloomfield were at the end of their careers and could not do a job for him. Forwards Alan Peacock and Alan Sealey were both injured. Friday before the Middlesborough game Bingham released a list of eight players to the press which he said he had circulated to other clubs in an attempt to beat the 16 March transfer deadline. On the Sunday Lawer, in his *Spectator* page, revealed that Bingham was looking for around £15,000 for Mike Everitt, Alan Sealey, Jimmy Bloomfield, Andy Nelson, Tony Rounsevell and John Leiper.

In a matter of weeks Bingham attempted to reduce Plymouth's playing-staff to fourteen full-time professionals and two apprentices. Frank Lord, who had joined Argyle as player-coach two months before Bingham had arrived, was told his services were no longer required. Part of Bingham's deal with the Plymouth board was to do his own training and coaching. Lord was told by the club that they were prepared to release him if he could find a suitable appointment elsewhere, but as events took Plymouth into division three Bingham briefly resurrected Lord's playing career with a run of nine games which produced two goals. Other economic measures instigated by Bingham included cutting some of the full-time ground-staff positions to part-time and at one stage, when Plymouth secretary, Graham Little, was recovering from a car accident, Bingham took over his job rather than bring in a temporary replacement. Logically and practically it was the most sensible thing to do, but it also illuminated the character of the new manager at Home Park. Bingham was the boss and he wanted everybody to know it.

The soccer world is often viewed with disdain by outsiders who can't understand why millions of people frequently suffer arctic conditions to get passionately involved in watching twenty-two people contesting a small ball on a large area of grass. Ironically, some players view managers similarly when they introduce the sort of punishing training schedules Bingham did when he arrived at Home Park. As a player Bingham believed that fitness was very important to him and when the Plymouth soccer press asked him if he would expect the same dedication from his squad he told them that 'the training which suited me would not suit everyone'. He said that it 'took more than fitness to make a side and that different players need different handling'.

As a soccer pragmatist and a disciplinarian Bingham inevitably clashed with several players. Among the first to suffer from this side of Bingham's management was David Burnside, an exciting and skilful player whom Bingham signed from Wolverhampton Wanderers for approximately £10,000 a few days before the transfer deadline. Burnside had agreed to become Bingham's first acquisition on the condition that he be allowed to live in Bristol –

near his relatives – and commute to digs in Plymouth. Burnside held a Football Association coaching badge and only agreed with Bingham's philosophy to a certain point. 'Dave had certain beliefs,' said one former Argyle player, 'and he wasn't quite prepared to knuckle down and become, as Billy wanted everyone to become, a worker. Being a player of skill Dave couldn't quite accept that type of thing and possibly didn't have the stamina to be able to do what Billy wanted. Dave needed good players around him to make him tick; he could make other good players tick, but Bingy wanted workaholics.' When Bingham took his players on a pre-season training trip with the local marines he told reporters that 'some of the exercises might not make them better footballers, but they will certainly help to conquer fears and build their confidence'.

Most of the players agreed that they had enjoyed the unusual training routine but they were baffled by Bingham's reasoning. Pat Dunne said that he 'enjoyed being put through that type of training' but that wasn't the problem. 'I think he treated everyone as if they didn't have ability,' said Dunne. 'No matter how long you spent on the training ground, doing hundred-metre sprints one after the other or weights or whatever, it wasn't going to make you a better player. The training with the marines didn't make us better players, it didn't make any of us better soldiers or commandos either!'

In the club programme, on the opening day of the new season – back in division three – Bingham told the supporters that the players had responded positively to the intensive 'physical and mental' training during the summer break and he felt it would set them up for 'a good season'. If the players believed that it helped conquer their fears and build their confidence they didn't show it on the field. They did, however, show how fit they were. In the third game, after beating Bournemouth and drawing with Crewe, they scored three goals in the last twenty minutes to beat Reading at Home Park. Lawer wrote: 'Players like Dave Burnside and Norman Piper, who had done so much foraging and running in the first half, seemed to be spent. Yet both came back astonishingly well to dispel fears that they had faded too early. This determination from them and success so late in the match must reflect credit on their manager, Billy Bingham, and his training.'

Bingham was aware that the opening results hid his real problem, that some of his players were not capable of mastering his system of breaking positively from a strict defensive formation. His fears became the supporters' moans when Swindon exposed this weakness in Plymouth's defence the following week. The following Saturday Shrewsbury made it two defeats in a row and Bingham's countrywide quest for a centre-half was imperative if Plymouth was going to challenge for promotion. Bingham's search had been thwarted on several occasions. Either his bid was too low or the players didn't want to go to Plymouth. The Swindon and Shrewsbury defeats seemed to stun the Argyle board and when Bingham asked them for approximately £7,000 to purchase centre-back Fred Molyneux from Southport, they were happy to concede. Plymouth's small-town mentality went in Bingham's favour as the club attempted to beat the new forty-eight-hour Football League regulation for players' registration – introduced in June that year. The Argyle board had a courier ready to drive through the night to the Football League headquarters in Lytham St Anne's with the necessary documents. Then the Head Postmaster of Plymouth assured the club that he could get the packet in the post in time for the 3 p.m. deadline on the Thursday.

Molyneux was one of Bingham's first signings as a manager at Southport and it is customary for a manager to return to former clubs for players who have adapted to their tactics and training. Bingham had gone up north to watch a winger, and he decided to take in a game at Haig Avenue. Molyneux had been on his list virtually from the day he had started at Plymouth but his bids for the defender had been too low. After the game Bingham was asked by a Southport director: 'How much will you give us for Molyneux?' Meanwhile Molyneux had left the ground and gone for a drink with some friends. As he relaxed in a nearby pub he was approached by a member of the Southport staff and asked if he was interested in going to Plymouth.

The following day Molyneux went to Plymouth and was immediately 'impressed by the set-up' and on the Wednesday Bingham signed him. Back in Southport the supporters were in revolt at the sale of one of their best players; the Southport manager accused Bingham of 'poaching' Molyneux even though it was his own board who had instigated the deal. 'I got the blame for us getting beat when we played Newcastle in the cup,' said Molyneux. 'There were eight minutes to go and I was supposed to have given away a penalty. They scored and we lost the chance to go to Newcastle where the club would've made some money. The Southport manager didn't want me to go, it was the board that sold me and he knew nothing about it.' Bingham would never have tolerated such interference.

Fred Molyneux's arrival at Home Park revived the club on the pitch. The team, with Molyneux forging a strong partnership with Bobby Saxton at the heart of the defence, strung three successive wins together. In the boardroom the directors tried to divert attention away from the club's financial crisis with a pitiful piece of propaganda in the programme for the Barnsley game on 23 September. They wrote that directors are not in football because there is any 'financial advantage'. 'Directors put considerable money into their clubs in shares, loans or other ways. At the present time the directors of this club have made interest-free loans to the club of over £40,000, quite apart from the money which they have in the club in shares. Directors also have to guarantee the club's bank overdraft and the mortgages on various houses bought for occupation by the players.'

There had been an optimistic feeling in the town since Bingham's arrival and, despite the drop to the third division, the supporters were now prepared to give the new manager the time he wanted. But they also needed to be persuaded. Gradually, Argyle's home gates began to climb and on the Monday night of the Barnsley game the attendance was just over 13,000 – an increase of 2,000 on the previous home match and a 3,000 increase from the opening day of the season. The last thing they wanted was a sermon from Plymouth's magnanimous directors. They also didn't appreciate Plymouth's pathetic efforts against Barnsley and the scoreless draw which resulted.

Some of the players felt that Bingham's tactics for home matches were wrong. Goalkeeper Pat Dunne believed that the team was not adventurous enough at Home Park, as did the supporters. Bingham also wanted the team to be positive and score goals, but his players were not responding – with the exception of Mike Bickle, who was averaging a goal every two games. When Ron Flowers' Northampton team came to Home Park and went away with two points, Bingham probably realized that his comment, that, with the arrival of Molyneux, 'the defence looks secure', was premature. Bingham tried to placate the Argyle support by telling them that Northampton's 'pure defensive football is a completely negative attitude which affects the players and the paying public'. 'I like good defensive football,' he said, 'but I always like my players to be positive and adventurous when we are in possession.'

No one at Home Park doubted his sincerity, they just doubted his wisdom. The local press, who were slowly beginning to get on his nerves, were only too delighted to tell anyone who read their columns that the Plymouth team just didn't have what Bingham required of them.

Defeats by Northampton, rivals Torquay (their first ever success at Home Park), Southport and Gillingham had taken the shine off Molyneux's early success. When Argyle failed to beat lowly Oldham at Home Park, the response was predictable. There was 'no method, no midfield control and no finishing. You name it – poor old Argyle didn't have it,' wrote Harley Lawer. However, he also wrote: 'Bingham does have the satisfaction of knowing that these same players can do better. He has seen that for himself this season, but the best must be consistent to keep the cash customers happy.'

The 'tremendous team spirit' which Bingham had talked about after Molyneux's signing had vanished, yet he wasn't despondent, just 'amazed' at the attitude of the local press. 'Every time we lose or draw it is a catastrophe, with either the manager, directors or team blazoned in headlines across the local papers. Argyle always seem to be put under the microscope,' Bingham wrote in his programme notes a few days later. He also tried to explain why Oldham had won a point. He said that Oldham had frozen the Plymouth wingers out of the game. 'They played their wingers behind ours on many occasions, with the result that when our winger received the ball he was faced with a winger and a full-back to beat. That's why I told Stephen Davey and Aidan Maher to come inside for the ball and put Norman Piper up front with Mike Bickle and Danny Trainor.'

It was almost as if Bingham had given Oldham a team talk before the game – such were their tactics. The result was unfortunate, because it was the first time Bingham had attempted to play with wingers in the old-fashioned manner – going down the line and getting crosses over from the byline. Bingham had been criticized for not using wingers and in his defence he reported that he had been searching for the right players. When he eventually paid £10,000 to Everton for Aidan Maher – an outside-left –it wasn't just the press who criticized him. Some of the Plymouth players thought that the five-figure sum was a scandalous price to pay 'for a limited player'. Bingham couldn't win. Despite his vivacious coaching and strenuous training the team was not consistent. Away from Plymouth Bingham thought 'our approach leaves a lot to be desired'. 'Team talks, tactics, training and £50 incentive does not seem to be enough for some players to raise their game away from home.'

Critics of Bingham's period at Plymouth believe his failure was caused by the club's poor financial standing and the location of the club. 'I don't think he was given the money that was necessary to buy players, although some of the players that he got didn't work,' said one former team member. 'There were a lot of honest players at the club and they gave what they had but it wasn't good enough. One of the biggest problems he probably had was the fact that players wouldn't come that far – without a financial incentive. Bingy wasn't the type of manager who would pay a lot of money to bring in a star.'

The newspaper writers had a similar attitude – the players Bingham had were just not capable of putting his theories into practice on the field. 'I think they grasped his tactics, all right, they just didn't like them and Bingham didn't seem capable of adapting his tactics to the players he had,' said Harley Lawer. 'He never seemed to me to want to succeed the way other people in football had succeeded or have succeeded since,' said Pat Dunne.

Then, unexpectedly, Bingham seemed to be vindicated, and the new year brought a revival as the team suddenly clicked. It was all the more interesting because Bingham had nearly left the club when first division Ipswich made him an offer of £6,000 a year in January 1969, to tempt him to Portman Road. Plymouth had ended 1968 in mid-table with twenty-four points from twenty-four games. In a new-year message to the Argyle supporters the Plymouth board said they 'were not satisfied' with the season. 'We are disappointed, but we do not intend to lose our heads. We have confidence in our manager and wish him well in his difficult task, a task which is not made easier for him by many critics who will not accept that a manager cannot perform miracles overnight but that he must build patiently and wisely.' On 4 January 1969, Brighton and Hove Albion visited Home Park and came away with a point. It would be the only point Bingham's team would drop in a seven-match unbeaten run in the league.

One of the most successful tactics Bingham perfected in his managerial career is the art of players covering for each other. To do this effectively players form triangles and as one goes forward one falls back, with the third player always available for a pass or in position to cover for the others. At Plymouth, Bingham was still trying to perfect these triangles, and it would only be many years later, with the Northern Ireland team, that they would become an intrinsic part of his team's play – involving a defender (full-back), a midfielder and a forward (winger). Bingham had been trying to get his players to do this before Christmas and Molyneux believed it 'just clicked' against Oldham, who they beat 2–0 on 11 January. 'I think you knew what you had to do every week,' said Molyneux. 'At the team talks Bingham laid it down that you helped each other, as one went forward, one dropped in. There were many times when I would just take off up the field, but I knew that somebody would fill in. I can remember him saying to me "Be positive and become a forward. Let somebody else drop in and fill the hole that you've left and you go all the way and finish with a shot if you can." I think it was a case of perseverance once we'd got it together and a few results makes it a good habit to get into.'

Bingham encouraged his players to go forward and play a positive game. 'At the end of the day it was only about working for each other, covering for each other and if you want success that's what you have got to do,' said Molyneux. The local press probably did not recognize the specific tactics but they did witness its effect. Harley Lawer reported:

Oldham 0–Plymouth 2 Dave Burnside was backed up by a sharper-moving attack, with Aidan Maher [winger] and Norman Piper [midfield]. Duncan Neale [defender], also a star, often appeared in attack and it was refreshing indeed to see Johnny Hore [defender] shaking off his defensive shackles to support his attack and shoot whenever he had a chance.

Eric Burgess [defender], strong in the tackle, was also more than useful in an attacking role. It was his overlap with Piper [midfield] that produced the second and deciding goal for Stephen Davey [winger].

Lawer reported that Burgess (defender), Piper (midfielder), Burnside (forward) and Maher (winger) had 'all figured' in the moves which brought Davey's goals. The following week, against Barrow, Davey hit two more and Lawer wrote: 'The way Davey shaped in turning up in the right positions to grab his goals must have been a great pleasure to Billy Bingham.' It was 19 January, slightly over two weeks since Bingham had told his forwards that they needed the following qualities to score goals:

A) Courage (To be challenged in the goal area where one has to accept the physical part of the game)

B) Positioning sense and anticipation
C) Coolness when the chance presents itself
D) Heading ability
E) Accuracy and strength of shot

A reporter's account of the first three goals against Barrow:

Shot 1: A beauty from Norman Piper, it was aimed with accuracy and pace. Knox (the Barrow goalkeeper) couldn't reach it.

Shot 2: A sizzler from Stephen Davey, who cut loose in midfield, shook off two tackles *en route* for goal and fired fiercely over the keeper's head. Knox got his fingertips to the ball but had no hope of stopping it.

Shot 3: A corker from Richard Reynolds, who took a short pass from Piper's free kick and smashed the ball home in glorious style. Knox couldn't have seen that one.

The unbeaten run – which also included a 1–0 win over Exeter in the Devon Bowl – produced seven victories and one draw, with a goals ratio of 13–2, and took Plymouth into the top four of the third division, four points behind leaders Watford. It was 22 February. Bingham had been at Home Park for exactly one year. Plymouth had won fifteen of their thirty-one league games and had thirty-seven points. The feeling was that Bingham was going to take them straight back into division two.

Bingham still needed a forward who could score goals. He decided to ask Terry Harkin to leave Southport. Bingham had brought Harkin, an Irish international, to the Lancashire club and he knew the player could do a job for him. Unfortunately, Harkin did not want to move to Plymouth.

Bingham's failure to persuade Harkin was to prove costly, yet, in his programme notes for the Tranmere game at the end of February, he said he had made 'the right decision'. Our terms were 'more than generous', Bingham told the supporters and 'infinitely better than he was receiving from Southport'.

It was a curious statement for Bingham to make. Harkin simply did not want to go to Plymouth because of the distance. 'I was very tempted,' said Harkin. 'I had been with him at Port Vale and I had built up a friendship with him. I really enjoyed listening to him. His training was smashing and there was a great variety. He couldn't get the players to go to Plymouth and I was an example. It was a bad mistake on my part and I have always regretted it.'

Despite the talents of goalkeeper Pat Dunne, defender Fred Molyneux, midfielder Norman Piper and forward Dave Burnside, Plymouth Argyle had a limited squad of players. Bingham had strengthened the side when he bought Burnside and Molyneux yet his insistence that Devon, Cornwall and Somerset 'must' be rich with 'untapped talent' was unrealistic thinking. The 'continual flow of youth players' he sought for the reserves and subsequently the first team did not materialize. For Plymouth to succeed he had to venture into the transfer market and to get players to move to south-west England – the motorway then ended 180 miles short of Plymouth – he had to spend money. 'I think he told the board, when he arrived, that he could get them promotion basically with what they had,' said Pat Dunne. 'I felt he had said to them, "those are the players we have, it's not going to cost you too much more for us to be where we should be."' Both Dunne and Molyneux felt that Bingham tried to make do with what he had. He had been successful at Southport on a shoestring, and he believed he could achieve the same at Plymouth.

Dunne believed that relegation was Bingham's greatest setback. 'That made it doubly hard, because you had twenty chances of staying in the second division and only two of getting back. I don't think he recovered from that. He thought he could motivate the players he had there enough to keep them up. It didn't happen and then we always had problems the following season from the very first game,' said Dunne. Twelve months later the financial restraints at Home Park and the relative failure of the youth system were beginning to make Bingham's job virtually impossible. He had brought local talent into the team but, according to Dunne and Molyneux, they weren't good enough. 'At one particular time we had nine locals in the side and to me that is never going to bring you success. The only foreigners were Pat and myself,' said Molyneux.

As Easter approached the season turned sour for Bingham, and the loss of six points from four games during the first eleven days of March effectively ended Plymouth's promotion hopes. Stephen Davey had lost his goal-scoring touch and it was left to Burnside to lead the attack, but his five goals in six games produced only five points. Burnside was at the end of his career and according to Molyneux needed someone 'to take the weight off him' in attack. Mike Bickle might have been the hero of the Devonport end of Home Park but his early season flourish had not been repeated and Molyneux felt that the player just wasn't good enough.

The season was almost over when Plymouth played at Stockport. Molyneux abandoned his defensive duties in an attempt to reduce Stockport's two-goal lead, which he felt was not a true reflection of the way the game was going. Molyneux accused Bickle of jumping out of tackles and called him a coward. 'We actually squared up and I flew at him and there was a bust up,' remembers Molyneux. 'I can't remember if the referee booked us but Bickle went off and scored two goals and it finished up a draw. Of course the press got hold of it – two team-mates fighting all over the headlines – and they had us in the manager's office after the game. As far as I was concerned I'd got what I wanted. We'd got a point and he'd done what he should have been doing, whereas otherwise we would have got nothing.'

It was the sort of leadership Bingham expected from Molyneux yet he was obviously embarrassed by the players' actions. Nevertheless Molyneux was sure that 'at the end of the day Billy was 75 per cent in my corner'. Molyneux believed that many players let Bingham down on the field. 'Once you step over that white line he can't play the game for you. He'll give you plans and each player has a certain job to do. During league games, possibly people were more relaxed, and they tried to do things they weren't capable of, whereas if they had just done what they had been told to do there would have been no problems.'

Unfortunately, Bingham didn't have enough players of Molyneux's calibre in his squad and his motivational qualities carried only a certain amount of credibility. 'He's either a man that you take to or you don't,' said Molyneux, 'there's no in-betweens. If the man is going to bring you glory you want to play for him, and you listen to him whether you believe in his tactics or not. If you want success then you have to listen and do as you're told.'

In soccer, whether it is at professional level in front of a 50,000 crowd or at amateur level in the park in front of a man and his dog, the game is the same. If you are winning the luck runs with you; if you are losing it goes against you. Although it didn't make any significant difference to Plymouth's League position, they lost a couple of points to Barrow and Watford following two freak incidents. In the Barrow game goalkeeper Pat Dunne wanted to pack it all in when a shot which was going 'at least five yards wide' struck the referee, who was running frantically away from the edge of the six-yard box, and curled over Dunne's head for the only goal of the game. Against Watford Molyneux hit a shot from twenty yards which he claimed was over the line despite rebounding from the underside of the crossbar. In the 1966 World Cup final Geoff Hurst was awarded a similar goal and England went on to win the game. In the European Cup semi-final in 1969 between Manchester United and AC Milan at Old Trafford, Denis Law watched in disbelief as the referee disallowed a goal with the ball clearly over the line. United, the holders, went out. Plymouth were beaten 1–0 and Watford went on to win the championship.

Plymouth Argyle finished the 1968/69 season in fifth position, fifteen points behind Watford; so near and yet so far. Bingham wrote that he was a realist and that Plymouth had got what they deserved. 'Good luck and bad luck balances itself out in a season,' he wrote. Not everyone agreed that the lack of goals and the poor home-form were the main reasons for Plymouth's failure. Bingham had attempted to blend the local talent with his small coterie of experienced players and it hadn't worked. Plymouth were still in division three and the experienced players knew why. Some of the players were recalcitrant about Bingham's training methods and team talks. 'If you want to play for the manager, he's halfway there,' said Molyneux. 'Some of the lads didn't want to roll up their sleeves and have a go for him. Either they didn't agree with the way he wanted them to play or they just weren't good enough to put his tactics into practice.'

Pat Dunne thought that, by the end of the '68/69 season, Bingham knew the job was virtually impossible and 'didn't have the courage to get out'. Bingham had faced his first managerial crisis and being the dogmatist that he was, was determined to complete his contract. 'Billy always came across as being straight down the middle and honest but I don't think he felt the same about the job twelve months after he took over,' said Dunne.

Bingham demanded loyalty from his players and was hurt when the reason he didn't get it reflected back on his methods. The test of loyalty at Plymouth would not happen until well into the '69/70 season, but the seeds were sown long before then.

During the summer in – by Plymouth's standards – a surprisingly extravagant plunge into the transfer market, Bingham increased the full-time playing-staff at Home Park to eighteen with the addition of two unexceptional forwards and a defender. He paid £5,000 to Leicester City for outside-left Don Hutchins and £9,000 to Coventry City for Trevor Shepherd. In a shrewd move, he obtained centre-back Winston Foster from Birmingham on a free transfer many other managers thought would have a fee involved. Neither Hutchins nor Shepherd would fit into the Home Park set-up and Bingham would prefer other forwards in their positions before the end of the year. Bingham's attempt to solve Plymouth's goal-scoring problems wouldn't end there. A few months into the season he would add winger Barry Rowan and striker Derek Rickard to the attack. By mid-December he would use eleven players in attacking positions, which would cause discontentment rather than competition among the first team squad.

The season began with the ignominious defeat by Devon rivals Torquay in the League Cup. Bingham's problems were not confined to his forwards. During the summer his successful centre-back partnership between Fred Molyneux and Bobby Saxton was unceremoniously severed when Saxton suffered a badly broken leg in a car accident, which would keep him out until January 1970.

By the end of August the pressure on Bingham intensified as David Burnside was added to the injury list. The loss of his silky skills and the failure of Hutchins and Shepherd in the forward line forced Bingham to try sixteen players in four games. He told Harley Lawer that it was too early to make quick assessments. 'Equally, if we had won all our matches it would have been too early to say that we were sure of doing well,' said Bingham.

Despite Bingham's permutations the team wasn't playing well. Heads had dropped and several players found that they couldn't raise the standard of their game, or remain consistent over a series of matches. The growing tension about Bingham's training methods was also beginning to affect team morale and when David Burnside defied an order to come to training it was the beginning of a three-month saga which would signal the end for Bingham at Plymouth Argyle.

Towards the close of the '68/69 season, Burnside asked Bingham if he could cut his training at Plymouth down to two days a week and make the rest up with one of the Bristol clubs so that he could spend more time with his family. There was no written agreement, and when Burnside refused to attend a Tuesday training session at the specific request of his manager, Bingham fined him. When the conflict between them reached the newspapers two weeks later Bingham told reporters that Burnside was not 'absolutely fit'. Yet Bingham also told the soccer press that Burnside trained hard. 'He is that type of player but it is often important for him to be with the rest of the players for training and tactical talks.' Inevitably Burnside asked for a transfer, which Bingham said was unfortunate because he didn't want to lose him.

It was a crucial incident in Bingham's managerial career and one in which he was determined to assert his authority as the boss at Plymouth Argyle, but it also prompted the board of directors to look more closely at the day-to-day running of their club. After all, they were paying Bingham a lot of money and the results were not coming. Bingham was, as ever, optimistic. He had revived the patient last season and, with positive thinking, he felt there was no reason why he couldn't do the same again. But there were many reasons – not least of all that the players he had were just not of the calibre to bring promotion and success to Plymouth. Another reason was the £100,000 debt the club would report to share-holders that autumn. The volcano was about to erupt.

On Saturday, 6 December, Plymouth were knocked out of the FA Cup in the second round by Peterborough. It was Argyle's third successive defeat and the team was slipping into a precarious position in the third division table, having taken only eighteen points from twenty-one games. Bingham had made David Burnside captain in the absence of Fred Molyneux, who had joined the injury list. The Argyle manager was also about to give another local player a chance in the first team. New acquisition Derek Rickard was to become the twenty-first player to pull on a first team shirt in twenty-seven League and Cup games. While Bingham was not visibly worried about his team's performance, the directors were. On the Monday after the FA Cup defeat, chairman Robert Daniel went looking for Molyneux.

It was Monday morning at Home Park and Molyneux was in the bath after an easy workout. The players were out training with Bingham. Daniel sent word to Molyneux that he should come up and have a chat with him when he was ready. The footballer found the director in the boardroom. The Plymouth chairman greeted the player sombrely.

'What's going on in the club?' Daniel asked Molyneux.

'I don't think it would be right for me to say anything without the boss,' replied Molyneux, aware of what Daniel was really asking.

Daniel reluctantly told Molyneux that was OK. 'We'll wait for

Billy to come back from training,' he said. But Daniel became impatient and asked Molyneux if there was any dissent between the players and the manager.

'Some of them aren't very happy with the boss's training,' Molyneux told him. As he said that, Bingham arrived outside the door.

'Billy heard me saying that the lads weren't happy with the training methods, put two and two together and came up with five,' remembers Molyneux. 'One thing led to another and then it blew up out of all proportion.' Bingham then called Molyneux, the club captain and Pat Dunne, the Players' Union's representative, into his office and asked them to organize a meeting of the first-team players. 'I want to know their feelings on my management,' Bingham told them. 'What he wanted us to do,' recalls Dunne, 'was to come back to him with a 100 per cent backing from all the players.' Dunne told him that he didn't think that was possible because some players disliked Bingham's training and others couldn't understand why they had been dropped.

Dunne and Molyneux eventually gathered the squad together and told them that Bingham wanted a vote of confidence from them. 'The feeling was that we couldn't give him 100 per cent backing,' said Molyneux, and with Dunne he returned to Bingham.

'You're not getting it, boss. People don't feel, they don't think you're the best for what's happening,' Dunne told him.

'Well, thanks, lads,' Bingham replied. The two players left.

'Training had finished that particular morning,' remembers Dunne, 'and so Fred and I went off for a cup of coffee, which was our normal practice, and then we got word that Robert Daniel wanted to see us. We told him the whole story, what Billy had asked us, and this was the first – definitely in hindsight – that I knew we were being manipulated. It's only in hindsight, twenty years later, but we told Daniel what had happened and of course that gave him, unknown to us at the time, all the information he wanted.'

Bingham was perturbed by this show of disloyalty from his

players, and in an impetuous moment asked the players if they would see him individually and sign a declaration of confidence in him as manager of Plymouth Argyle. Pat Dunne was particularly annoyed at this request and told Bingham that he would not sign. 'I got very uptight,' said Dunne, 'and told him that I felt he was putting pressure on the younger lads.' Both Dunne and Molyneux felt that Bingham's declaration caused friction amongst the players, and ultimately between the players and the manager. 'Everybody felt they were being got at and that put everyone on tenterhooks,' said Dunne.

'He called all these players in individually and the outcome of it was that these lads who'd voted no confidence in him had gone and signed a petition that they backed him,' said Molyneux.

Bingham had confronted his players because he believed that they had staged a mutiny against him when, in the cold light of history, everyone – directors, manager and players – merely reacted to what was no more than a bad run of results and, according to Pat Dunne, a whispering campaign in a narrow setting. It is unlikely that a manager of Manchester United, for example, would capitulate to similar pressures at Old Trafford – a larger-than-life setting – whereas in Plymouth Bingham had a local press which covered every move he made.

Molyneux and Dunne were not the only players to think that the whole dispute was a club matter which should have been solved without the drama, but it was more complicated than that. Without the drama the directors could not draw attention to their dilemma which Dunne described succinctly as being 'small-minded people in a small-minded fishing-town with a big potential and not being able to see that'. Bingham was threatening to take their club to places they had never been before. Molyneux was even more acute when he said that they 'wanted success but were frightened to death to pay for it in case it never came off and they were going to be stuck with all sorts of debts around their necks'.

Bingham is probably too modest to admit today that his methods were too modern for Plymouth and that they didn't understand them. If Bingham's experienced players could see what was wrong at Home Park so could Bingham. Whether the directors decided to get rid of Bingham because of the players' discontent, or because he was not bringing them the success they said they so desperately wanted or for other reasons will never be known, because they will never tell their stories. There was never any argument about training methods because Bingham already knew that his players were unhappy with some of his training methods. Molyneux said the players 'just wanted to do a little more ballwork instead of just running around the track and we'd already had a meeting over that and Billy had agreed to do that and change it'.

Pat Dunne said that he felt the board wanted to get rid of Bingham because he was not bringing them the results they wanted. Dunne's implication was wrong. It was entertainment the board wanted and, as Dunne already knew, if the results came that was fine – if they didn't, it was hoped there would not be too many defeats.

Bingham eventually released a statement to the press which he knew the club directors would also take note of:

I will go to the last month, the last hour, the last minute and the last second of my contract to get this club right. I will not bother whether people love me or hate me. I know my wife and two children love me and all that bothers me is whether people give me 100 per cent in training and on the field.

That's all that matters to me and I made this clear to my players before today's game. I told them I didn't care whether they hated my guts or not. All I am concerned with is what they do on the field.

These are professionals paid by the club and if they do not give me 100 per cent effort then I don't want them at Home Park.

I am the manager here and that's that. I am not worried whether managers are popular or not. It is a well-known fact that most successful managers are not.

Those cold words did not hide what Bingham really felt about the game and consequently about the players. Fred Molyneux, whom Bingham had bought twice, believed that Bingham 'felt very let down by what I did'. Like Dunne, Molyneux was caught in the middle. 'He made me club captain but I had to do what was right by the players. It didn't matter whether I backed him or not, I was still out-voted at the beginning because that is the way they felt,' said Molyneux.

'I think the Plymouth board had made up their mind that if the players were behind them in wanting to get rid of Bingham, they would have backed us. They wanted to get rid of him without it costing them anything,' said Dunne, who believed that some of the board had managed to instigate a whispering campaign which Bingham picked up and then went to the players, as if there was real dissension among the squad. 'If Bingham was prepared to accept that he didn't have the full backing, which he had asked us for, and he still didn't resign, then the spokesmen were in trouble because they were seen to lead a rebellion, which we hadn't,' said Dunne.

The board thought Bingham would react and honourably offer his resignation, as soccer managers usually do under such pressure. Instead Bingham shuffled the papers in his desk drawer and pulled out his contract. There was nothing in it about having to resign because of a fabricated scandal. As Pat Dunne was known to say, 'end of story'. Bingham was staying.

When everyone at the club eventually took control of their emotions it became only a matter of time before the exodus began. Bingham, not surprisingly, had decided that he couldn't stay at a club that really didn't want him, and less than three months later both the manager and the chairman found a way out.

While all this was going on, Bingham was still the part-time manager of Northern Ireland. The events of autumn 1969 probably did more to persuade him that the occasional three-day intensive schedule with the Northern Ireland squad was preferable to the frantic seven-day-a-week pressures as a league manager. Even the unfortunate defeat by the Soviet Union which ended Northern Ireland's 1970 World Cup hopes was readily forgotten. There would always be the next time!

In January 1969, shortly after the Plymouth directors had persuaded Bingham not to accept the Ipswich offer, Bingham was given their permission to accept an additional position with the

Irish FA – running their new under-23 international squad. Throughout that year Bingham made several trips with Northern Ireland's full international team and, much less frequently, with the U-23 team.

Following the December hiatus the team managed to get back to playing soccer and in an astonishing display of positive football Argyle beat Torquay 6–0 in the Devon derby at Home Park on 26 December. Victories over Fulham and promotion-chasing Luton followed and then the team slumped back into a bad run, which produced only six points from seven games. Plymouth had thirty-one points from thirty-three games and were seventeenth in the third division table.

There was no real threat of relegation, but the best the club could hope for was a respectable placing by the end of the season. Bingham was, as ever, optimistic, although he was being forced to reduce his playing-staff to cut the wage bill before the transfer deadline. Argyle's longest-serving players, Duncan Neale and Mike Reeves, were listed and they were joined by Bingham's first Plymouth signing, David Burnside, and Barry Rowan. Bingham said he would, reluctantly, listen to offers for Fred Molyneux. Hutchins and Shepherd, who couldn't settle at Home Park, were not on his list but they were also expected to leave.

It was Saturday evening, 1 March, and Plymouth had lost at Home Park to Bradford City. Although Argyle had three games during the coming week Bingham was thinking about the Northern Ireland U-23 squad and their game with Wales at Wrexham on 4 March. The Plymouth chairman approached Bingham and told him they were unable to give him 'leave of absence from Monday to Thursday to look after the Irish U-23 team'. Bingham refused to stay and told Daniel that his contract allowed him to manage the 'Northern Ireland teams', with the emphasis on the plural. Daniel told Bingham that if he went he 'would have to suffer the consequences'.

On the Monday Bingham travelled to Chester to meet the Irish U-23 squad. At the last moment the game fell victim to the weather and was cancelled. Bingham returned to Plymouth. The following day, Thursday, 5 March, the Plymouth board told him he had been suspended from his duties. Later that afternoon Bingham fell victim to the cold-hearted businessman's approach to football. Daniel said he was keeping to his decision that if Bingham went with the Irish team he would sack him. Bingham left Home Park with eleven months of his contract still to run, and said he would sue the club for breaching it. Some time later Plymouth made him a settlement, reputed to be in the region of £5,000.

Bingham's dream was over, yet, in an interview with Harley Lawer, he said that his admonishment had been premature. 'It's hard,' Bingham said, 'because I really thought I could succeed – even after the last troubles, before Christmas. The lack of money was obviously a serious handicap and when I took the job it made it doubly difficult to attract players down here. The potential is still here, waiting to be tapped. I have always maintained this and one must ask, after all the troubles and dismissed managers, whether it can be always the manager's fault. I felt we were on the right road. Everyone in any job thinks he is doing the right things. I did.'

CHAPTER EIGHT

'FORTUNE FAVOURS THE BRAVE'

BINGHAM THE BOSS

I so wanted to gather-in that great triumph and be the centre of all the nation's wonder and reverence. Besides, in a business way it would be the making of me; I knew that.

The Boss; Mark Twain, *A Connecticut Yankee at King Arthur's Court*

Billy Bingham had not been involved in Irish League football for twenty years. Wiser and wealthier than the fresh faced nineteen-year-old who had set off for soccer glory in 1950, Bingham returned from exile to manage Northern Ireland's most successful football club: Linfield. More than a football team, Linfield are an institution, and it would be impossible to overestimate their significance in Irish soccer. The unique importance of 'The Blues' is described by Malcolm Brodie, sports editor of the *Belfast Telegraph* and club biographer, in the opening paragraph of *Linfield: 100 Years*:

There is no other football club in Ireland quite like Linfield. They are loved and hated. Loved by thousands of fans – some of whom have had their ashes scattered at Windsor Park, while others were buried in their Linfield regalia. Hated down the years by the opposition for an implacable enmity, a fierce and relentless sporting rivalry has always existed between Linfield and all other teams.

Yet the adoration and animosity that Linfield evoke are not confined to Northern Ireland's soccer community. Existing in a society divided politically and traditionally, Linfield is all things to all people. Founded in 1865 by workers from a Belfast linen mill, from which the club took its name, Linfield FC grew to represent, for some, a sectarian institution that discriminated against Catholics; for others it was the epitome of Ulster Protestantism, with the true blue of the Linfield jersey cut straight from Union Jacks. For Billy Bingham it was just another job.

The tradition and grandeur was all very well but Harry Wallace, Linfield club secretary in 1970, knew it would take something more to entice Bingham back to Irish League football. 'The IFA had just reviewed their salaries,' said Wallace, who believed that the national manager's wage, 'together with what Linfield could afford in a combined salary would certainly equal what Bingham might expect in English football'. Bingham was entering his fourth season as Northern Ireland manager when Wallace phoned him with the offer of a combined post. Bingham, by a twist of fate, was already preparing to come to Belfast to visit his ailing father. A meeting was arranged for later that August in Belfast Castle. Wallace said, 'When we sat down and added it up Bingham certainly showed an interest.'

Wallace, up to now, had been acting for Linfield on his own initiative: 'The thinking behind it was my own,' he confessed, yet the secretary was bound to report his progress to the club's directors. Their initial reaction was one of surprise and dismay. 'Oh no, we couldn't afford that!' they said, but when Wallace explained the feasibility of Linfield and the IFA sharing Bingham, the board were, in Wallace's words, 'overwhelmed by the idea'.

The psychology behind Harry Wallace's move was impressive. 'Bingham,' he maintained, 'had his fingers burnt as Plymouth manager' and Wallace doubted if Bingham 'could be tempted back to English club football'. If Billy, after twenty years, really had learnt that the grass was no greener on the other side of the Irish Sea, then Linfield and the IFA were only too willing to welcome their prodigal son back to the emerald isle. As the Linfield secretary explained, 'The national manager on your own doorstep was good for the club, good for local players keen to impress him and good for the Northern Ireland team.' It was also, as they say in Belfast, 'good for Billy'.

Bingham signed for Linfield in time for the start of the 1970/71 season on the condition, explained Wallace, that 'we would release him at any time for the Irish FA and for whatever reason.' Bingham told reporters: 'I'm extremely happy about the appointment and as long as Ireland want me I'm available.' Tommy Armstrong, the Linfield chairman, considered the appointment a 'wise step by the IFA', and Wallace went on to describe it as 'a shot in the arm for Irish football'.

From the grounds of the castle, where the negotiations began and ended, Bingham could look across Belfast Lough to the streets of Ballymacarret, where he grew up. Twenty years, but only a few miles, separated the two points. For a small boy playing football in those same streets in post-war Belfast the distance would have seemed much further. Belfast Castle for Bingham then was no closer than Camelot. Yet here he was now, as a guest of honour. In a building more appropriate for a coronation than a contract negotiation, Bingham pledged to serve Linfield dutifully for the next twelve months. The curious combination of business and an aristocratic setting probably appealed to Bingham's entrepreneurial streak and his aspirations to join soccer's nobility. If Billy Bingham was not yet the king of Irish football, to many people it must have seemed like he was working hard at it.

With the pomp and ceremony over, it remained to be seen if Bingham, the most professional of managers, could adapt to a semi-professional side. As it happened, a semi-professional side was forced to adapt to a most professional manager. Ivan McAllister, who had signed from Bangor just before Bingham's arrival, remembers the efficiency of the new manager's approach. 'He treated it as a business; he was the managing director and he had to make a profit.' Bingham's position in that business was indisputable. 'You had to call him boss,' said McAllister, 'and that was the first thing he told me.' Yet Bingham's autocracy was gained at the expense of his personal popularity. Asked by another Irish League manager, 'Do the boys like you?' Bingham replied caustically, 'The boys aren't paid to like you,' and there is certainly no evidence to suggest that they did. 'Some of the semi-professionals were only getting £6 a week, and calling somebody "Boss" for £6 might have stuck in some of their throats,' said one player.

Bingham's part-timers were expected to train as often as five nights a week. It was to prove a heavy burden for many. A day's work and an evening's training was a testing combination, especially for the Linfield players who were members of the security forces in 1970. Players found themselves forfeiting their annual leave to meet the demands of Bingham's training schedule and to accommodate match commitments. 'If you want success in football you've got to have a certain mean streak in you,' said Len Hiller, the Linfield physiotherapist, who recognized that particular facet of Bingham's character. 'This is the criterion for people who want to be at the top in football,' said Hiller. Bingham met this criterion admirably and expected everyone around him to do the same.

Yet initial dismay at Bingham's ruthless efficiency was tempered by a determination to succeed with the remodelled Linfield. Eric Bowyer was one of only six first-team players who remained from the previous season. Bowyer could appreciate that Linfield was under pressure to get the season off to a good start in order to appease their army of fans who would never settle for second-best. 'We'd taken a bit of stick the previous year because we'd only won one trophy,' said Bowyer. 'When you're with the Blues you have to achieve success, so at the start of the season we were very keen and didn't mind the training too much.' A good result was needed to keep the fans happy with the team, and the team happy with the manager. Bingham's reputation as a footballer impressed few of Linfield's hard cases. 'He spent more time on his arse than on his feet,' was one synopsis of Bingham's international career. For many people he still had to prove himself as a manager.

It was vital that Linfield should not only get a good result from their first game of the season but that they should do so in style. A difficult opening fixture had Linfield travelling to Shamrock

Park to face Portadown, who had finished the previous season's league campaign only two points behind the Blues. Two early goals from Billy Millen and Dessie Cathcart gave them not only the game but the confidence that Bingham and the Blues needed. The local papers voiced their approval that night. 'Billy Bingham has got the Blues on the boil. The new Linfield – vote them a big hit,' wrote one reporter. Yet Portadown were considered by many as no better than unpredictable opposition and the true mettle of Bingham's team was still to be tested. Judgement was reserved in anticipation of the first 'Big Two' clash of the season, obligingly arranged for the following week at the Oval – the home of Glentoran.

The Glens had won the '69/70 Irish league championship by a comfortable seven-point margin. Linfield simply had not rated. A Belfast derby was always the occasion for a battle royal, but the clash between a Linfield side, determined to prove themselves against the defending league champions, augured something even more special. Glentoran themselves were keen to improve on a false start to their season, after suffering an embarrassing 1–0 home defeat by Crusaders. Approximately 13,000 spectators assembled at the Oval in the bright summer sunlight that August afternoon. They came expecting something special. In spite of their opposing loyalties not a single one left disappointed.

Bingham could appreciate the rivalry between the teams. For him, it was a strange sort of homecoming. Glentoran, the team he had supported as a child and played for as a youth, now became a formidable enemy in a battle for hearts and minds, as much as Ulster Cup points.

Bingham's men marched onto the field with the stern order 'not to react' to the tense atmosphere of the all-Belfast joust. The manager's warning fell on deaf ears when, after only twenty minutes, Linfield's midfield general, Billy Sinclair, was ordered off. It was an emotional moment for the former Glentoran player who had left the club after being told his career was finished. Sinclair was described as the 'brain in the middle of the park' by Len Hiller, who had worked on the player for four months before he was eventually brought to Windsor Park for £400 at the start of the season.

Linfield went a goal up when Sinclair embarrassed the Glens' defences, setting up Dessie McAteer's charge through an army of Glentoran shirts and subsequent close range score. Shortly after this, Sinclair was sent off by the aptly named Maurice Fussey, for what Bingham judged 'a simple retaliatory foul. The chap involved had committed three fouls before Sinclair took action.' The 'chap involved' was Roy Coyle, the present Linfield manager. The legions of Linfield supporters watched in disbelief as Sinclair left the pitch in disgrace, his team a goal up and a man down. Bingham smiled. With eleven men apiece, never mind Glentoran's home advantage, it was a game that Bingham felt was too easy. 'With eleven men I could have sat back and enjoyed myself. I think we would have had the winning of this game easily,' he said. Bingham did not merely rise to the new challenge; he welcomed it: 'I thought justice was done when Sinclair went off; it meant that we had a bigger fight on our hands.' It was a case of 'the fewer men, the greater share of honour'.

Here was a real chance for the 'new Linfield' to prove themselves. 'In the second half, I had to adopt a policy of containment,' said Bingham. 'I pulled them back, but Millen and Cathcart were really deadly in the breakaways. They could have got a couple of goals.' As it happened, it was Phil Scott who headed Linfield's second from a corner ten minutes into the second half. The league champions launched attack after attack. Despite a Glentoran goal from Tommy Morrow in the sixty-third minute, and a penalty which the Linfield keeper, Derek Humphries, saved, the Blues, with ten men, held out. If Bingham and his team were on trial, they acquitted themselves superbly.

Ewan Fenton, the former Linfield manager, watched the battle from the terraces and must have asked himself what had happened to the side he had left languishing in mediocrity months earlier. For the reporters who watched the game that day the answer was clear – 'it was Bingham'. Linfield, after only eight days of the new season, were already being tipped to sweep the boards. 'To achieve victory with ten men is something of which manager Billy Bingham can be proud. His players, superbly trained, gave everything they possessed. Every ounce of energy was drained from their bodies as they went for a victory which maintained their 100 per cent Ulster Cup record,' wrote the *Ireland Saturday Night*.

What the reporters failed to mention was that the nucleus of the 'new Linfield' had been brought to Windsor Park by Fenton, who was not given the chance to watch his new players develop. He had been forced to release several older players because they had outlived their usefulness. A former Linfield official said that Fenton 'was the best manager we ever had, his team was just starting to click when Billy took over'. It will always be debated whether Fenton would have achieved success with those players had he stayed. They had the talent; did Bingham simply arrive at the right moment?

There is no doubt that Bingham's training methods brought the best out of the players. That they should be congratulated on their stamina came as no surprise to Bingham or to the players themselves. Sinclair, now manager of Cliftonville, experienced Bingham's training programme as a player at Linfield, but also as an observer, when he later visited him at Everton to study coaching methods. 'I was surprised at what little difference there was between what we did as part-timers and what they did as professionals at Everton,' said Sinclair. 'The Boss' was a hard taskmaster. 'A fitness fanatic,' explained Sinclair, 'who based his training on the amount of running an individual would do in a match – usually a midfielder, the most-worked player in the team – and this was broken down into yards.' Bingham estimated the total to be about seven miles (12,320 yards). This figure represented 100 per cent on a sliding-scale that was introduced to the Linfield players, who were expected to achieve certain levels of effort in a given training session.

Eric Bowyer had been attending an American university during the summer of Bingham's arrival and remembers returning after Linfield's pre-season training had begun. 'The first session I attended we were already up to about 50 per cent on the scale and I can remember looking at the charts on the changing-room wall that went up to 100 per cent and thinking, "Oh no!"'

Bingham's training, while 'always very hard, but short, intense and very competitive', as Bowyer put it, was nothing if not varied. Weights were a common feature of the programme, while the use of a rubber suit represented one of Bingham's more unorthodox approaches to fitness. Phil Scott, a player who Bingham liked and respected, was forced to run wearing a wet-suit in order to sweat off weight. By his colleague's admission, Bingham 'probably gave "Scotty" a few more playing years', even if the benefits were not immediately appreciated. 'Those wee legs of his were going about four million to the gallon,' said Bowyer, remembering one session when Scott, who had been running solidly for almost half an hour, looked up and gasped, 'I . . . don't want . . . to be in the first team . . . any . . . more!'

Bingham's methods at Linfield earned him the nickname, 'the stopwatch king' because, as Ivan McAllister explained, 'everything you did was timed. There was no bluffing him.' Yet Bingham could only obtain the desired effort from his players if he had their respect and confidence. What was good enough for his subjects was good enough for him! And to a man Bingham's players were 'impressed by the amount of running he did for someone nearly in his forties'. While the effort Bingham himself put into training sessions was impressive it was, at times, too impressive. 'Out of the blue he'd say, "Right, we are going to have a match, lads", and you'd think "thank Christ!"' said McAllister. But Bingham very often was a little over-zealous. 'He used to love to score goals in the five-a-sides,' said one player. Friendlies between the team would often develop a distinctly unfriendly complexion because of the manager's eagerness to score goals. Bingham had earned a reputation for being something of 'a glory hunter'.

If the players felt they knew their boss well, then it was clear 'The Boss' had no illusions about them. 'Bingham,' said McAllister, 'knew you were never going to get the perfect player and you just have to use the skills you've got.' Bingham was aware of his players' limitations, yet he got his men to believe in their abilities to such a degree that he could make their very real failings redundant. Bowyer appreciated just what a fine motivator Bingham was, even if it meant he bent the truth a little: 'He could be a bit of a con man in two ways – he could get beyond the pale and make players think they were better than they were. He was a good psychologist and he worked a set-piece to death. We would practice a free-kick 99 per cent of the time, until we got it right just once, and then come away thinking we could do it.' Yet Bingham's players did do it!

Linfield were a less than perfect football team, but to all intents and purposes they played perfect football. In the '70/71 season Linfield won the Ulster Cup, the Gold Cup, the Championship and the All-Ireland Cup. Linfield's 3–0 victory over Distillery on 19 September 1970, gave them the season's first trophy and the press congratulated them for their achievement. The *Ireland Saturday Night* wrote: 'It was a triumph for the manager who has made such an impact on Irish league football since his arrival last season.' Bingham said: 'This was a superb show. Remembering they had a terrifically hard game on Wednesday, the way they finished so strongly today was a sure sign of the rhythm and determination of the club.'

'The terrifically hard game' that Bingham referred to, without exaggeration, was Linfield's European Cup-Winners' Cup clash with holders Manchester City. Under Joe Mercer and Malcolm Allison, two of English football's most influential managers, City had won the second division championship in 1966, the first division championship and the Charity Shield in '68, the FA Cup in '69, the European Cup-Winners' Cup and the League Cup in 1970. Linfield, as the holders of the Irish FA Challenge Cup, had earned themselves the right to play City in the first round of the Cup-Winners' Cup. It was not a pleasant prospect.

Linfield had suffered their first serious slump at the wrong time. A five-goal victory for Ballymena United at Windsor Park only five days before the Blues were to play Manchester City at Maine Road served to highlight the apparent futility of Linfield's cause. 'I'll be delighted if it's close,' wrote a reporter in the *Belfast Newsletter*, 'but I visualize something along the lines of 4–0. Manager Billy Bingham is no fool. Though he cannot admit it he must have abandoned any thoughts of winning this tie. His first priority is survival. At all costs a massacre must be avoided. This is a must for two reasons: one – the closer Linfield make it, the bigger the gate will be for the return leg at Windsor Park; two – a reasonable showing will not further dent morale which must be tender to say the least of it.'

That the best that many people were hoping for was a few pounds for Linfield, at the expense of a slightly damaged pride, revealed the enormity of the task which faced Bingham and his team. If the *Newsletter* journalist had known what Bingham was hoping for, the description 'no fool' might not have been so readily applied. Bowyer remembers his manager's attitude on the night before the big game. 'He seemed to be really confident and that rubbed off – most of us were expecting a hiding.' Malcolm Brodie described the attitude of Bingham's knight errants as they set off for England. 'Bingham had them believing they were the equal of the highly valued first division stars. His chirpiness permeated everything; the mood was just right, but behind the wise-cracking joviality was a grim determination to show that the Irish league part-timers were anything but chopping-blocks.'

The manager who knew his players so well knew their limitations, knew their abilities and knew they could do it. Bingham had spent two hours in training before the game, on a 'dress rehearsal', going over his strategy. Any attempt to outplay City stars of the calibre of Colin Bell and Francis Lee would have proved pointless. Bingham instead settled on a policy of containment. With enough faith in Linfield's defenders, Bingham knew the Belfastmen had an ally in the unpredictable temperament of the Manchester City professionals. Tight marking and hard tackling would lead to frustration among the English. If Linfield could hold out against City at Maine Road then anything was possible on the return leg in Belfast. A united Linfield, could just possibly conquer a divided Manchester City.

Linfield came within seven minutes of succeeding and the sports writers were forced to admit that Bingham had been right. 'The Northern Ireland team boss, whose assessment of the tie was spot on all down the line, maintained that his team would "run" City. Few people believed him, putting it down to a manager attempting to boost his players, but nobody's laughing now, least of all City,' said one paper.

Linfield held out for eighty-three minutes. Bowyer, the captain, said: 'It was a typical game against any good English side. We just kept plugging away and they got frustrated.' City laid siege to the Linfield defence but could not penetrate it. As the game wore on, the Windsor men stood as strong as the castle their home was named after. For the 'stopwatch king' it was all going like clockwork. 'It was all going to plan,' said Bingham. 'City became frustrated and anxious. We wanted this to happen.'

With only ten minutes remaining, Isaac Andrews, who had played so well for Linfield, left the field with blood 'jetting' from a wound above his eye. The absence of the teenage star had an unsettling effect on Linfield's back four. Ivan McAllister, at the centre of the Linfield defence, failed to intercept a high ball from Manchester City wing-half Alan Oakes. It fell instead to England inside-forward Colin Bell, who headed-in for the only goal of the game. McAllister later revealed that he had been blinded by the Maine Road floodlights, preventing him from clearing a ball with his name on it. The *Belfast Telegraph* in its match report commented: 'It was the one time when the Linfield defensive blockade, devised by manager Billy Bingham with all the meticulousness of a military operation, had looked vulnerable.' The glare of a floodlight had beaten Linfield, not Manchester City's shining reputation.

Harry Wallace described the game as 'Our proudest hour (and a half)' in European competition. 'For eighty-three minutes we withstood the might of English first division football and but for an unfortunate injury to Isaac Andrews I firmly believe we would have held out for a o–o draw.'

After the game Bingham remained philosophical and determined. 'The boys did exactly as they were told. No manager could wish for more than that.' If the boys did exactly what they were told for the return leg in Belfast in two weeks, who knew what might happen!

Northern Ireland in September 1970 was experiencing some of the worst violence in its recent history. Windsor, for those seeking sanctuary from the rioting in the streets around Belfast, proved the wrong place to be. The Manchester City party had been warned of the possibility of an early kick-off. 'We understand fully that the fresh outbreak of trouble over the weekend may cause certain alterations and there is a possibility that the kick-off may be brought forward,' said Albert Alexander, the Manchester chairman. Joe Mercer, the City manager, was less concerned about the violence on Belfast's streets: 'The only thing we're frightened of is this man they call Billy Bingham. It's his tactics and nothing else we've got to worry about.'

This man they call Billy Bingham, meanwhile, was sticking to his guns, fielding the same team that had worked so hard in Manchester; Billy Oliver, the *Newsletter* soccer writer, was also sticking to his, writing: 'Last time I said Linfield would lose 4–0. I still believe they will lose, but they can give City a game to remember.' Windsor Park was set for a shootout.

Bingham had led his team in a training session early that morning in full view of the Manchester squad, who had arrived to inspect the field of battle. 'The City team,' said McAllister, 'came out to look at the pitch and we were running around the track training and this was the morning of the match.' Whether Bingham was attempting to lull the English professionals into a false sense of security by presenting his side as a bunch of hopeful amateurs desperate to catch up on some some training, or merely loosening the limbs of his part-timers in preparation for the game that evening is unclear. Either way, the City players, some then earning more than £10,000 a year, could not have expected the onslaught that came from Bingham's £6 a week semi-professionals.

Four minutes after Welsh referee, Bill Gow, started the contest

Linfield scored. Billy Millen intercepted a nervous back-pass to City goalkeeper, Joe Corrigan, and tapped the ball towards the net. Despite a frantic attempt to clear by City winger, Tony Towers, the ball was adjudged to have crossed the goal line. Linfield were 1–0 up. Outside Windsor Park the latecomers heard the roar that heralded only one thing. But by the time the stragglers had found places on the terraces, City's Francis Lee had equalized. A shot from twenty yards skidded through the Blues rearguard and under keeper Derek Humphries. A disappointed Humphries complained later that he was 'completely unsighted. Isaac Andrews was smack in front of me and I never saw the ball until it was too late.'

It was to be a bad night for goalkeepers. Joe Corrigan, at the Spion Kop end in the second half, came under a hail of bottles from the hooligan element in the crowd and grew increasingly nervous as missiles fell around his goalmouth. The referee appealed to Bingham to do something. 'I was asked to speak to the police but decided to see what I could do on my own,' he said.

Bingham, standing like King Canute in front of a sea of blue, demanded obedience; Billy had better luck. 'The referee told me he would have to stop the match if the crowd did not stop throwing things. I saw bottles lying around the goalmouth when I went round. I shouted at them until I was hoarse and it seemed to work, for there was no further trouble.'

After Bingham's impressive display of authority Corrigan was still shaken and mis-hit a goal-kick straight to Linfield's Bryan Hamilton. In his haste to retrieve the situation, the giant goalkeeper handled just outside his box and a free kick was awarded. In a deadball routine that Linfield had practised long and hard, Dessie Cathcart took the one in a hundred free-kick that Eric Bowyer had talked about. A simple double bluff, with first Cathcart and then Sinclair feinting the kick, left the City defence confused and powerless to stop Cathcart rolling the ball to Millen, who blasted it into the net. It gave Linfield the lead on the night and a 2–1 victory over the European Cup-Winners' Cup Champions.

Despite the victory, and an aggregate score of 2–2, Linfield

were out of the competition. The away-goals rule meant that
City's Belfast goal counted as two and earned them a place in the
second round. (City went on to the semi-finals of the competition
only to lose to the eventual winners, Chelsea.)

The Linfield motto – *Audaces Fortuna Juvat* (Fortune Favours
the Brave) – took on a cruel irony. No braver side than Linfield
had been beaten by such a luckless technicality. Yet Linfield's
achievement was undeniable, and Joe Mercer was quick to give
them praise. 'That City team was a great side ... We won
everything except the Grand National, but we couldn't beat
Linfield,' said Mercer.

Victory over Manchester City had been Bingham's grail. 'It
was the match he wanted to win most,' said Ivan McAllister, but
now Linfield's crusade in Europe was over.

It would be unfair to the players to credit Bingham solely with
the glory. Eleven men had done the fighting, not just in the
European clash, but throughout the season. Bingham was
genuinely delighted with his team's dedication. 'I'm getting a
greater response from these players than all the others I've worked
with in cross-channel football,' he said, a week after their exit
from the European Cup-Winners' Cup. 'I can honestly say that
the Linfield lads have already given me a lot more in effort and
loyalty.'

Yet the goal that gave Linfield victory that night was as much
the product of the manager's strategy as the team's application.
Mercer could have avoided the embarrassment of a Linfield
defeat by a closer study of the Belfast team. 'I didn't believe in
going to watch them,' he said. 'I thought, we'll just play our
own game.' While fully understanding Bingham's positive philosophy, the City manager, to his cost, failed to appreciate Linfield's industrious approach. 'He's a happy kind of fellow and
very optimistic, who's going to lick us,' he probably thought,
and thought rightly, Mercer might have added. 'I didn't expect
such quality and we were lucky. It's not that we took them to
be easy. We had no game plan, but they beat us 2–1 and beat
us fair and square,' he said.

Linfield had lost to Ballymena before the first leg of the
European tie. Two weeks later a similarly poor result against
Bangor raised doubts about Bingham's ability as a trainer and
motivator. While Linfield could match the skills of an English
First Division side and finish their Ulster Cup campaign with a
stylish and indisputable victory over Crusaders, it became increasingly uncertain if the Blues could sustain a successful Irish
League campaign on a week-to-week basis. Three successive
home defeats and some uninspired away performances shook the
confidence of the Linfield team between October and November 1970. And as Bingham put it, 'confidence is the name of
the game'.

Following a 3–1 defeat, at Windsor Park on 24 October, by
bottom-of-the-table Portadown – the team that the Blues had
disposed of so efficiently at the start of the season – Bingham
pleaded guilty to the same charges levelled against Mercer after
City's lucky escape. 'We obviously went out there too complacently
and probably some of us thought that Portadown would not present many problems. These teams do raise their game when they
come to Windsor Park but certainly Portadown deserved their
win.' With the enthusiasm of the start of the season gone and the
European challenge over, King Billy's reign at Windsor had
somehow lost its appeal. In the corridors of power at Linfield
there was even talk of treason.

The demands of Bingham's training schedule began to take
their toll on the over-worked part-timers. There were 'mutterings
and grumblings about a strike', said Ivan McAllister. Bingham, as
Len Hiller described him, was 'a hard-training wee man'. 'He
took a hell of a lot out of them; he was training them four nights a
week and that's what all the resentment was about.' Yet 'The
Boss' managed to avoid any serious confrontation by relaxing his
training sessions sufficiently in order to get his team working
again. Eric Bowyer doubted 'if Bingham would have got the same
effort if he had stayed for a second year'. The 'stutter between
October and December when we weren't winning', said Bowyer,
had left an impression on the team. Everyone was happy as long

as Linfield were successful, yet Bowyer wondered if Bingham's methods would have continued 'if we weren't winning'. Football teams, for whatever reason they play, or rather play well, don't play just for their managers' sake. Bingham alone was not suffcient motivation for his players. Linfield, more than any Irish League club, needed the impetus of hard competition more than a hard competitive manager.

Bingham's assessment of his players' 'loyalty and effort' on 12 October displayed singular bad-timing. 'Bingham was forced to ease off training', said Len Hiller. 'He had to because the players were just about getting up to their necks in it.' The Linfield 'stutter', however, was to prove to be a mixed blessing. The new year saw a new attitude from the team and 'The Boss'. Bingham had been forced to relax his training schedule and make a more realistic assessment of what his players could and were prepared to do. The team had been shocked out of the complacency that had come from their early successes. Bingham was not prepared to let his players rely on an established reputation, especially when he was not allowed to rely on his.

Linfield lost only once in January, and averaged three goals a game. Bingham continued to drive his team and would not tolerate complacency. Ivan McAllister remembers one match when Linfield had gone five goals up against Crusaders, when the centre-half, who had scored that day, relaxed 'and started to tap the ball about a bit'. Bingham caught McAllister's eye and shouted, 'there's ten other players on the team with a job to do and that's theirs, get on with yours'. McAllister heeded the warning and got back in position. Before the ninety minutes were up Linfield had scored again.

The successes continued, with Linfield taking the Gold Cup; by the end of the season they were one point clear of Glentoran at the top of the table with one game remaining.

That game was against Glentoran at the Oval.

'Glentoran needed two points and we needed one,' remembers McAllister. 'It was a match more like a cup tie than a league game.' Bingham made clear the importance of the last game of the competition. 'Winning the league is the most important thing, it is the trophy we all wanted to go for,' he said.

Bingham had worked on his players' confidence before the match. Using an image of apples on a tree, Bingham asked them the rhetorical question: 'There's only one apple left on the tree, who's going to take it, Glentoran or Linfield?' Ivan McAllister came away thinking, 'there was no way I could ever see us getting beaten'.

McAllister was right. A Phil Scott goal for Linfield after only four minutes meant that Glentoran simply could not settle. Manager Peter McParland admitted: 'We had no penetration today worth talking about. It was a great run into the championship but we blew it all in ninety minutes.' The *Ireland Saturday Night* wrote that evening: 'We couldn't agree more.'

Two goals following predictably from set-pieces in the second half, from Eric Magee and Bryan Hamilton – named before the match as 'Ulster Player of the Year' – crowned Linfield Irish League Champions 1970/71.

Almost all the one thousand Linfield fans who had journeyed across Belfast to the Oval climbed the battlements dividing the ground from the stands, and invaded the pitch. 'It was a complete sea of Union Jacks,' wrote the *Ireland Saturday Night*. Bingham watched while the triumphant fans celebrated Linfield's twenty-ninth title victory, singing 'You'll Never Walk Alone' and, almost incongruously, 'God Save The Queen'. It was as if, for the Loyalists in the crowd, William of Orange had come down from his portrait on the gable walls around the Sandy Row area. It was only 1 May but it could have been 'the Twelfth of July'. The Linfield supporters were celebrating their new champion. King Billy was back again.

CHAPTER NINE

IN THE LAP OF THE GODS

BILLY THE GREEK

This is your last chance, the lies are over now. I cannot understand how a player can move brilliantly with his local club on a Sunday, yet with the national team he cannot even run ten metres. If even one of you doesn't go out there this evening and fight for this team, I can only promise you that from here on in the national team is closed.

The Greek team trainer, Miltos Pappastolou, before the Greece–East Germany game in Athens on 26 March 1986. The Greeks won!

Billy Bingham left Ireland again for the same reason that he had returned to it: money. His departure in August 1971 was not dissimilar to his leaving for Sunderland in the winter of 1950. Following an approach from the Greek Football Association Bingham sought permission from Linfield and the Irish F A to break his contract. As his parents had done twenty-one years earlier, the Irish officials gave him their blessing: 'Bingham the Brave' set off for Greece in search of his fortune.

When Bingham arrived at Linfield the club were disgruntled Irish Cup holders. When he left a year later they had won four trophies and were All-Ireland champions – holders of the trophy the club and the supporters had desperately wanted to win. Even if Bingham didn't admit it, he realized that he could not improve on his achievements at Linfield, but unlike Southport there were, according to several people at Windsor Park, 'sighs of relief' when he left. Bingham had got his timing right, once again.

The Greeks had also got their timing right and in Bingham they had the perfect man for the job of national coach. When the president of the Greek F A, George Dedes, and the Greek minister for sport, Aslanides, approached Bingham on the recommendation of Allen Wade, they could not have known that the forty-year-old Irishman would become a national hero in Greece after only two years. 'I read in the paper that Bingham had been trainer of the Irish national team. We wanted an English coach and I flew to England, where I spoke to Allen Wade about this. My basic choices were Brian Clough, Dave Sexton and Billy Bingham. The Greek board had a clear preference for Bingham. I asked the Irish FA whether they would release him and when this looked possible, I approached him,' said George Dedes.

'I got the appointment,' said Bingham, 'when I was attending an international managers' conference in Zurich. The Greek FA president, I discovered later, made some discreet inquiries of Harry Cavan and Bill Drennan and the upshot of it was that the job was offered to me.'

Aslanides had told Wade that he wanted all the Greek first division clubs and the national team trained by qualified British coaches. 'They wanted a strong man, a person who would be able to control the Greek temperament – an iron fist in a velvet glove you could say; someone who had credibility,' said Wade. The description typified the Bingham attitude, and on 8 August 1971 he watched his last Linfield game against the Republic of Ireland side, Shelbourne, in a friendly. The Blues confirmed their status as All-Ireland champions by giving him a winning send-off.

Bingham arrived in Athens with the knowledge the he could learn about Greek football from the coterie of British coaches already established in the country. Les Shannon, who had been at Everton with Bingham, had joined the northern Greek first division club, POAK Salonika, in February of that year and his Anglo-Saxon insights would be invaluable to the Irishman. Bingham had enjoyed working with the tolerant temperaments of the Linfield players. The Greek players would be his greatest test.

'The Greek footballer is a star, a virtuoso in his own right,' said Greek journalist, Emmanuele Mavromatis. 'It is very difficult to persuade him to do anything he doesn't want to. He can also be rather lazy, so when it comes to hard physical exercise you are in trouble.' In *World Soccer*, shortly after Bingham's appointment, Eric Batty wrote that the Greeks' inability to control their emotions is 'one of the strangest quirks in sport'. What was even more strange, he wrote, is 'that this was the country which began the Olympic movement, with its emphasis not on winning but on participation'.

'Yet the fact remains that the Greek temperament is particularly unsuited to football today, and for years the Greek authorities have recognized this. As a result, they have a unique system in their national league that has no parallel anywhere else in the world. Only in Greece do the winners of a league match get three points and the losers one. For drawn matches the points are shared evenly, two each.'

The Greek FA was forced to introduce this system as an incentive to stop players having tantrums when a penalty or free-kick was awarded against them, or worse, when they were sent off. Games would end prematurely because players who had been ordered off refused to leave the field, causing the game to be abandoned. The Greek FA decreed that the losing team would take away one point if the game was played to its natural conclusion. Temperament, however, was not the only problem Bingham would have.

Alkis Panagoulias had been assistant coach of the national team for some months before Bingham came to Greece. Panagoulias was in New York coaching the Greek-American team when the Greek FA asked him if he wanted his old position back – this time under Bingham.

'I worked with Billy, not just as assistant coach, but as translator on the field during training. There was some confusion at first; I speak English with a strong American accent, and Billy has a strong Irish one. I liaised between Billy and the other players, and made their ideas more communicable to each other. We also introduced a more gymnastic approach into the training, helped by Alekos Sofianides, a former international and AEK player, and a lecturer at the athletic college in Athens,' said Panagoulias.

Bingham made the Greeks aware of set-pieces and, said

Panagoulias, 'emphasized that 40 per cent of goals are scored in this way. This more technical approach to play around the penalty box was all quite new to Greek football, and something the players did not encounter so much in their local teams.'

Takis Econoumopolis, a former international goalkeeper with Panathinaikos, said that the players learned much from Bingham 'which they took back to the local clubs. He cared a lot for the physical condition of his players; they were poorly trained in this respect by their local teams. All the clubs had different methods, and Billy tried to bring them all up to the same standard.' This, however, did not completely please the clubs. 'The governors of Panathinaikos reacted very badly to Billy,' said Econoumopolis. 'The team was at the zenith of its career at that time, and they disliked the fact that players came back tired from national-team practice.'

Suddenly, Bingham found himself at the centre of an age-old problem in Greek football. 'The conflict between local and national teams stemmed not from the players, but from the managers,' said Panagoulias. 'Before Billy, we would sometimes call twenty-four players for national-team training, and get twelve telegrams of apology.' Emmanuele Mavromatis, a journalist with the Greek daily paper *Ta Nea*, also stressed that 'there was very little incentive for the players at national level. There had been times when players even had to pay for their own transport to international matches – a ludicrous situation. Everyone respected the national team, and it was a great honour to be selected for it, but there were so many obstacles in the way of its success.'

Bingham and Panagoulias introduced a system of incentives. 'We called them "moral" and "material",' said Panagoulias. 'For instance, each player was offered 25,000 drachmas for winning the Italian game. A major obstacle to our gaining the full commitment of the national team players was the comparatively small rewards the players received. From the start Billy pushed for more money for the players.'

The story of how Bingham talked Aslanides into giving him £1,000 per man for the Italy game has become a favourite anecdote since the Irishman returned from Greece. Although there is some difference in the amounts Bingham is supposed to have received, it was the response that mattered. 'I went into the dressing-room before the game and told the team. They stood up and clapped,' said Bingham. 'At half-time it was 1–1. I was going down the tunnel when the minister stopped me.' Bingham remembers that Aslanides said he would double the amount. 'When I passed this on to the players the applause was deafening. In Greece it is the fans who have the pride; the players are motivated only by what they can get out of it.'

'But money aside,' said Panagoulias, 'they played for Billy because they respected him enormously. It was a great honour to play for the national team, and the moral incentives were just as important. We would spoil a player who worked particularly hard in training, and Billy made a point of maintaining social contact with the players.

'We made a serious effort to have all our national-team players for training at least one day a week, and for five or six days before an international. This was all fairly new. I said it was a great honour to play for the national team, but the managers put a great deal of pressure on the players not to take risks or tire themselves in national-team playing. Local teams were also where the real money was.'

Greek international morale was low, even with Panathinaikos' success in the European Cup in 1971. Despite the conflict between the local clubs and the national team the Greeks realized that Bingham could harness the temperamental energy of the players available to him and boost their confidence. 'Billy had a great effect on the psychological state of the players: we all suffered a massive feeling of inferiority towards the other international teams, and he simply told us to have confidence in ourselves, that with his methods we would be just as good as the others,' said Econoumopolis.

Allen Wade has said that Bingham probably learned more about management from his years in Greece than all his time in British football. 'They were enormously skilful players and he learned all about separating the players' real capabilities from their assumed (and usually unrealistic) potential.' Yet the description of Bingham's methods by the former Greek and Panathinaikos centre-forward, Antoniades, might have been made by any of Bingham's Irish players. 'Billy preferred discipline and strategy to creativity. He had a passion for physical fitness and for tall and strong strikers. He preferred consistency in his team line-up and tried not to experiment too much.'

Bingham changed the formation of the Greek team, to suit his opposition, but with strong forwards like Antoniades at his disposal, 4–4–2 became the obvious choice. Antoniades remembers that it was Bingham who introduced the 4–4–2 system, which was taken back to the local clubs by the players. 'That is when we learned to interchange the roles of the two strikers,' said Antoniades. 'I remember the game on 4 March 1972, when we beat Italy, the World Cup finalists at Mexico. I remember that Italy's centre-back, Burgnich, was a short guy, so the Italian coach placed Facchetti against me, an unfamiliar set-up for the Italian team. Bingham explained how I should face him, and I recall that I scored the first Greek goal and, applying a certain trick he taught me, I set up the second goal. When we kicked a corner, I had been instructed to stand in front of the opposing goalkeeper. I had height and a strong head, so when my colleague kicked the corner. I would run towards the ball and then head it back to the mid-penalty area, where the second striker would try to score. This is exactly what happened in the second Italy game goal, which Pomonis scored.'

As the players at Linfield knew, this was not an atypical goal from a team managed by Bingham. Panagoulias said that Bingham had drilled the players in these set-pieces until they got them right. This meticulousness was not confined to tactics, and Bingham's ability to work with each player individually enabled him to control their moods. Bingham also invited other Greek coaches to watch his training sessions. They came, said Panagoulias, 'not just from the big clubs, but also from the small village teams'. This was the Bingham style; such individual attention was unusual for foreign coaches in Greece, and this was the reason most of them failed. 'The players felt very close to Bingham,' said Nikos Katsaros, a Greek TV-journalist. 'They felt that he followed the progress of each individual. Greek players need their morale kept high, otherwise they feel insecure, which makes them moody, and then they do not cooperate on the field.'

'Bingham paid a lot of attention to Antoniades, and made him a lot more aware of his aggressive possibilities than he had been at Panathinaikos,' said Panagoulias. 'He was a big, gangling man of around six foot, and Bingham impressed on him how a man of his height could really dominate the penalty area.' As the Italians had found to their cost, Bingham did not treat their game as just a friendly; to the Greeks it was a triumph over the World Cup finalists and the result elevated Bingham to the status of a Greek national hero. As the fans treated the players as gods, it seemed suitable for Bingham to be regarded as the supreme deity of a modern-day football pantheon.

Kolonaki is a wealthy district in central Athens, a built-up area of narrow, steep streets leading to the hilltop monastery of Lykavitos. It was here Bingham first settled. Though he would later leave the area for the beaches and the comparative quiet of Glyfada, it was a fortunate choice for a man who would become a well-known figure in Greece. Football is enjoyed by the widest spectrum of Greek society and nowhere is this more obvious than in Kolonaki itself.

Kolonaki Square is a park, ringed with pavement cafés where Athens' sports people, artists and writers congregate. Bingham and Panagoulias would frequently meet in these cafés and discuss tactics, or subjects totally unrelated to football. 'I had just had my old Chevron shipped over from New York, and we used to drive around Athens in that, like real American big-shots. We would talk every day, often meeting in Kollonaki Square where we would see journalists and other coaches as well,' said Panagoulias.

Despite the language problem, Bingham was clearly enjoying his time in Greece. 'I go to school twice a week, and although I have an interpreter at my disposal, I can now talk to the players in their own language and make myself understood,' he told reporters when he returned to Belfast, ostensibly to move his family, rather than to take a break from Greece. Bingham had left less than a day after he had watched his new team lose 5–0 to Holland, and his sudden departure prompted eager Irish journalists to speculate that he had problems. 'I am very happy out there,' he told them, 'and they seem to be happy with me. The team that played against Holland was an experimental one. We are trying out a group of young players, to assess their potential.'

That defeat came two weeks before the Italy game. Bingham was probably not surprised that only the British press reacted to the Dutch defeat. Their Greek counterparts certainly did not believe that Bingham was doing anything wrong, and when he masterminded the success over Italy, they felt confident that the Irishman could lead their national team to victory over Yugoslavia and Spain in the 1972–74 World Cup qualifying games.

Unfortunately, Bingham's greatest asset to Greek football was to be his presence and his methods. His tactics would be diligently carried out by the players, despite the belief, inherent in their make-up, that only individual brilliance won games. 'He didn't stifle the players' creativity,' said Mavromatis. 'He could not; it's in the nature of Greek football that games are won or lost on the performance of a single individual, and a single player has been known to rally the morale of a whole team, and save it from defeat. They were all strong individualists, but under Billy they forgot all this and tried to cooperate.'

That cooperation meant that Bingham could stress to his players that they work to his plan. 'In international games there is no room for mistakes,' he told them, and he was adamant that they obey his instructions to the letter. 'He always used the blackboard in coaching,' said Takis Econoumopolis, 'taking the team out to the pitch to try out his methods, then back to the blackboard to analyse the results. He was very much against the short-pass style which dominated most of the penalty-box play in Balkan football.

Bingham looking pensive and worried after England have snatched victory with a Mark Hateley goal in the World Cup qualifying game in Belfast, February 1985 (*Duncan Raban All-Action Photographic*).

The Northern Ireland team that took three points out of four in their last two games with Romania and England to qualify for the Mexico finals: *Back row (left to right)*: Norman Whiteside, Alan McDonald, John O'Neill, Pat Jennings, Mal Donagh Jimmy Quin, Stephen Penney; *Front row (left to right)*: Ian Stewart, Sammy McIlroy, David McCreery, Jimmy Nicholl (*Michael King Allsport*).

John McVey, the Leicester City and Northern Ireland physio (*Dave Cannon Allsport*).

Bingham celebrates the 0–0 draw with England at Wembley in November 1985 that gave Northern Ireland the point they needed for Mexico.

With long-serving goalkeeper Pat Jennings, who had performed heroics on the night (*Billy Stickland*).

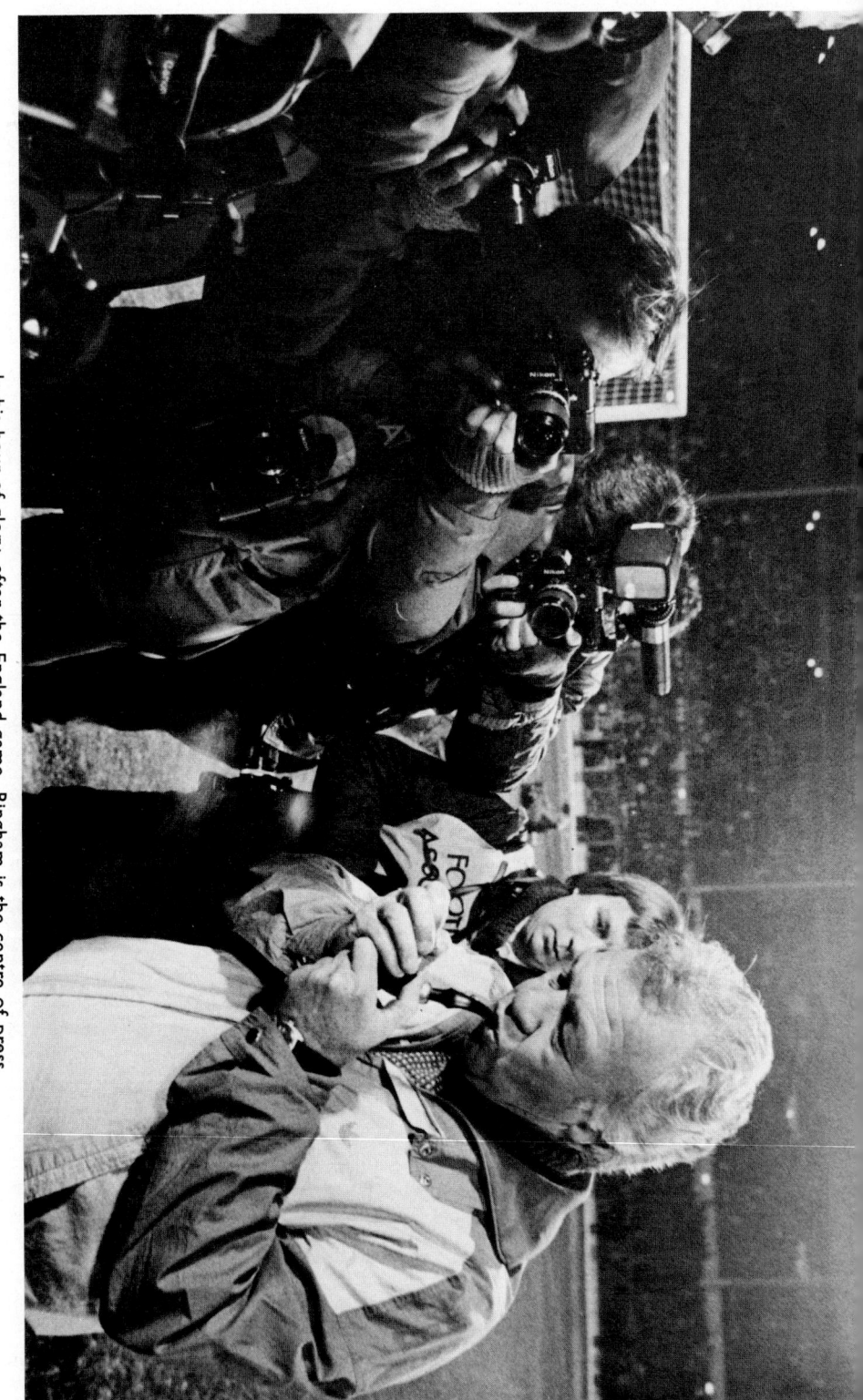

In his hour of glory, after the England game, Bingham is the centre of press attention (*Billy Strickland*).

Rather, he encouraged long-shots and diagonals, and he put a lot of emphasis on free-kicks.'

Yet in the opening World Cup game, against Yugoslavia in Belgrade on 19 November 1972, it was Bingham who got it wrong, when an unfortunate quirk of soccer psychology deprived Greece of the draw they deserved. What happened is told by Antoniades.

Because the ground was wet, Billy told me I would be substituted by Kritikopoulos, as he was lighter than I was. But because the Yugoslavian centre-backs had played for Red Star Belgrade, and because Red Star had been taken out of the European Cup the year before by Panathinaikos, when I scored two goals, they were afraid of me. When they heard that I wasn't going to play they were very relieved, and by half-time, we were losing 1–0. Then Billy decided I should play the second-half, and the two backs fell into a panic. But they were really saved by their goalkeeper. I had one shot against the post and three shots and one header which were stopped by him.

Antoniades' colourful account seems to be fairly accurate. The Yugoslav press also believed that the result might have been different if Antoniades had played from the start. One paper wrote that 'only the result in this vital World Cup qualifying match was bad [for Greece]. After surviving an early battering, the Greeks were unlucky not to have returned with a point.'

The idea that Bingham would leave Greece when his contract ended in August 1973 was hinted at, three days after another experimental selection threw away a two-goal lead against Bulgaria, to draw 2–2, and a fortnight after a defeat by Spain virtually ended Greece's expectations in the '74 World Cup. Bingham believed it was likely that the Greek FA would offer to renew his contract, and it seemed likely that AEK Athens, whom he had coached for a short period, would ask him to join them full-time. But in February 1973 he was linked to Panathinaikos and, more curiously, to Linfield. 'If offers are made I'll consider them,' he said, stressing that he would make a decision before the summer. 'So far I haven't decided what to do. My family are with me in Greece and we are happy, but two years is rather a long time to be away from Britain.' In answer to speculations that he would return to Linfield, he said: 'They are a club I admire. Let's say my ear is always open.'

Bingham, in fact, did keep his ears open for possible offers, and he decided to join the royal blues in the end, but it was the 'Blues' of Everton rather than of Linfield, when the Merseysiders' chairman, John Moores, approached Bingham in May 1973. The Greeks were reluctant to let him go, but they appreciated that the offer to join a top-class, English first division club was a challenge Bingham could not ignore. However, he came running back to Greece when Everton sacked him three and a half years later.

Then he joined Les Shannon's old club, PAOK of Salonika and, in an attempt to escape English football, accepted a one-year contract. In an interview with Bill Clark of the *Sunday Mirror* on 31 July 1977, Bingham explained why he had returned to Greece. 'I think English football is a good thing to get out of right now. There's almost anarchy among the players. Managers haven't got a chance. There are troublemakers at just about every club. It's so different in Greece. My Salonika players are mostly local boys and they are emotionally involved with the club. They aren't mercenaries.'

Bingham also told Clark that he had only agreed to a one-year contract because he believed a year away from England would 'be enough time to decide what I want to do. At present I'm disillusioned with football [in England] but who knows what I'll feel like twelve months from now?'

In searching for an escape from English football, Billy looked for a place which was totally different. In doing so he ignored his own instincts, which previously had helped him to survive in the tough world of soccer. His interview with Clark was very strange, in that, during his time at Salonika, he was not totally happy. Nor did he mention his major tactical mistake in the Greek championship decider against Panathinaikos, when PAOK drew and surrendered their title.

'PAOK has the most fanatical fans in the country,' said Mavromatis. 'If they don't like the team's performance they really let them know, and they are prepared to humiliate those they hold responsible. Expectations were running high during Billy's time there; the season prior to his arrival had been very successful and it's typical of northern Greek football that if the team does well, the players get all the credit; if it fails it's the board and trainer that are under pressure. And Billy was very sensitive to that pressure. I'd say that he had never been so lonely in his life.'

PAOK had accommodated Bingham in a local hotel, but the Irishman was living there without his family and had made no close friendships as he had with Panagoulias. 'When I was up in Salonika,' said Mavromatis, 'I went to visit Billy and he was always delighted to see me. I was a friend from the old days. Billy used to choose restaurants outside town which had simple food – all much to his taste. We didn't discuss football, more politics, and the Anglo-Irish conflict, which seemed to concern him a lot at that time. I remember him drinking red wine on these occasions, which was unlike him; it seemed to make him melancholy. There were players that he knew and got on well with, Apostolides in particular, but apart from that he had no friends up there. He had a translator, but he was not really a friend or a partner as Panagoulias had been. He could ask for anything he wanted, but he was still isolated from everything. I used to tell him that he was suffering from "poetic" loneliness.'

Whatever Bingham suffered from, his methods at PAOK were still the same. Koulis Apostolides, a midfield player with PAOK, remembers that Bingham tried to change the style the team had used with their German coaches. PAOK was more familiar with the German system of play, and right before Bingham we had two coaches who used this style: Branco Stankowitz and Guila Lorant. Bingham was insistent on the Anglo-Saxon style of football – forms of attack which would pass from defence to the centre-forward and then back to the half-backs, to break to offence through the wings. But to be successful, that kind of tactic needs the right kind of players, and although he had first-class material, that kind of tactic cannot be learned overnight. It needs a few seasons and there was just no time.'

Mavromatis said that Bingham 'didn't meet expectations, perhaps because the expectations were too high'. It seemed ironic that Bingham was under the same pressure in Salonika that he had left England in order to avoid. It is also strange that Bingham persevered with a club that was largely unprofessional and had an interfering president. 'The financial structure of club football is different over here,' said Mavromatis. 'Often the president's own money is involved and this can make him panicky and interfering. It can make him feel he is somehow qualified to take the part of trainers. I do not think the president of PAOK was at all supportive of Billy; in fact he expected too much from him, because he was British.'

Then, in October, it became too much for Bingham, and he packed up and left, which prompted PAOK to threaten to report him to FIFA. In the end nothing came of this, simply because they probably knew the reason he had left. 'Foreign coaches usually don't stay long with Greek clubs,' said Apostolides. 'Boards and managers usually treat foreign coaches like gods as long as things are going well. When they don't, everyone tries to get in the act, like it's some god-given opportunity for them to take over the training.' In Bingham's book that just wasn't on.

CHAPTER TEN

BACK TO EVERTON
BINGHAM THE PRAGMATIST

His tactics were always geared towards the team, and had more to do with organization than with individual creativeness.
Martin Dobson, former Everton player, later manager of Bury

Howard Kendall had been manager of Everton for two and a half years when the annual shareholders' meeting came round in the winter of 1983. Goodison Park was a sad place, and the Evertonians who had once cheered and lauded Kendall, when Everton won the championship in 1970, now wanted him sacked. For weeks Kendall could not pick up the local papers without reading vilifying remarks about his management in the letters pages.

'There was a minority of supporters handing out leaflets at one particular game,' remembers Kendall. 'When the gates go down to between 12,000 and 13,000 at Everton they are bothered. We weren't scoring goals and we weren't winning matches. We could produce it on the training ground, we just couldn't on the field. You could feel the pressure, but it was a question of why, not when, would I be sacked.'

Everton were doing relatively well in the first division, but the championship seemed destined to remain in the Anfield trophy-cabinet, where it had become a familiar part of the furniture throughout the '70s and early '80s. Liverpool had won the title seven times since 1970 and Evertonians were disgusted that their once-great club, with all its resources, could not wrest the championship away from them. Kendall was getting nowhere except the Milk (League) Cup quarter-finals, where Everton travelled to the Manor Ground to face Oxford United, who had already knocked out championship contenders Manchester United. In

January, after a fortunate draw, Everton thrashed Oxford United
4–1 at Goodison Park. The following night, also in a fifth-round
replay, Liverpool were three goals better than Sheffield Wednesday. If both clubs avoided each other in the draw for the semi-
finals, an all-Merseyside cup final was possible for the first time
in history. They did, and Everton beat Aston Villa 3–0 over two
legs, while Liverpool beat Walsall 4–2 on aggregate.

Kendall had been reprieved, and despite losing to Liverpool in
the final after a replay, the Everton fans had seen enough to
convince them that Howard Kendall was, after all, the man to
bring success to Goodison Park. Two months later, in the final of
the FA Cup, Everton beat Watford 2–0 to win their first trophy
for fourteen years. And just to show that there was more to come
the club's younger players won the FA Youth Cup. Exactly one
year later Kendall's team missed out on a glorious treble of League
championship, FA Cup and European Cup-Winners' Cup when
Manchester United beat them at Wembley. The man the fans
wanted to get rid of had taken them to four finals and three
trophies in fourteen months.

Billy Bingham had been at Everton for three and a half years
when the annual shareholders' meeting came round in December
1976. League results had been poor and in November the Everton
chairman, John Moores, said that he had considered resigning
from the board. The supporters were disenchanted and when a
shareholder asked what the board were going to do about 'another
mediocre season', Moores took his point, and agreed that
Bingham's position was in jeopardy. Bingham's only hope seemed
to be the League Cup where Everton had reached the semi-finals
following an impressive 3–0 victory over Manchester United in
the fifth round. Everton had lost their previous two games and
were not expected to defeat United at Old Trafford. After the
game, Bingham told reporters that football management was a
'pressurized business' and that every manager has to expect the
supporters to be disenchanted if their team loses two or three
games in a row. 'If we had lost against United, everyone would

have been chasing me and not Tommy Docherty (Manchester United manager at the time),' said Bingham. Despite the result, the Everton board had already decided to dismiss Bingham, and on 10 January, after an FA Cup third-round victory over Stoke City, which suggested a double assault on Wembley, Bingham was sacked!

Some of the players and supporters were surprised by the board's reaction, after seeming to endorse Bingham's position in December, by giving him £380,000 to buy Bruce Rioch from Derby, and Duncan McKenzie from Anderlecht. However, a larger percentage of Evertonians welcomed Bingham's removal from Goodison Park, and several players could not disguise their delight that the Irishman was leaving. The national soccer press reacted as they do to the sensational sacking of a first division manager, although a couple of reporters felt that Bingham had been made a scapegoat by the Everton board. Derek Wallis in the *Daily Mirror* asked why what was acknowledged to be a 'collective failure' had resulted in only Bingham's dismissal. Moores had said that Everton were not playing the sort of football 'he and the crowd liked and remembered', but Wallis rhetorically asked why Bingham had been 'kicked out, when the team he had so painstakingly and patiently reconstructed might, just might, be on the threshold of something big'. He suggested that Moores should do what he had threatened to do in November and resign. 'Isn't it time,' Wallis wrote, 'that directors recognized that although football might be a hobby to them, it is a way of life and a living to the manager.' The truth behind Bingham's sacking was, of course, much more complicated, and Everton player, Mike Bernard, seemed to touch on it when he flippantly said: 'It seems a very funny time for a manager to leave a club, just as they're in the semifinal of the League Cup and the fourth round of the FA Cup.'

Few soccer reporters chose to analyse why Bingham had been dismissed and those who did, like Colin Malam of the *Sunday Telegraph*, described the relationship between the club, once known as 'the School of Science', and the huge Littlewoods Pools, mail-order and chain store empire. In 1977, when Bingham left

Everton, John Moores was the head of this empire, and was reputed to be one of the richest men in Britain. Moores had joined Everton as a director in 1960 – the same year Bingham came to the club as a player – at a time when they were still the top club in Merseyside. By 1973 Liverpool, under Bill Shankly, had changed all that, and Moores' business philosophy of hard work, value for money and an unwillingness to accept second-best, made it extremely difficult for anyone to manage Everton. Despite Catterick's success in the '60s, Moores felt he had no choice but to replace him when the club slumped to fourteenth, fifteenth and seventeenth place after winning the championship in 1970. Was Howard Kendall really the 'truly remarkable manager', Malam wrote Everton would need after Bingham had been paid off, or were there other reasons why Kendall succeeded where Bingham failed? After all, Bingham's team went on to the League Cup final and in his second season as manager he came closer to the championship than Kendall did, until Everton eventually won it at the end of the Englishman's fourth season as manager.

The former Scottish international full-back, Alex Parker – who played with Bingham at Everton and under him at Southport – believed that the Irishman failed at Everton because 'he made the mistake of treating Everton as though it were Southport'. Parker referred to Len Shackleton's blank page which, in his autobiography, he headed 'The Average Director's Knowledge of Football'. Parker said: 'Maybe he could pull the wool over the Southport directors' eyes, but the Everton directors have more status and they're more powerful. The Southport directors took Billy's word as gospel, because they were doing better than they had done for years, whereas Everton wanted immediate success.'

That wish for immediate success, which Everton's impatient fans and demanding directors wanted so desperately, was like a malignant disease which Bingham thought he could cure. Parker also thought that Bingham wanted to manage Everton and when Moores offered the Irishman the position on Saturday, 26 May 1973, the mood among the directors, players and supporters was optimistic.

Moores said that Bingham, 'as a true Evertonian', was ambitious for the club to achieve the success the supporters 'so richly deserve'. Bingham said he was 'dying to have a go' at 'The Job'. 'I've blue blood in my veins and I want to have a hand in putting them right back on top. Otherwise I would not become their manager,' said Bingham. It was emotional stuff, and the press and the fans lapped it up.

Such euphoric comments are common when a new manager joins a club, and when it is a first division club down on its luck, the promises and superlatives flow like the champagne everyone expects to drink from the trophies when they are won. Bingham, affable and cheerful with the soccer press, had the predictable answers for the predictable questions, but when it came down to brass tacks, his answers reflected his character as a positive thinker, a cautious optimist, a pragmatist.

He told the soccer writers that he felt he was 'ready to take on a first division appointment', and referred to his experience with Southport and Plymouth in the second, third and fourth divisions of the English league, Linfield in the Irish league and the national teams of Northern Ireland and Greece. 'I was not ready before I went to Greece, and if I had been offered a first division chance when I was at Southport or Plymouth I would have turned it down,' he said. (Ipswich were in the first division when he turned down their offer in January 1969.)

Bingham had climbed the ladder of soccer management adroitly, and despite a few slips on the way, his experience of English, Irish, Western and Eastern European soccer was unparalleled by any of his counterparts in the first division. He expected to take Everton back into Europe, where his experience would be 'of great assistance to the club'. The Everton challenge was immense, he admitted, and added that he was 'not afraid of it'. Evertonians believed him, and the press wrote of his 'silver tongue and obvious sincerity'. Two of his former playing colleagues, Parker and Brian Labone, warned Bill Shankly that Bingham would use his 'gift of the gab' to rival the Liverpool manager in the propaganda war. 'He's like Shankly in the way he whips up enthusiasm among his players,' said Parker. 'When he was at Southport, he had us believing that there was no team as good as we were.' Labone said that Everton's facilities were ideal for Bingham and 'it was up to him to get to grips with the task of putting the team together'.

Getting to grips with that task was not something Bingham thought would wait. Like the monsoon rains, he swept away the detritus which had gathered at Everton over the previous three years. Unfortunately, the heavy tropical rains flood the land and leave a lot of mud behind. Bingham's desire to run the club his way was not the way to manage Everton FC politically.

Horace Yates, the *Daily Post* soccer writer, knew what to expect from Bingham. Six days before he eased into the manager's chair at Everton, Yates wrote that Bingham had qualities that stood out in a crowd. 'He is a stickler for discipline and it is only his Irish charm that takes the sting out . . . I have no doubt at all that Bingham will prove an amiable boss – so long as his aims are achieved.' The Everton players would soon find out what Yates meant.

Yates first heard the Bingham philosophy of football in the sedate surroundings of the seaside town where Bingham had arrived as a messiah seven and a half years before. 'I have no magic wand to wave,' Bingham told the reporter, emphasizing that Fleet Street could interpret his blarney any way they liked. 'I'm no messiah. I come as a hard-working manager, dedicated to motivating the players to work for me and the club. I promise nothing but a lot of hard work. Everything I have achieved has been done by hard labour. As a player I worked and trained hard and I will accept nothing less than that from anybody.'

Four weeks later the Everton stars would know what Bingham meant when he told Yates that he had his own ideas about training; 'the methodical and scientific approach to fitness' and how to bring players 'to a peak at the right time'. Bingham had already said that he wanted to enhance Everton's reputation 'for playing attractive football', but he also emphasized that he wanted his team to win matches with a mix of 'attractive football, strength and determination'.

Throughout his managerial career Bingham has treated all his players as equals. There are no stars in his team and, more significantly, there are no prima donnas. Alex Parker believes this was why he had difficulty getting some of the Everton players to work for him. 'He treated Everton's players like he treated Southport's players and the difference is that, although they weren't doing well, they were first division players,' said Parker. 'Fourth division players will listen to you and accept what you are saying without thinking of questioning you, but his mistake was that first division players won't.' Parker was referring mostly to tactics, but it was at Bellefield, Everton's training ground, and on the beach at Ainsdale that Bingham's first division players would start to react to his methods.

By the time the players reported for training on Friday, 13 July 1973, Bingham had already drawn up his training schedules and organized graph-sheets for each player. At Plymouth the players had complained that Bingham did not do enough ballwork. After Bingham's experience in Greece – where players walked off in tantrums if they weren't given a ball to play with – he integrated ballwork into his scientific programme of stamina and speed-work. 'Distances covered and times taken by individual players are all charted in graph form,' said Bingham. 'My aim is to bring the players to 100 per cent fitness, mentally and physically, by 25 August.' This was the opening day of the season, and a tough game at Leeds. Bingham had also ordered weight-training equipment, but hoped that he wouldn't 'put the fear of death in the players' by doing so. Bingham felt that some players needed 'building up' and he would put those on 'some weight-work', which was 'essential for those whose physique will benefit'.

Martin Dobson, signed by Bingham from Burnley, said he found the change to this type of training very difficult. 'Billy's coaching and tactical approach was so different from what I was used to. For the first year or so I felt that the training was too hard. Having to run 3,000 metres a day and meet the weight targets he set us, and then play a match with the reserve in the evening – it just felt like his methods were not geared to the

Saturday game. By the time that came along, I felt physically jaded, all the spark was gone.'

However, Dobson admits that he had thought he was fit. 'I wasn't and we all reaped the benefits of Bingham's training programme in the end.'

Dobson's tall, angular build made it difficult for him to meet Bingham's weight requirements, yet he now feels it was all worth it. 'I'm thirty-eight years old and I'm still registered as a player – I'm sure this is to do with Billy's training methods.'

Bingham had already stressed to the players that he wanted 'to bring warmth to the links between us' and establish a strong relationship. He had not forgotten his playing days and Sunderland, and the inconsistent treatment he had received from the directors of the club and the manager, Bill Murray. Although Sunderland tried hard to impress the players, it was only Murray who made them feel part of something special. When Bingham went to Everton as a player he had a similar love for the club, but he and the other players felt it wasn't reciprocated. As manager of Everton, he was determined that his players would feel they were appreciated. 'I want them to feel a real part of a club that is going places,' said Bingham.

Bingham also wanted to enforce a mutual honesty between himself and the players, so that there would be no misunderstandings. 'There is no reason why there should be any coldness, although this doesn't mean that if I have to take some firm decision which may not please a player, I will shrink from it. When I have anything to say or do with the players, they'll not be left under any illusions about what I mean. If someone lets me down I can be ruthless.' When Bingham changed the sign on his Bellefield office door from 'Manager' to 'W. L. Bingham, Manager' no one was left in any doubt who was the new boss at Everton. However, Bingham endeared himself to the players when he scrapped Everton's infamous 'clocking-in book', which all the squad had had to sign every day when they reported for training.

Bingham told his players that he didn't intend to make any drastic changes until they had shown him what they could do on the field. His words to them were simple and demonstrated exactly what he expected of them. 'They'll have to show an all-out effort to me and the fans,' he said, 'and if any of them hint that they are not proud to wear an Everton shirt, I'm perceptive enough to see it and take action.'

As a track-suit manager Bingham had no use for some of the backroom staff he had inherited from the Catterick regime. Tommy Eggleston, the coach under Catterick, left soon after Bingham's arrival and as a magnanimous gesture from the directors for his services, Catterick – according to chairman John Moores, 'Everton's most successful manager ever' – was given a scouting and spying role for Bingham, who had already brought in Ray Henderson as his second-team trainer. Bingham had been at the club two months.

At the club's annual shareholders' meeting Moores told the gathering that 'the king is dead, long live the king. And I think we have a good king in Billy Bingham.' Moores had said the same when Catterick replaced John Carey while Bingham was still at Goodison Park in the early '60s. Alan Waterworth was elected the new chairman and he told the shareholders that Bingham 'is an extrovert and I think we can look forward to a very promising season, because we have a side of greater potential than last season'. Although Bingham had been told there was 'at least £300,000', if he needed it to buy players, he had not moved into the transfer market. The squad was exactly the same.

Moores told the shareholders that there was a 'tremendous feeling of optimism and enthusiasm in the club already. The players feel the manager is one of them and will not ask them to do anything he cannot do himself.' This clearly impressed Moores. The scene was set for the '73/74 season and Bingham's first game as a manager of a first division club – against his old Sunderland colleague, Don Revie, now manager of Leeds.

Everton's playing season actually began with a pre-season three-match tour of Sweden in August, which Bingham said was not the ideal preparation that he had hoped for. If he learned little from the tour, the players learned that their new manager was not known as a disciplinarian for nothing. When Joe Harper, Roger Kenyon and Mike Bernard broke Bingham's eleven p.m. curfew, they were fined £100 each.

Unlike Bingham's flamboyant arrival at Goodison Park, the team's early-season performances were tentative. Bingham brought Dave Clements, one of his former Northern Ireland midfield players, from Sheffield Wednesday, and sold Henry Newton to Derby. Catterick's championship-winning team of 1970 gradually began to leave Goodison Park; full-back Tommy Wright retired, goalkeeper Gordon West joined Tranmere, and Jimmy Husband moved to Luton. In their absence, Bingham quietly took Everton up the first division table, and in November was awarded Bell's Whisky's 'Manager of the Month' for October. In August, Leslie Duxbury had written in the *Observer* that Bingham 'clearly sees managing Everton, not so much as the unrelenting slog it seems to be, but as an exciting journey into the unknown, with an even chance of stumbling across the promised land'. Duxbury also wrote that it remained to be seen if Bingham 'will be allowed enough time to complete the journey'. As the winter nights approached, and Britain's soccer-faithful prepared to wrap up for the colder days ahead, Bingham had no illusions about the promised land, but Evertonians were warming to their new manager's revival of their team.

After ten games Everton were in sixth position and Bingham was pleased, 'When you consider that we have been without [midfielders] Howard Kendall and Colin Harvey, [full-back] Tommy Wright and [forward] Joe Royle for most of those games.' 'Yet those injuries have also helped to prove the depth of talent at the club. Youngsters like Terry Darracott, Mike Lyons and Mike Buckley have come into the side and done extremely well,' he added. Bingham told reporters that his immediate task was to rebuild, and that would take time and patience. Bingham's positive thinking and his ebullience had characterized his first six months at Goodison Park. The players respected his knowledge of the game and the directors revelled in his ability to attract young players to the club. The half-term report was encouraging.

Bingham had emerged from his probationary period as a first division manager with credit.

Then in February 1974 Bingham brought Bob Latchford from Birmingham in a deal which took Howard Kendall, who had lost his place through injury, in the opposite direction in part-exchange. It was to be a mistake which Bingham would openly regret. It also seemed to be a contradiction of Bingham's philosophy. In an attempt to improve his goal-scoring rate, he had sold a player who created and scored the goals Bingham expected from players in midfield positions.

The '73/74 season ended as it had begun for Everton – quietly – and the club finished seventh in the league. Their defeat by West Bromwich Albion in the fourth round of the FA Cup was the only real sore point, because the trophy finished up across the park which separates Liverpool's two first division clubs. Bingham knew he had achieved more than was expected of him. He also knew that he had to 'sustain the initial impetus' after his arrival, and motivate his players to greater heights. Although Bingham said he wasn't going to aim too high – 'I'll be happy to qualify for Europe' – he knew that nothing less than the championship would satisfy Evertonians.

Bingham had just turned forty-three when the new season began, in August 1974. He had been involved in senior football in Ireland, England and Greece for almost twenty-seven years, and his objective was to win what many observers have described as the greatest and most demanding league in the world – the English first division championship. Not surprisingly, Bingham wanted to do it his way. 'You like to win it in style, and to win it with something you have built yourself. You get more satisfaction out of it then,' he said.

He had taken Everton back into the top half of the league, with several young players who he expected great deeds from, in a championship-winning side. Bingham still needed more experience in the midfield and with Colin Harvey still injury-prone, the Everton boss tempted Martin Dobson from Burnley and immediately compared him with Danny Blanchflower. 'He's a

classical player and he plays like Danny . . . only faster!' said
Bingham. With Clements, Buckley (an English youth international who would go on to gain three under-23 caps) and
Dobson, Bingham had his own midfield. He added Jim Pearson
from a Scottish club, St Johnstone, and by Christmas Harry
Catterick had tipped Everton to win the league and cup
double.

Catterick said that Bingham had found the right blend. 'He's
bought well in Dave Clements, Martin Dobson and Bob Latchford, and he's organized a tight defence,' said Catterick. 'He's
also winning games attractively.' Not everyone agreed. After
Everton had beaten Derby County at the Baseball Ground in
December 1974 to go top of the league, the Derby assistant manager, Des Anderson, called Bingham's team 'robots'. The game
had been a typical, physical encounter between two tough English
teams, played more on mud than on grass. Bingham said that such
conditions merited a 'physical game', and his team had adapted
better and won. Latchford had scored the winner in the second
half, after Bingham had told his players to cool their tempers.
'Players were squaring up to each other and I told them if this
carried on somebody would be sent off,' Bingham commented
after the game.

He shrewdly used this criticism to his advantage. After each
article appeared, lambasting his team, Bingham pinned it up on
the wall outside his Bellefield office. It was an unusual method of
motivation.

Bingham was confident that his team could win the championship. He stoutly defended his tactics, and what one reporter
described as, 'his team's twelve draws, their 4-4-2 formation,
their back-passing and their growing image as non-footballers'.
Bingham argued that the loss of Bob Latchford had dulled the
steel in their attack, and that many of the draws were not drab
affairs, as the reporter had suggested. Other soccer writers were
equally critical, and one wrote that Everton were 'a colourless
team who don't lose too often but don't win too often either'.
They asked why, with players like Dobson, Clements and

Latchford, Everton lacked adventure. Bingham was finding that it was tough at the top, but he asserted that Everton would be there at the finish, 'because we can hold our own in any situation – against skilful teams and against physical teams – on heavy ground and without key players, because we have the necessary depths.'

In the mid-seventies the top of the first division was like Clapham Junction – teams didn't stop there for long. By February 1975, at least ten clubs were still in contention for the title, and most of them had reached the pinnacle – albeit briefly – during the opening half of the season. Everton, because they had lost only three of their twenty-seven league games, were favourites for the title and Bingham pleaded with the critics to look at the way the English game was developing and not single out his team because they were consistent while others were not. He suggested they consider the extra tension that the three-up, three-down system had brought to the promotion and relegation struggles and then question why there was a more negative approach to the game. He might also have said that you only play as well as the opposition allows.

Bingham has always believed that a solid defence is intrinsic to the success of any soccer team. As his success with Northern Ireland has shown, he is not a man to allow his teams to go forward 'like a cavalry charge, with flags flying and bugles blowing'. Bingham has said on numerous occasions that he does not 'contribute to the belief that it does not matter how many goals the opposition score as long as we score one more'. His philosophy proved correct for Northern Ireland when Bingham the pragmatist replaced Danny Blanchflower the romantic. 'A lot of players who I played with were attacking-players,' said Blanchflower, 'and Bingy was an attacker; what they were looking for was a way to stop themselves; it's easier for them to be defensive, because they knew what the tricks were.'

When Peter Corrigan of the *Observer* interviewed Bingham in February 1975, these sentiments were prevalent in Bingham's answers, and the Everton manager's arguments were water-tight:

We have had to use twenty-four players in the first team this season. Of the team which played in our first match [of the season] only two played against Spurs last week. That's a big turnover. We've had to put a lot of responsibility on very young shoulders, and yet we have managed to keep picking up points, home and away. People say we are negative because we have had so many draws, and they say we are hard to beat in a way which does not sound like a compliment. But we have scored twenty-two goals in away matches, which is hardly a defensive sign. Seven of these draws have been at home, which is not usually where a team plays negatively. Five of the draws happened when Bob Latchford was injured, and he is so important to us when it comes to getting goals. We are a developing side. We work hard at perfecting a tactically flexible game, at summing up opponents, because we know you don't become a good side without this. If you analyse the good teams – Leeds for instance – they all went through hard, formative years. It is a hard game to learn and you have to learn it within the team framework. It is the vogue to cry for the aesthetic, for the individual skills, but football is a team game after all, and the only freedom comes from being in a good team. We are too much in a hurry, and Don Revie is right when he says we have to learn patience.

Corrigan suggested that perhaps Everton had made 'an unscheduled stop at the top of the league' on their way to becoming a good team. Corrigan would be proved right by the end of the season, but Bingham got little sympathy from Evertonians in his cry for patience as Derby County stole in to take the championship and left Everton in fourth place. Yet, in only his second season as a first division manager, Bingham had achieved more than he could have realistically hoped for. His progress was consistent with Moores' belief that Everton should achieve success under Bingham within three years. But Bingham believed that Everton was still rebuilding and was under-strength in several key positions. Everton lost the title because they drew games they should have won, dropped points against lesser teams, suffered several bad injuries at crucial stages in the season, lacked that little bit of flair, or magic, when it mattered, and had not had the run of the ball on several occasions. In other words, Bingham's tactics had produced a better league placing than could have been expected from the players he had in his squad. The cavaliers of entertaining soccer had attacked Bingham's team for their negative football, when it was obvious to experienced coaches that the Irishman was getting a better response out of his players than other first division managers were getting out of theirs. Unfortunately for Bingham, what should have been a perfect foundation to build on for the following season was to become his downfall, and he would not repeat his success of the '74/75 season. As Steve Burtenshaw, who would become Bingham's chief coach, said, 'Only one team can win the title each season.' Evertonians just wished it wasn't Liverpool!

Bingham had benefited immensely from his years in Greece, where he had adapted a wintry coaching manual to the summery skills of the flamboyant Greeks. At Everton, Bingham was still trying to coax his players to force the maximum out of their actual abilities and to get them to play for each other.

Bingham's experience as a player with Sunderland had taught him that skilful, 'star' players do not necessarily make a club successful. Bingham knew that he could only make Everton successful if he gathered together the right type of players, who would assume an unselfish approach to the game and accept their responsibilities to the team. Many observers of Bingham's Everton era have said that his failure was born out of his inability to get the right type of players, who would play to this system; hence Alex Parker's comment that Bingham did not treat some of the players as they wanted him to. 'We are first division players and demand to be treated as such.' 'No,' Bingham might have said, 'you are the individual parts of a machine that will only function successfully when they are propertly synchronized.'

Inevitably, transfers followed, as Bingham moved into his third season with Everton. He had sold his hapless striker, Joe Royle, to Manchester City, and had added Welsh international, David Smallman, to the forward line, remarking that the acquisition was an important addition to the squad. With winter approaching and the pressure mounting on Bingham, Bryan Hamilton was bought from Ipswich and Martin Murray from Home Farm in Dublin. Bingham said he wanted midfield players who could score goals. 'Bryan certainly fulfils that requirement,' said Bingham. Hamilton was perfect in many other ways. He had played under Bingham at the Irish league club Linfield, as a twenty-six-year-old part-time footballer, with no prospect of becoming a professional. Within a season of Bingham's arrival at Linfield, Hamilton was transferred to Ipswich for approximately £20,000 – a substantial fee for an Irish league player. To justify the amount, Ipswich put Hamilton straight into their first team, and the Irishman was forced to make the grade or go back to part-time soccer in Ireland. Bingham needed that same sort of dedication and determination at Everton if he was going to achieve the success Moores had expected of him by the end of the '75/76 season.

Although there was no daily or weekly pressure on Bingham, there was pressure on him to get results, as there is on all managers. By Christmas 1975, several reporters began to tighten the screws. One soccer writer said that Bingham needed 'a win more desperately than at any time during his two and a half years at Goodison, to relieve the mounting pressure on him'. Admittedly the season had started badly for Bingham. Elimination from Europe by A. C. Milan, defeat by Notts County in the League (Milk) Cup and several embarrassing league results, which had pushed Everton into mid-table, had affected the attendances and Bingham's position. 'Many clubs would not regard that as a slump, but at Everton it is, because of the pressure always on us, as a club in a city so wrapped up in football,' said Bingham. The gates had dropped from an average of 40,000 to less than 30,000 which, reporters claimed, meant that Everton were losing £3,000 a week.

It seemed that instead of a heavenly sojourn, someone had given Bingham the wrong set of maps and he was now descending into hell. Steve Burtenshaw's arrival had allowed Bingham to alter the coaching methods. 'Billy wanted a different outlook,' said Burtenshaw, 'and he wanted me to provide a few different thoughts.' Bingham said the change in the training pattern was one of many 'different things' they had tried, to bring the team out of what he described as 'a rut of poor results – the first we have had since I became manager'. Yet the press and the supporters didn't seem to believe that the rut had been caused by 'a considerable number of injuries to first-team players', which meant he was unable to field a settled side, and 'a loss of form by some players at the same time'. Two months later, Everton's spoilt footballers would react to Bingham's methods. Bingham, sadly, had heard it all before.

Several close observers of Bingham's career as a club manager believe he accepted the positions at Plymouth and Everton before he was ready for them. At Plymouth he was too professional, too soon, and at Everton he tried to ignore the politics. 'You have to be a politician at Everton,' said one soccer writer. 'I don't think he was ready for Everton,' said Allen Wade. 'He was intimidated by them. In Liverpool, Everton are the class club, despite Liverpool's success, and players are put on pedestals. That makes it harder to manage, because players talk to directors and fans talk to players. It was not like Liverpool's boot-room, where, if you didn't do as you were told, you'd get a clout across the ear.'

It became apparent to the supporters that Bingham was not the manager they thought he would be. Several expected his team to play the kind of entertaining football they had become accustomed to when he was at Everton in the early '60s. Tom Cannon, an Everton supporter since the '50s, could see the creative side of Bingham as a manager but he felt that he was 'trying to do more with Everton than was possible at the time'. Cannon felt that Bingham lacked a 'hard man' in the team. 'They were open and creative, but all good teams need a hardness in their team and I don't think Bingham had that. I always had the feeling that he was picking the right players, but they weren't doing it on the pitch, and at the end of the day the manager can only put them on the pitch, he can't play the game for them.' Cannon also felt that Bingham was changing the team for no underlying reason and 'it seemed he was doing this because he was reacting' to the pressures around him.

The people on the terraces can often see that something is

wrong in a football club without being able to identify the problem. Cannon was not alone in realizing that several players were disenchanted with Bingham's management. Reporters on the Liverpool papers could not fail to notice this, and one wrote that 'every Everton fan has his own stock of stories about discontent among the playing staff' and that there must be 'some substance' to these rumours.

Everton, of course, is no ordinary club. Bingham is no ordinary manager, but when he was faced with the demands of players who thought their contracts were inadequate, the crisis at Goodison Park raced out of his control. Bingham could tell his players at Southport and Plymouth that they were being paid an adequate wage; at Everton it wasn't as simple as that. First division players sign contracts, when they are transferred from club to club, that guarantee them a wage they believe is commensurate with their talent. Bingham's problems at Everton began when several players came to him at the beginning of the '75/76 season, looking for better contracts. Bingham, in his inimitable manner, assured them that they were being paid a fair wage, but as the season ground on and Everton flopped out of the F A Cup and began to slip further down the first division table, the frustrations of both the manager and the players became public knowledge.

Bingham had constantly changed his injury-hit team in an attempt to find the right balance, and when he left Gary Jones and Mick Buckley out of the team to play Manchester City, at Maine Road, on 21 February the dam burst. Outside the ground a small group of Everton supporters demanded his resignation. Inside Maine Road, Jones and Buckley spoke to reporters about their disillusionment and said they were going to request a move.

Buckley told reporters that he had 'been dropped, brought back and then dropped again. This kind of thing can really affect my career.' The England under-23 international's response was not atypical of a player with a first division club, who feels his career is more important that the success of the team. Jones simply wanted a better contract. 'I'm not trying to cause a rift,' he told reporters, 'but if I don't speak up, then nothing will be done. A lot of things have caused this. Partly it's financial, because I've not been happy with my terms since the start of the season. There are some players on better terms – which I resent. We haven't won anything again this season and I can't see anything being won in the near future.'

On the Monday after the game Bingham and Burtenshaw held a conference with the players and the training-ground was barred to the press. Bingham was disturbed by the leakage of information from Goodison Park and Bellefield. But he had bolted the door too late!

Everton ended the season eleventh in the league – a respectable enough position for most clubs going through a transition. Bingham had weathered the storm remarkably well, although he admitted that he had been hurt by the internal disputes and the external taunts. Those who were close to him knew that his heart and soul were in Everton Football Club. 'I want to be successful here,' he told local reporter Charles Burgess. 'I am a little sad over it all because one person starts something and others pick it up. I am an Evertonian like them, and there is nobody who wants the team to do well more than me.' Bingham added that he was doing his best, yet that, and his undoubted loyalty, did not seem to be enough. The three years Moores had given him to bring success to Goodison Park were to become Bingham's watershed. It was May 1976. Bingham was optimistic that the new season would bring success. He was right; it would, but he wouldn't be there to enjoy it.

It is a matter of conjecture whether Bingham would have brought the League Cup to Goodison Park. He had taken the team to the semi-finals when he was sacked on 10 January 1977. The team which his successor, Gordon Lee, led out at Wembley was not significantly different from the selection Bingham would have made. The Irishman's success in knock-out competitions suggests that he would have brought the trophy back to Liverpool.

Bingham had said it was ironic that 'just as the team is beginning to take shape, I have to leave it on the verge of the Wembley turf in the League Cup'. He had accepted the Board's decision calmly, for a man whose ambition was about to be realized by someone else. It was a blow that Bingham would never really recover from. To the end, Bingham stood by his methods, and told reporters: 'I have had pressures from every quarter, and I have tried to do the job as well as I could. Some people may debate whether that was the right way, but it was the best I could do.'

Bingham was philosophical about his dismissal. 'It's bound to come sooner or later in management,' he said. Bingham was proud of his record in management, at Southport, Plymouth Argyle, Linfield, the Greek F A and Everton, and he was confident that he would 'pick up another manager's job in the Football League'. Bingham knew that his semi-retirement would not last long, and it was no surprise when John Church, his former chairman at Southport, suggested that a place on the board at Haig Avenue might suit him. Bingham considered it and on 11 February he bought £1,000 of shares at Southport and became a director. He had promised, some weeks before, that if he did become a director he would dedicate himself to 'being nice to the manager'. He never got the chance, and John Church thought it was February 1968 again when Bingham took off for Greece to manage PAOK Salonika at the end of April.

Bingham had stayed in England long enough to watch Gordon Lee lead Everton out for the League Cup final at Wembley.

By rights, it should have been me leading Everton onto the field. It is my team – the same players I spent three and a half years bringing together. I'm pleased for the players that they're at Wembley, because they strove to get there. But I have my pride. I was appointed manager to get them somewhere and having got them to the verge of it, I had to leave. But I'm professional and philosophical enough about football and its ups and down to try to overcome the feelings one gets.

Those feelings were just enough to persuade him to stay in Greece for what Bingham described as a 'breathing space', away from the English football scene. The move to Salonika, however, was premature, and Bingham was back in England six months later, bemoaning the fact that Greek clubs didn't give their managers freedom to manage. The ghost of Everton had remained with him and he was determined to exorcize it for ever.

Bingham returned to an English autumn and immediately began to canvass for a manager's position. 'I'm a proud man and I want the chance to prove that I am a good manager,' he told a soccer writer. For several months his name was linked to various clubs, mostly in the first division, and then on 28 February 1978, Arthur Patrick, the chairman of second division Mansfield Town, announced that Bingham had replaced Peter Morris, who had joined Newcastle United, as manager of the club.

Bingham said his 'appetite for management' had been restored, and all he wanted was the right opportunity. 'Mansfield approached me and they need me as much as I need them,' said Bingham. Mansfield Town were at the bottom of the second division. Bingham said he was going to try his best to improve their placing. 'I'm very optimistic,' he said. 'I believe that faith can move mountains. You look at teams like Blyth Spartans and wonder how they can win at Stoke and get a result at Wrexham. It's a question of making the players believe they can do it.' The philosophy was still the same; dedication, determination and motivation. Bingham was back. 'I know Mansfield are not in a good position, but then Everton were not in a very good position when I took them over,' he said. This time Bingham was more cautious and agreed to stay at Mansfield until the end of the season, and then talk terms!

It is difficult to know what motivates football managers, the money or the challenge. Not all are honest about their reasons; for Bingham it was both. He started at Southport as a trainer–coach on a meagre salary and, when the board realized they had something special, they increased it to match any offers other clubs might make. But the money wasn't enough, because Bingham felt he could not improve on what he had already achieved at Southport.

At Plymouth, the money and the challenge could not be ignored; at Linfield, he had something to prove and plenty to gain; at

Everton and in Greece he was offered the best money and the hardest challenges – in one he succeeded beyond even his own dreams and became a national hero in the process, while the other became a nightmare when time ran out on him.

Yet the posts he took were not easy, all his clubs were going through crises when he joined them, with the exception, perhaps, of Southport, who could only improve on their lowly position in the fourth division. It was a challenge that Bingham relished, but it wasn't quite enough to satisfy his craving for a club he could take to the stars.

Plymouth were struggling to consolidate their newly acquired second division status, but they had the resources to go places. Bingham failed because he could not get players to go there and because the club had virtually no money. The greatest irony of those days is that Plymouth pioneered the football lottery system as it is known today, but were unable to make it work in the late '60s for various reasons. In 1984 the club reported a profit of £189,000 from their lottery scheme – money which would have realized many of Bingham's dreams if the system had worked when he was there.

Everton were one of the country's top clubs, with a reputation which was being undermined by their neighbours, Liverpool, when Bingham became manager. His dismissal almost broke his heart. Mansfield Town ... well, Mansfield were like Plymouth Argyle, only ten years on. They were struggling to hold on to their newly acquired second division status when he joined them in February 1978. Like Plymouth, nothing less than relegation seemed to be their fate, yet Bingham nearly pulled them away from the edge. He failed because his players could not score from the penalty-spot. Bingham tried to placate the Stags' fans who couldn't understand why the team was losing important games simply because it could not score from a dead-ball situation:

I am sure it is a great deal to do with tension and pressure. In other words, it is psychological. Just as it is with the scoring of goals anyway. If a side is doing well, if everything is going smoothly and the ball is running for you, then there is no anxiety and the confidence is there. On the other hand, when everything is against you, results are wrong, injuries crop up – and the rest; then over-anxiousness creeps in. One thing I can assure you; in training sessions there is no sign of penalty nerves.

Bingham attempted to do at Field Mill what he had done at Haig Avenue. At Southport he had the backing of a sympathetic board and several good players, who knew him and his methods. Terry Harkin had played with Bingham at Port Vale, and Bingham then rescued the Derryman from Notts County when he joined Southport.

'I really enjoyed listening to him, and his training was smashing. There was a great variety, we did something different every day, and the great advantage was the salt-baths at Southport, where he took us to relax after a session,' remembers Harkin.

At Mansfield, Bingham had a reasonably decent squad when he arrived. The addition of several players, including Belfast-born John McClelland, whom Bingham bought for £10,000 from the Northern Premier League club, Bangor City, suggested that Mansfield could bounce straight back to division two. The chairman, Arthur Patrick, certainly thought so.

After the signing of McClelland, he said: 'This is just the first of several positive moves to strengthen our first-team squad.' Referring to the three-year contract Bingham had signed a month earlier, Patrick said: 'We made sure of the most important factor, ensuring a long stay at Field Mill for one of the top managers in the game, Billy Bingham.

'Now we shall make certain he has the facilities, and we are confident that he will be in a position to build up the squad and take us back into division two.'

Patrick's optimism was not atypical of a Football League chairman. Bingham was delighted that he had another chance to prove himself in English football, but the gods had turned against him. The winter of '78/79 fell hard on the Pennines, and Bingham found himself with a disgruntled squad and a back-load of games to play in the spring of '79. Then fate intervened. Bingham and

Patrick quarrelled over the signing of Luton's Steve Taylor, who joined Mansfield as part of a deal which took Bingham's centre-half Mick Saxby to the Bedfordshire club. On 9 July 1979 Bingham and Mansfield Town agreed to mutually terminate their arrangement. It was the storm before the calm. There was only one place Bingham could go.

CHAPTER ELEVEN

MEXICO

BINGHAM THE MOTIVATOR

Complacency is the only thing we have to fear.
Billy Bingham

Karl Heinz Rummenigge stepped onto the pitch at Windsor Park and looked at what might have been a scene from a gothic novel. Barbed wire embraced the perimeter of the ground. Pieces of litter flapped in distress as a cold northern wind blew down from the Black Mountain. The German stared in disbelief at the ramshackle stadium. The old Railway Stand, silhouetted against the arc of the floodlights, looked like the carcass of some huge and rotting animal. A skeleton of steel struts and stanchions poked through wounds in the shelter's corrugated skin. Rummenigge shivered. The wind and rain brought a surreal quality to the ground, while the faithful marched through the turnstiles and brought the stands to life. The guttural cries of the Northern Ireland supporters matched the ferocity of the November weather. Rummenigge listened to the unintelligible obscenities that served as a welcome to Belfast, while the Irish supporters waited for their team to appear.

From the gloom of the players' tunnel a pair of small but shining eyes peered out from under distinctive, slanted brows. Billy Bingham watched as Rummenigge stood alone and thought to himself, 'My God, he thinks he's landed on the moon. He doesn't want to play.' Bingham turned on his heels and ran to the players' changing-room. The great Rummenigge and West Germany were frightened of lowly little Northern Ireland, and Bingham couldn't wait to tell his players. 'They don't fancy it,' he said. 'Get stuck in, make sure they know we know that they don't fancy it.'

The story of how Northern Ireland had West Germany shaking in their football boots is one Bingham likes to tell. Yet it is unclear if it was the lack of hospitality in the Belfast weather and the Belfast fans, rather than Billy Bingham's reputation, which sent a shiver up Rummenigge's spine.

Either way, the Germans had good reason to be afraid. Northern Ireland had not lost at home for three years and, as British champions, were rated as one of the top six European teams. 'It was,' as Bingham said, 'not too bad for a nation that wouldn't fill Birmingham.' To these considerable achievements Bingham could add another home victory, against the Germans on that cold November night, in the 1982–84 European Championships.

The sight of Rummenigge looking decidedly apprehensive about the prospect of facing Northern Ireland was, for Bingham, the perfect illustration of the team's growing international stature. It was what Bingham needed to instil confidence into his players. 'It's funny, but that night I was struggling a bit for my team talk. I believe you've got to have one little item to hit the players with,' he said. The Northern Ireland team was, quite naturally, in awe of the European champions' reputation but 'that one little item', courtesy of Rummenigge, was proof of the Germans' respect for Northern Ireland's achievements.

If Bingham had been concerned by the lack of confidence in his team before the Belfast game, it was over-confidence that could prove a destructive force in Hamburg, almost a year to the day later, the scene of the return leg with Germany. Bingham, as always, had no illusions about the task facing his team. The West Germans had beaten Northern Ireland 5–0 in Cologne in 1977, and would be desperate to gain revenge for their Belfast defeat. Bingham told his team, in no uncertain terms: 'These Germans can turn you over, like the last time we were here. They can leave you looking for holes to crawl into.' Then Bingham gave the team 'the good news'. 'Run when you feel like dropping, concentrate till it hurts and maybe, just maybe, you'll get out of this with a bit of pride.' Norman Whiteside's goal, together with Pat Jennings obeying Billy Bingham's pre-match instructions to the letter, meant Northern Ireland had officially improved their international ranking and that they need fear no one in the European arena. 62,000 fanatical German supporters applauded the Irish achievement and even chanted, 'Northern Ireland, Northern Ireland'.

Bingham was genuinely delighted with his team's performance. 'I'm happier now than I've ever been. I'm manager of a successful international side. We haven't lost at Windsor Park for three and a half years. We've been British champions, we reached the quarter-finals of the World Cup and I feel that during all that, both the team and myself have matured, developed and improved.' Northern Ireland had come a long way in international football, but it had taken them just a little longer than Billy Bingham had anticipated.

'The immediate goal is a place in the last sixteen of the World Cup in Mexico,' said Bingham. It is a curious irony that Northern Ireland should achieve Bingham's 'goal' by qualifying for the 1986 Mexico finals and not those in 1970 which he had referred to; it is also a valuable insight into the way Bingham achieves success.

The present Northern Ireland team does not suffer from an over-abundance of individual talent; the squad Bingham took charge of in the summer of 1967 did. It has been said that none of the present Northern Irish team would be selected for an all-United Kingdom side. George Best in October 1968 was the only player from Britain to be selected for a World XI to face Brazil.

Bingham could remember his own glory-days as a World Cup player alongside Charlie Tully, Bertie Peacock, Jimmy McIlroy and Danny Blanchflower, and he looked to the 1970 finals with his hopes pinned firmly on the talents of his new players. 'We reached the last eight in Sweden when I was one of the team,' he recalled, 'and I'm sure we can do it again, now that we have players like George Best, Derek Dougan, Pat Jennings, Alex Elder and Johnny Crossan to call on.' Yet Bingham could not 'do it again'. Not immediately, anyway.

Football is a team sport. No manager has a greater conception of a team working together as an indivisible unit than Billy Bingham. That conception was made known right from the beginning of his career as an international manager. Bingham said that he wanted to build up team spirit and some kind of system. Players were to be part of that system first and individuals second. 'Everything is to be sacrificed for the team,' he said. Northern Ireland's victories over West Germany are examples of that sacrifice. Bingham recalled: 'Gerry Armstrong spent a long time pinning down Briegel. It wasn't a great assignment for a proud, attacking player. But eventually it was the baffled Briegel chasing Gerry. My players have taken criticism, but they've swallowed their pride and stuck by me.'

Bingham brought the Ulster, Protestant work-ethic to football. Hard work was to be its own reward but initially Bingham won few converts. In October 1967, George Best had 'beaten Scotland on his own at Windsor Park', wrote one newspaper. It was not good enough. Bingham wanted Best to win as a team member. The strategy was to play Best, not as an out-and-out striker, but as a work-horse in the middle of the field. 'Best would have kept the backs busy and given his forward colleagues more goal-scoring chances,' said Bingham. However, Bingham was not a disciplinarian for discipline's sake. It was in Best's own interests to play in formation, and within the team's strategy, for the temperamental Irishman found himself increasingly being marked or fouled out of internationals.

Bingham's tactic of attacking in formations of three players at a time would have drawn pressure off Best by dividing the opposition. Yet Best could not, or would not, run along the wings in Bingham's favoured style, and often found himself, with no cover, playing across the field. If Best was having to 'win matches on his own' it was in defiance of his manager, and because he did not play the same style of football as the rest of the team.

The present Northern Ireland side's greatest asset is their teamwork. Bingham recognizes that his squad of the '80s, while lacking the individual flair and enigmatic talent of Best and Dougan, more than compensates for it with, as he puts it, 'guts, loyalty, pride and honesty'. Yet while Bingham's players have changed over the years, his philosophy has remained constant. A soccer realist who works with limited resources, he has the ability to make players believe in themselves and play to the best of their – often limited – abilities. 'With no big money to throw around, you don't attract glamour-boys, unwilling to work,' said Bingham, while manager of Southport. The same may be equally true of the Northern Ireland team situation. 'Lads who come here are often rejects from other, bigger clubs, who have lost faith in themselves, but have plenty of genuine ability, if not of first division standard.'

The Northern Ireland side that drew with England at Wembley on 13 November 1985, to qualify for Mexico, consisted of six players who belonged to, either lower division clubs, or the reserve ranks of first division sides.* Mexico '86 may see Northern Ireland's attack spearheaded by Colin Clarke and Jimmy Quinn, players with lower division clubs.

Bingham's achievements are all the more laudable for the fact that his team is drawn from a nation of only one and a half million people. Those limited resources have proved to be a positive advantage rather than a disadvantage. England manager Bobby Robson has said of the Northern Ireland team that 'The whole is better than the parts.' Bingham might ask, 'What parts?' Individuality is sacrificed in Bingham's teams for team effort. Paddy Agnew, formerly of the Dublin *Sunday Tribune*, provides a useful insight into Bingham's ability to organize his teams into a unit. Northern Ireland's success is not

attributable to any moment of individual magic or flair, but rather, to the fact that they kept on playing their own game, that they stuck to their system. Old habits, familiar moves, knowing that if you move forward, Martin [O'Neill] will drop back to cover for you, knowing that if you cut inside, Mal [Donaghy] will pull out wide to make the overlap for you. A team knows these things out of habit, because they have been rehearsed, because they are organized, because they are professional.

* See Appendix.

Bingham is responsible for that professionalism. Bingham is also quick to point out that his system of covering for each other, of knowing who will move into whose place should anyone move forward, that such a system is the product of practice and rehearsal. Bingham feels that he needs every moment of the three days he has before an international to remind his players both of one another and of what they are expected to do.

While Bingham exploits the limited resources available to him, he creates the confidence that comes with familiarity, and 'Confidence,' says Bingham 'is the name of the game.' A nucleus of players have been consistently successful through two consecutive World Cup campaigns. The Northern Ireland team that reached the Mexico finals did so on the strength of a panel of only twenty players. In Bingham's first term as Irish manager, thirty-five players were used over fourteen matches, between October 1967 and April 1970. In twenty-three games, between November 1982 and November 1985, he used just twenty-six.

While Billy Bingham's team has remained relatively unchanged over seven years, it is not the result of a sedentary, pipe-smoking, Southport antiques dealer, set in his ways. A creature of habit Bingham may be, but he knows that a team cannot function methodically and successfully if they are subject to a constant influx of new players and complicated tactics.

In man-to-man play, Northern Ireland will inevitably come out the worst against most top European sides. Yet Bingham stacks the odds in his favour by avoiding that one-to-one confrontation, and having his players attack and defend in formation. He has been trying to achieve this with his players for over twenty years, and it is only the understanding he now has within the present squad that makes him successful. Bertie Peacock has said that Bingham 'very seldom brings in players in untried positions', yet when he has done, his experience and his instincts have told him that it will work. The inclusion of centre-back Alan McDonald for the crucial World Cup qualifying game against Romania in Bucharest, in September 1985, showed that Bingham is a shrewd judge of players. McDonald not only won his first cap, he finished the game as though he had played for Northern Ireland all his life. For Bingham it was simple. McDonald had height and would be more than adequate cover for John Mc-Clelland's absence. McClelland watched the game from the BBC studios and commented how well McDonald fitted in. Many other managers would have moved Mal Donaghy from his full-back berth. Bingham simply could not do that because it would have been like removing an important part of a machine and replacing it with a similar, yet slightly different, part from another section of the same system. McDonald was a shiny new part who could do the job. Bingham did not need to disrupt his tight-knit unit, and Northern Ireland won the game – taking away two vital points. It was easier to go to Wembley needing one point rather than two.

Bingham builds on his team's strongest natural talent. His players are prepared to work, and the manager sets them specific tasks. The understanding within the team, cultivated by Bingham, is exploited, with each player working with the others in set-pieces and formations that are drilled to perfection.

His training schedule demanded a very high level of fitness, but was always placed 'in the context of the game', said a former Linfield player. There are similarities between the training that the Belfast club experienced and the schedule that Bingham de-livered to his international squad in their preparations for Mexico. The special insulated suits that Bingham requires his players to jog in probably owe much to the rubber wet-suit that Linfield's Phil Scott first modelled in 1970.

Bingham, both as a club and international manager, knew his players well. He knew what they could and could not do, when to encourage and when to criticize. That knowledge, as he admits, is gained only by trial and error. 'I think the sum total of my experiences over many years enables me to make better decisions now,' said Bingham. 'I used to make more mistakes in my first period as manager of Northern Ireland in the late '60s, but today I am more sensitive about when to face things at team talks and when not to – I never labour deficiencies, I boost morale, and I know enough about the game to be credible to players.'

That understanding of his players is probably his greatest asset. 'The thing with Billy,' said Robert Armstrong, 'is that he concentrates an awful lot on practising the strengths and assets of particular players in particular situations; for example with Jimmy Quinn, he will get him to stand at the near post and have corner after corner kicked at him and get Jimmy to do a back-flicked header into the goalmouth. He ignores the weaknesses.'

Bingham's ability to capitalize on his players' strengths and exploit them within the confines of the game is in contrast to the efforts of his predecessor, Danny Blanchflower. Trying to get to Gerry Armstrong to improve his dribbling skills, Blanchflower gave him two balls to practise with. Armstrong tried for half an hour until Blanchflower looked at the ground and shook his head and said, 'You're better dribbling with two balls, Gerry, than you are with one.' Bingham relates all his training to within the context of the game.

If you add to that Bingham's undoubted ability as a motivator, with just the right word at the right time or a clever piece of psychology, like the Rummenigge story, then his players stroll onto the field with enough confidence to beat anybody. Unfortunately, anybody usually means somebody with a reputation, and that has now become a problem: Northern Ireland themselves now have a reputation.

Despite successive home wins against Germany, Turkey, Albania and Austria, Bingham's team consistently failed against technically inferior opposition away from Belfast. That 1–0 defeat by Turkey in October 1983 ended Northern Ireland's very real hopes for a place in the finals of the European Championship. Martin O'Neill, the team captain, was despondent after the Turkish game. 'Making the European finals would have been a fantastic follow-up to the World Cup. Now for some of us, that chance has gone for ever,' he said. 'We appear to have a phobia about away-games. Yet again we lost when we shouldn't have. We do well against the big teams and fail against the others.'

While Bingham's teams were always capable of achieving the impossible, it was the mundane tasks that proved to be increasingly difficult. Bingham could motivate his team sufficiently to challenge the odds and defeat the soccer greats, but ten men beating the World Cup hosts in Valencia was only one side of the Billy Bingham story. When the referee tossed a coin to begin Northern Ireland's games against Honduras, Albania and Turkey, all supposedly inferior teams, Bingham's luck invariably landed face down.

Billy Bingham suggests his team's poor performances are the product of his players' inability to travel well: 'I have three men who play like tigers at home, but are timorous away. That's not good enough,' and the simple fact that Northern Ireland, while they can create opportunities and can control a game, cannot take goals: 'Our problem is that we have never had a prolific goal-scorer. Only Gerry Armstrong and Billy Hamilton of our squad have managed double figures in a season. I can't teach my men how to finish. I can only coach them how to create. They must do the final bit themselves.' Yet Bingham's players *can* do 'the final bit themselves'. Eight goals from three consecutive World Cup games in 1984 against Romania, Israel and Finland is proof.

Bingham has no doubt about the reason for Northern Ireland's success. 'It's really quite simple. We've a squad who respond to motivation and obey orders.' The terms that Bingham lays down for success are the real reason why the team sometimes fails.

The impetus of the home advantage is all-pervasive. If Rummenigge should feel apprehensive about travelling to Belfast, then the acid test of Bingham's players is clearly their performances away from home. Bingham's ability, both as a manager and a motivator, is that he can get his players to believe in themselves and perform the specific tasks that he requests. That belief has never been shaken by a hostile environment, but it has been shaken by a lack of commitment by some players.

Against Albania and Turkey, Northern Ireland displayed a distinct lack of urgency and commitment. Against Finland, in the opening game of the 1984–86 World Cup qualifying campaign, only days after Northern Ireland had taken the British Championship, Bingham's normally highly motivated players set themselves up on a pedestal and were knocked back down. Northern Ireland earned a reputation for having a will to win when they had nothing to lose.

That situation was reversed with the Finnish game. Finland's Ari Valvee, who scored the winning goal in Pori in May 1984, compared beating the Irish to Northern Ireland's own double success over West Germany. 'It was marvellous to defeat a team like Northern Ireland,' said Valvee. 'Complacency is the only thing we have to fear,' said Bingham.

There are many theories why Bingham has achieved his success with Northern Ireland rather than with his league clubs. The answer has more to do with Bingham's own temperament than his ability as a coach. He needs to be 'The Boss' because only he can make his ideas work and the Northern Ireland set-up is an ideal vehicle for that, and for his industrious and pragmatic approach to the game. Everywhere Bingham has worked, he has tried to impress on the club his ideas and his methods, which have included building new training-grounds and encouraging a youth system based on his coaching.

His present contract takes him up to 1989 and he has said he would like to be appointed full-time manager of Northern Ireland with responsibility for all teams, from schoolboy to senior. In some ways, he is already doing that. He habitually holds coaching sessions for the younger players and no one knows better than Bingham who is doing what at every level in Northern Ireland football. He has been described as a mercenary, yet he has turned down many lucrative offers to manage other national sides. The job he is doing for Northern Ireland is all the more remarkable because it is part-time. The Irish FA official who, some years ago, said that Bingham was being paid a full-time salary for a part-time job was talking nonsense; Bingham's value to Northern Ireland is priceless. When Bingham was awarded the MBE in Queen Elizabeth's Birthday Honours in June 1983, the MP for east Belfast, Peter Robinson of the Democratic Unionist Party, said he should have been knighted.

'Sir Boss' is probably a title Bingham would like. If he is allowed to continue the job he is doing, perhaps as director of coaching, with an appropriate salary, there is no reason why Bingham's Northern Ireland success should not continue. I wonder how Mexicans sing 'Here we go, Here we go'?

APPENDIX

NORTHERN IRELAND INTERNATIONAL
TEAMS 1946–86 (April)

Substitutes in brackets † World Cup final stages * World Cup qualifying games involving Bingham as a player and manager

1946 England	1946 Scotland	1947 Wales	1947 Scotland	1947 England
1 Russell	1 Hinton	1 Hinton	1 Hinton	1 Hinton
2 Gorman	2 Gorman	2 Gorman	2 Martin	2 Martin
3 Aherne	3 Feeney	3 Carey	3 Aherne	3 Carey
4 Carey	4 Martin	4 Sloan	4 Walsh W.	4 Walsh W.
5 Vernon	5 Vernon	5 Vernon	5 Vernon	5 Vernon
6 Douglas	6 Farrell	6 Farrell	6 Farrell	6 Farrell
7 Cochrane	7 Cochrane	7 Cochrane	7 Cochrane	7 Cochrane
8 McAlinden	8 Carey	8 Stevenson	8 Smyth S.	8 Smyth S.
9 McMorran	9 Walsh D.	9 Walsh D.	9 Walsh D.	9 Walsh D.
10 Doherty P.	10 Stevenson	10 Doherty P.	10 Stevenson	10 Doherty P.
11 Lockhart	11 Eglington	11 Eglington	11 Eglington	11 Eglington
Belfast	Hampden	Belfast	Belfast	Everton
28 Sept: 2–7	27 Nov: 0–0	6 April: 2–1	4 Oct: 2–0	5 Nov: 2–2
Lockhart 2		*Stevenson, Doherty*	*Smyth 2*	*Doherty, Walsh D.*

1948 Wales	1948 England	1948 Scotland	1949 Wales	1949 Scotland
1 Hinton	1 Smyth W.	1 Smyth W.	1 Moore	1 Kelly P. M.
2 Martin	2 Carey	2 Carey	2 Carey	2 Bowler
3 Gorman	3 Martin	3 Keane	3 Aherne	3 McMichael
4 Walsh W.	4 Walsh W.	4 McCabe	4 McCabe	4 Blanchflower D.
5 Vernon	5 Vernon	5 Vernon	5 Vernon	5 Vernon
6 Farrell	6 Farrell	6 Walsh W.	6 Farrell	6 Ferris
7 Cochrane	7 O'Driscoll	7 Cochrane	7 Cochrane	7 Cochrane
8 Smyth S.	8 McAlinden	8 Smyth S.	8 Smyth S.	8 Smyth S.
9 Walsh D.	9 Walsh D.	9 Walsh D.	9 Walsh D.	9 Brennan
10 Doherty P.	10 Tully	10 Doherty P.	10 Brennan	10 Crossan
11 Eglington	11 Eglington	11 O'Driscoll	11 O'Driscoll	11 McKenna
Wrexham	Belfast	Hampden	Belfast	Belfast
10 Mar: 0–2	9 Oct: 2–6	17 Nov: 2–3	9 Mar: 0–2	1 Oct: 2–8
	Walsh D. 2	*Walsh D. 2*		*Smyth 2*

1949 England	1950 Wales	1950 England	1950 Scotland	1951 Wales
1 Kelly H.	1 Kelly H.	1 Kelly H.	1 Kelly H.	1 Hinton
2 Feeney	2 Bowler	2 Gallogly	2 Gallogly	2 Graham
3 McMichael	3 Aherne	3 McMichael	3 McMichael	3 Cunningham
4 Bowler	4 Blanchflower D.	4 Blanchflower D.	4 Blanchflower D.	4 McCabe
5 Vernon	5 Martin	5 Vernon	5 Vernon	5 Vernon
6 McCabe	6 Ryan	6 Cush	6 Cush	6 Dickson
7 Cochrane	7 McKenna	7 Campbell	7 Campbell	7 Hughes
8 Smyth S.	8 Smyth S.	8 Crossan	8 McGarry	8 McMorran
9 Brennan	9 Walsh D.	9 McMorran	9 McMorran	9 Simpson
10 Tully	10 Brennan	10 Brennan	10 Doherty P.	10 McGarry
11 McKenna	11 Lockhart	11 McKenna	11 McKenna	11 Lockhart
Maine Road	Wrexham	Belfast	Hampden	Belfast
6 Nov: 2–9	8 Mar: 0–0	7 Oct: 1–4	1 Nov: 1–6	7 Mar: 1–2
Smyth S., Brennan		*McMorran*	*McGarry*	*Simpson*

1951 France	1951 Scotland	1951 England	1952 Wales	1952 England
1 Hinton	1 Uprichard	1 Uprichard	1 Uprichard	1 Uprichard
2 Graham	2 Graham	2 Graham	2 Graham	2 Cunningham
3 McMichael	3 McMichael	3 McMichael	3 McMichael	3 McMichael
4 Blanchflower D.	4 Dickson	4 Dickson	4 Blanchflower D.	4 Blanchflower D.
5 Vernon	5 Vernon	5 Vernon	5 Dickson	5 Dickson
6 Ferris	6 Ferris	6 McCourt	6 McCourt	6 McCourt
7 Bingham	7 Bingham	7 Bingham	7 Bingham	7 Bingham
8 McGarry	8 McIlroy	8 Smyth S.	8 D'Arcy	8 D'Arcy
9 Simpson	9 McMorran	9 McMorran	9 McMorran	9 McMorran
10 Dickson	10 Peacock	10 McIlroy	10 McIlroy	10 McIlroy
11 McKenna	11 Tully	11 McKenna	11 Lockhart	11 Tully
Belfast	Belfast	Villa Park	Swansea	Belfast
12 May: 2–2	6 Oct: 0–3	20 Nov: 0–2	19 Mar: 0–3	4 Oct: 2–2
Ferris, Simpson				*Tully 2*

1952 Scotland	1952 France	1953 Wales	1953 Scotland	1953 England
1 Uprichard	1 Uprichard	1 Uprichard	1 Smyth W.	1 Smyth W.
2 Graham	2 Graham	2 McCabe	2 Cunningham	2 Graham
3 McMichael	3 McMichael	3 McMichael	3 McMichael	3 McMichael
4 Blanchflower D.	4 Blanchflower D.	4 Blanchflower D.	4 Blanchflower D.	4 Blanchflower D.
5 Dickson	5 Dickson	5 Dickson	5 McCabe	5 Dickson
6 McCourt	6 McCourt	6 McCourt	6 Cush	6 Cush
7 Bingham	7 Bingham	7 Bingham	7 Bingham	7 Bingham
8 D'Arcy	8 D'Arcy	8 McIlroy	8 McIlroy	8 McIlroy
9 McMorran	9 McMorran	9 McMorran	9 Simpson	9 Simpson
10 McIlroy	10 Peacock	10 D'Arcy	10 Tully	10 McMorran
11 Tully	11 Tully	11 Tully	11 Lockhart	11 Lockhart
Hampden	Paris	Belfast	Belfast	Everton
5 Nov: 1–1	11 Nov: 1–3	15 April: 2–3	3 Oct: 1–3	11 Nov: 1–3
D'Arcy	*Tully*	*McMorran 2*	*Lockhart*	*McMorran*

1954 Wales	1954 England	1954 Scotland	1955 Wales	1955 Scotland
1 Gregg	1 Uprichard	1 Uprichard	1 Uprichard	1 Uprichard
2 Graham	2 Montgomery	2 Graham	2 Graham	2 Graham
3 McMichael	3 McMichael	3 Cunningham	3 McMichael	3 Cunningham
4 Blanchflower D.	4 Blanchflower D.	4 Blanchflower D.	4 Blanchflower D.	4 Blanchflower D.
5 Dickson	5 Dickson	5 McCavana	5 McCleary	5 McCavana
6 Peacock	6 Peacock	6 Peacock	6 Casey	6 Peacock
7 Bingham	7 Bingham	7 Bingham	7 Bingham	7 Bingham
8 Blanchflower J.	8 Blanchflower J.	8 Blanchflower J.	8 Crossan	8 Blanchflower J.
9 McAdams	9 Simpson	9 McAdams	9 Walker	9 Coyle
10 McIlroy	10 McIlroy	10 McIlroy	10 McIlroy	10 McIlroy
11 McParland	11 McParland	11 McParland	11 Lockhart	11 McParland
Wrexham	Belfast	Hampden	Belfast	Belfast
31 Mar: 2–1	2 Oct: 0–2	3 Nov: 2–2	20 April: 2–3	8 Oct: 2–1
McParland 2		*Bingham, McAdams*	*Crossan, Walker*	*Blanchflower J., Bingham*

1955 England	1956 Wales	1956 England	1956 Scotland	1957 Portugal*
1 Uprichard	1 Uprichard	1 Gregg	1 Gregg	1 Gregg
2 Cunningham	2 Cunningham	2 Cunningham	2 Cunningham	2 Cunningham
3 Graham	3 McMichael	3 McMichael	3 McMichael	3 McMichael
4 Blanchflower D.	4 Blanchflower D.	4 Blanchflower D.	4 Blanchflower D.	4 Blanchflower D.
5 McCavana	5 Blanchflower J.	5 Blanchflower J.	5 Blanchflower J.	5 Blanchflower J.
6 Peacock	6 Casey	6 Casey	6 Casey	6 Casey
7 Bingham	7 Bingham	7 Bingham	7 Bingham	7 Bingham
8 McIlroy	8 McIlroy	8 McIlroy	8 McIlroy	8 McIlroy
9 Coyle	9 Jones J.	9 Jones J.	9 Shields	9 Coyle
10 Tully	10 McMorran	10 McAdams	10 Dickson	10 Cush
11 McParland	11 Lockhart	11 McParland	11 McParland	11 McParland
Wembley	Cardiff	Belfast	Hampden	Lisbon
2 Nov: 0–3	11 April: 1–1	6 Oct: 1–1	7 Nov: 0–1	16 Jan: 1–1
	Jones	*McIlroy*		*Bingham*

1957 Wales	1957 Italy*	1957 Portugal*	1957 Scotland	1957 England
1 Gregg	1 Gregg	1 Gregg	1 Uprichard	1 Gregg
2 Cunningham	2 Cunningham	2 Cunningham	2 Cunningham	2 Keith
3 McMichael	3 McMichael	3 McMichael	3 McMichael	3 McMichael
4 Blanchflower D.	4 Blanchflower D.	4 Blanchflower D.	4 Blanchflower D.	4 Blanchflower D.
5 Cush	5 Cush	5 Cush	5 Blanchflower J.	5 Blanchflower J.
6 Peacock	6 Casey	6 Casey	6 Peacock	6 Peacock
7 Bingham	7 Bingham	7 Bingham	7 Bingham	7 Bingham
8 McIlroy	8 Simpson	8 Simpson	8 Simpson	8 McCrory
9 Jones	9 McMorran	9 McMorran	9 McAdams	9 Simpson
10 Casey	10 McIlroy	10 McIlroy	10 McIlroy	10 McIlroy
11 McParland	11 Peacock	11 Peacock	11 McParland	11 McParland
Belfast	Rome	Belfast	Belfast	Wembley
10 April: 0–0	25 April: 0–1	1 May: 3–0	5 Oct: 1–1	6 Nov: 3–2
		Simpson, McIlroy Casey	*Bingham*	*McIlroy, McCrory, Simpson*

1957 Italy	1958 Italy*	1958 Wales	1958 Czechoslovakia†	1958 Argentina†
1 Gregg	1 Uprichard	1 Gregg	1 Gregg	1 Gregg
2 Keith	2 Cunningham	2 Cunningham	2 Keith	2 Keith
3 McMichael	3 McMichael	3 McMichael	3 McMichael	3 McMichael
4 Blanchflower D.	4 Blanchflower D.	4 Blanchflower D.	4 Blanchflower D.	4 Blanchflower D.
5 Blanchflower J.	5 Blanchflower J.	5 Keith	5 Cunningham	5 Cunningham
6 Peacock	6 Peacock	6 Peacock	6 Peacock	6 Peacock
7 Bingham	7 Bingham	7 Bingham	7 Bingham	7 Bingham
8 McIlroy	8 Cush	8 Cush	8 Cush	8 Cush
9 McAdams	9 Simpson	9 Simpson	9 Dougan	9 Coyle
10 Cush	10 McIlroy	10 McIlroy	10 McIlroy	10 McIlroy
11 McParland	11 McParland	11 McParland	11 McParland	11 McParland
Belfast	Belfast	Cardiff	Halmstad	Halmstad
4 Dec: 2–2	15 Jan: 2–1	16 April: 1–1	8 June: 1–0	11 June: 1–3
Cush 2	*McIlroy, Cush*	*Simpson*	*Cush*	*McParland*

1958 W. Germany†	1958 Czechoslovakia†	1958 France†	1958 England	1958 Spain
1 Gregg	1 Uprichard	1 Gregg	1 Gregg	1 Uprichard
2 Keith	2 Keith	2 Keith	2 Keith	2 Keith
3 McMichael	3 McMichael	3 McMichael	3 Graham	3 McMichael
4 Blanchflower D.	4 Blanchflower D.	4 Blanchflower D.	4 Blanchflower D.	4 Blanchflower D.
5 Cunningham	5 Cunningham	5 Cunningham	5 Cunningham	5 Forde
6 Peacock	6 Peacock	6 Cush	6 Peacock	6 Casey
7 Bingham	7 Bingham	7 Bingham	7 Bingham	7 Bingham
8 Cush	8 Cush	8 Casey	8 Cush	8 Cush
9 Casey	9 Scott	9 Scott	9 Casey	9 McParland
10 McIlroy	10 McIlroy	10 McIlroy	10 McIlroy	10 McIlroy
11 McParland	11 McParland	11 McParland	11 McParland	11 Tully
Malmo	Malmo	Norrkoping	Belfast	Madrid
15 June: 2–2	17 June: 2–1	19 June: 0–4	4 Oct: 3–3	15 Oct: 2–6
McParland 2	*McParland 2*		*Cush, Peacock, Casey*	*Bingham, McIlroy*

1958 Scotland	1959 Wales	1959 Scotland	1959 England	1960 Wales
1 Uprichard	1 Gregg	1 Gregg	1 Gregg	1 Gregg
2 Keith	2 Keith	2 Keith	2 Keith	2 Elder
3 McMichael	3 McMichael	3 McMichael	3 McMichael	3 McMichael
4 Blanchflower D.	4 Blanchflower D.	4 Blanchflower D.	4 Blanchflower D.	4 Blanchflower D.
5 Cunningham	5 Cunningham	5 Cunningham	5 Cunningham	5 Cunningham
6 Peacock	6 Peacock	6 Peacock	6 Peacock	6 Cush
7 Bingham	7 Bingham	7 Bingham	7 Bingham	7 Bingham
8 Cush	8 McIlroy	8 Cush	8 Crossan	8 McIlroy
9 Simpson	9 Cush	9 Dougan	9 Cush	9 Lawther
10 McIlroy	10 Hill	10 McIlroy	10 McIlroy	10 Hill
11 McParland	11 McParland	11 McParland	11 McParland	11 McParland
Hampden	Belfast	Belfast	Wembley	Wrexham
5 Nov: 2–2	22 April: 4–1	3 Oct: 0–4	18 Nov: 1–2	6 April: 2–3
1 o.g., McIlroy	*McParland 2, Peacock, McIlroy*		*Bingham*	*Bingham, Blanchflower*

1960 England	1960 W. Germany	1960 Scotland	1961 Wales	1961 Italy
1 Gregg	1 McClelland	1 Gregg	1 McClelland	1 McClelland
2 Keith	2 Keith	2 Keith	2 Keith	2 Keith
3 Elder	3 Elder	3 Elder	3 Elder	3 McCullough
4 Blanchflower D.	4 Blanchflower D.	4 Blanchflower D.	4 Blanchflower D.	4 Harvey
5 Forde	5 Forde	5 Forde	5 Cunningham	5 Neill
6 Peacock	6 Peacock	6 Peacock	6 Nicholson	6 Peacock
7 Bingham	7 Bingham	7 Bingham	7 Stewart	7 Bingham
8 McIlroy	8 McIlroy	8 Bruce	8 Dougan	8 Dougan
9 McAdams	9 McAdams	9 McAdams	9 McAdams	9 Lawther
10 Dougan	10 Hill	10 Nicholson	10 McIlroy	10 McAdams
11 McParland	11 McParland	11 McParland	11 McParland	11 McParland
Belfast	Belfast	Hampden	Belfast	Bologna
8 Oct: 2–5	26 Oct: 3–4	9 Nov: 2–5	12 April: 1–5	25 April: 2–3
McAdams 2	*McAdams 3*	*Blanchflower D., McParland*	*Dougan*	*Dougan, McAdams*

1961 Greece	1961 W. Germany	1961 Scotland	1961 Greece	1961 England
1 McClelland	1 McClelland	1 Gregg	1 Gregg	1 Hunter
2 Keith	2 Keith	2 Magill	2 Magill	2 Magill
3 Elder	3 Elder	3 Elder	3 Elder	3 Elder
4 Cush	4 Blanchflower D.	4 Blanchflower D.	4 Blanchflower D.	4 Blanchflower D.
5 Neill	5 Neill	5 Neill	5 Neill	5 Neill
6 Peacock	6 Peacock	6 Peacock	6 Nicholson	6 Nicholson
7 Bingham	7 Bingham	7 Wilson	7 Bingham	7 Bingham
8 McIlroy	8 Cush	8 McIlroy	8 McIlroy	8 Barr
9 McAdams	9 McAdams	9 Lawther	9 McAdams	9 McAdams
10 Dougan	10 McIlroy	10 Hill	10 Cush	10 McIlroy
11 McParland	11 McParland	11 McLaughlin	11 McLaughlin	11 McLaughlin
Athens	Berlin	Belfast	Belfast	Wembley
3 May: 1–2	10 May: 1–2	7 Oct: 1–6	17 Oct: 2–0	22 Nov: 1–1
McIlroy	*McIlroy*	*McLaughlin*	*McLaughlin 2*	*McIlroy*

1962 Wales	1962 Netherlands	1962 Poland	1962 England	1962 Scotland
1 Briggs	1 Irvine R.	1 Irvine R.	1 Irvine R.	1 Irvine R.
2 Keith	2 Keith	2 Magill	2 Magill	2 Magill
3 Cunningham	3 Cunningham	3 Elder	3 Elder	3 Elder
4 Blanchflower D.	4 Harvey	4 Blanchflower D.	4 Blanchflower D.	4 Blanchflower D.
5 Neill	5 Blanchflower D.	5 Hatton	5 Neill	5 Hatton
6 Nicholson	6 Nicholson	6 Nicholson	6 Nicholson	6 Nicholson
7 Humphries	7 Humphries	7 Humphries	7 Humphries	7 Humphries
8 Johnston W.	8 Lawther	8 Barr	8 Barr	8 McMillan
9 O'Neill	9 McAdams	9 Dougan	9 McMillan	9 Dougan
10 McLaughlin	10 McIlroy	10 McIlroy	10 McIlroy	10 McIlroy
11 Braithwaite	11 McParland	11 Bingham	11 Bingham	11 Bingham
Cardiff	Rotterdam	Katowice	Belfast	Hampden
11 April: 0–4	9 May: 0–4	10 Oct: 2–0	20 Oct: 1–3	7 Nov: 1–4
		Dougan, Humphries	*Barr*	*Bingham*

1962 Poland	1963 Wales	1963 Spain	1963 Scotland	1963 Spain
1 Irvine R.	1 Irvine R.	1 Irvine R.	1 Gregg	1 Hunter
2 Magill	2 Magill	2 Magill	2 Magill	2 Magill
3 Elder	3 Elder	3 Elder	3 Parke	3 Parke
4 Blanchflower D.	4 Harvey	4 Harvey	4 Harvey	4 Harvey
5 Neill	5 Campbell	5 Neill	5 Neill	5 Neill
6 Nicholson	6 Neill	6 McCullough	6 McCullough	6 McCullough
7 Bingham	7 Humphries	7 Bingham	7 Bingham	7 Bingham
8 Crossan	8 Crossan	8 Humphries	8 Humphries	8 Humphries
9 Dougan	9 Irvine W.	9 Irvine W.	9 Wilson	9 Wilson
10 McIlroy	10 McIlroy	10 Crossan	10 Crossan	10 Crossan
11 Braithwaite	11 McLaughlin	11 Braithwaite	11 Hill	11 Hill
Belfast	Belfast	Bilbao	Belfast	Belfast
28 Nov: 2–0	3 April: 1–4	30 May: 1–1	12 Oct: 2–1	30 Oct: 0–1
Crossan, Bingham	*Harvey*	*Irvine W.*	*Bingham, Wilson*	

1963 England	1964 Wales	1964 Uruguay	1964 England	1964 Switzerland
1 Gregg	1 Jennings	1 Jennings	1 Jennings	1 Jennings
2 Magill	2 Magill	2 Magill	2 Magill	2 Magill
3 Parke	3 Elder	3 Elder	3 Elder	3 Elder
4 Harvey	4 Harvey	4 Harvey	4 Harvey	4 Harvey
5 Neill	5 Neill	5 Neill	5 Neill	5 Neill
6 McCullough	6 McCullough	6 McCullough	6 McCullough	6 McCullough
7 Bingham	7 Best	7 Best	7 Best	7 Best
8 Humphries	8 Crossan	8 Crossan	8 Crossan	8 Crossan
9 Wilson	9 Wilson	9 Wilson	9 Wilson	9 Wilson
10 Crossan	10 McLaughlin	10 McLaughlin	10 McLaughlin	10 McLaughlin
11 Hill	11 Braithwaite	11 Braithwaite	11 Braithwaite	11 Braithwaite
Wembley	Swansea	Belfast	Belfast	Belfast
20 Nov: 3–8	15 April: 3–2	29 April: 3–0	3 Oct: 3–4	14 Oct: 1–0
Crossan, Wilson 2	*McLaughlin, Wilson, Harvey*	*Crossan 2, Wilson*	*Wilson, McLaughlin 2*	*Crossan*

1964 Switzerland	1964 Scotland	1965 Netherlands	1965 Wales	1965 Netherlands
1 Jennings	1 Jennings	1 Briggs	1 Irvine R.	1 Jennings
2 Magill	2 Magill	2 Parke	2 Parke	2 Magill
3 Elder	3 Elder	3 Elder	3 Elder	3 Elder
4 Harvey	4 Harvey	4 Harvey	4 Harvey	4 Harvey
5 Campbell	5 Neill	5 Neill	5 Neill	5 Neill
6 Parke	6 Parke	6 Nicholson	6 Nicholson	6 Parke
7 Best	7 Best	7 Humphries	7 Humphries	7 Best
8 Crossan	8 Humphries	8 Crossan	8 Crossan	8 Crossan
9 Irvine W.	9 Irvine W.	9 Irvine W.	9 Irvine W.	9 Irvine W.
10 McLaughlin	10 Crossan	10 Clements	10 McLaughlin	10 Nicholson
11 Braithwaite	11 Braithwaite	11 Best	11 Clements	11 Braithwaite
Lausanne	Hampden	Belfast	Belfast	Rotterdam
14 Nov: 1–2	25 Nov: 2–3	17 Mar: 2–1	31 March: 0–5	7 April: 0–0
Best	*Best, Irvine W.*	*Crossan, Neill*		

1965 Albania	1965 Scotland	1965 England	1965 Albania	1966 Wales
1 Jennings	1 Jennings	1 Jennings	1 Jennings	1 Jennings
2 Magill	2 Magill	2 Magill	2 Magill	2 Magill
3 Elder	3 Elder	3 Elder	3 Elder	3 Elder
4 Harvey	4 Harvey	4 Harvey	4 Harvey	4 Harvey
5 Neill	5 Neill	5 Neill	5 Neill	5 Neill
6 Parke	6 Nicholson	6 Nicholson	6 Nicholson	6 Nicholson
7 Humphries	7 McIlroy	7 McIlroy	7 McIlroy	7 Welsh
8 Crossan	8 Crossan	8 Crossan	8 Crossan	8 Wilson
9 Irvine W.	9 Irvine W.	9 Irvine W.	9 Irvine W.	9 Irvine W.
10 Nicholson	10 Dougan	10 Dougan	10 Dougan	10 Dougan
11 Best	11 Best	11 Best	11 Best	11 McLaughlin
Belfast	Belfast	Wembley	Tirana	Cardiff
7 May: 4–1	2 Oct: 3–2	10 Nov: 1–2	24 Nov: 1–1	30 Mar: 4–1
Crossan 3, Best	*Douglas, Crossan, Irvine W.*	*Irvine W.*	*Irvine W.*	*Irvine, Wilson, Welsh, Harvey*

1966 W. Germany	1966 Mexico	1966 England	1966 Scotland	1967 Wales
1 Jennings	1 McClelland	1 Jennings (McFaul)	1 Jennings	1 McKenzie
2 Magill	2 Magill	2 Parke	2 Parke	2 Craig
3 Parke	3 Elder	3 Elder	3 Elder	3 Elder
4 Harvey	4 Harvey	4 Todd	4 Harvey	4 Harvey
5 Napier	5 Neill	5 Harvey	5 Neill	5 Neill
6 Neill	6 Nicholson	6 McCullough	6 Nicholson	6 Nicholson
7 Welsh	7 Welsh	7 Ferguson	7 Wilson	7 Welsh
8 Crossan	8 Ferguson	8 Crossan	8 Crossan	8 Trainor
9 Wilson	9 Irvine W. (Johnston)	9 Irvine W.	9 Irvine W.	9 Dougan
10 Dougan	10 Dougan	10 Dougan	10 Dougan	10 Bruce
11 McKinney	11 Clements (Todd)	11 Best	11 Clements	11 Clements
Belfast	Belfast	Belfast	Hampden	Belfast
7 May: 0-2	22 June: 4-1 *Johnston, Elder, Nicholson, Ferguson*	22 Oct: 0-2	16 Nov: 1-2 *Nicholson*	12 April: 0-0

1967 Scotland	1967 England	1968 Wales	1968 Israel	1968 Turkey*
1 Jennings	1 Jennings	1 Jennings	1 Jennings	1 Jennings
2 McKeag	2 Parke	2 Craig	2 Rice	2 Craig (Stewart)
3 Parke	3 Elder	3 Elder	3 Jackson	3 Harvey
4 Stewart	4 Stewart	4 Harvey	4 Stewart	4 Nicholson
5 Neill	5 Neill	5 Todd	5 Neill	5 Neill
6 Clements	6 Harvey	6 McKeag	6 Harvey	6 Clements
7 Campbell	7 Campbell	7 Irvine W.	7 Sloan	7 Campbell
8 Crossan	8 Irvine W.	8 Stewart	8 McMordie	8 McMordie
9 Dougan	9 Wilson	9 Dougan	9 Dougan (Gaston)	9 Dougan
10 Nicholson	10 Nicholson	10 Nicholson	10 Irvine W.	10 Irvine W.
11 Best	11 Clements	11 Harkin	11 Ross	11 Best
Belfast	Wembley	Wrexham	Jaffa	Belfast
21 Oct: 1-0 *Clements*	22 Nov: 0-2	28 Feb: 0-2	10 Sept: 3-2 *Irvine W. 2, Dougan*	23 Oct: 4-1 *Best, McMordie, Dougan, Campbell*

1968 Turkey*	1969 England	1969 Scotland	1969 Wales	1969 USSR*
1 Jennings	1 Jennings	1 Jennings	1 Jennings	1 Jennings
2 Craig	2 Craig	2 Craig	2 Craig	2 Rice
3 Harvey	3 Harvey (Elder)	3 Elder	3 Elder	3 Elder
4 Nicholson	4 Todd	4 Todd	4 Todd	4 Todd
5 Neill	5 Neill	5 Neill	5 Neill	5 Neill
6 Stewart	6 Nicholson	6 Nicholson	6 Nicholson	6 Nicholson
7 Hamilton	7 McMordie	7 Best	7 Best	7 Campbell
8 McMordie	8 Jackson	8 McMordie	8 McMordie	8 McMordie
9 Dougan	9 Dougan	9 Dougan	9 Dougan	9 Dougan
10 Harkin	10 Irvine W.	10 Jackson	10 Jackson	10 Clements (Jackson)
11 Clements	11 Best	11 Clements	11 Clements (Harkin)	11 Best
Istanbul	Belfast	Hampden	Belfast	Belfast
11 Dec: 3-0 *Harkin 2, Nicholson*	3 May: 1-3 *McMordie*	6 May: 1-1 *McMordie*	10 May: 0-0	10 Sept: 0-0

1969 USSR*	1970 Scotland	1970 England	1970 Wales	1970 Spain
1 Jennings	1 Jennings	1 Jennings	1 McFaul	1 McFaul
2 Craig	2 Craig	2 Craig	2 Craig	2 Craig
3 Harvey	3 Clements	3 Clements	3 Nelson	3 Nelson
4 Hunter	4 Todd (O'Kane)	4 O'Kane	4 O'Kane	4 Jackson
5 Neill	5 Neill	5 Neill	5 Neill	5 Neill
6 Nicholson	6 Nicholson	6 Nicholson	6 Nicholson	6 O'Kane
7 Hegan	7 Campbell (Dickson)	7 McMordie	7 Campbell (O'Doherty)	7 Sloan
8 Jackson	8 Lutton	8 Best	8 Best	8 Best
9 Dougan	9 Dougan	9 Dougan	9 Dickson	9 Dougan (Todd)
10 Harkin	10 McMordie	10 O'Doherty (Nelson)	10 McMordie	10 Harkin
11 Clements	11 Best	11 Lutton (Cowan)	11 Clements	11 Clements
Moscow 22 Oct: 0–2	Belfast 18 April: 0–1	Wembley 21 April: 1–3 *Best*	Swansea 25 April: 0–1	Seville 11 Nov: 0–3

1971 Cyprus	1971 Cyprus	1971 England	1971 Scotland	1971 Wales
1 Jennings	1 Jennings	1 Jennings	1 Jennings	1 Jennings
2 Craig	2 Craig	2 Rice	2 Rice	2 Rice
3 Nelson	3 Clements	3 Nelson	3 Nelson	3 Nelson
4 Hunter	4 Harvey	4 O'Kane	4 O'Kane	4 O'Kane
5 Neill	5 Hunter	5 Hunter	5 Hunter	5 Hunter
6 Todd	6 Todd (Watson)	6 Nicholson	6 Nicholson	6 Nicholson (Harvey)
7 Hamilton	7 Hamilton	7 Hamilton	7 Hamilton	7 Hamilton
8 McMordie	8 McMordie	8 McMordie (Cassidy)	8 McMordie (Craig)	8 McMordie
9 Dougan	9 Dougan	9 Dougan	9 Dougan	9 Dougan
10 Nicholson	10 Nicholson	10 Clements	10 Clements	10 Clements
11 Best	11 Best	11 Best	11 Best	11 Best
Nicosia 3 Feb: 3–0 *Nicholson, Dougan,* *Best*	Belfast 21 April: 5–0 *Dougan, Best 3,* *Nicholson*	Belfast 15 May: 0–1	Hampden 18 May: 1–0 *1 o.g.*	Belfast 22 May: 1–0 *Hamilton*

1971 USSR	1971 USSR	1972 Spain	1972 Scotland	1972 England
1 McFaul	1 Jennings	1 Jennings	1 Jennings	1 Jennings
2 Craig (Hamilton)	2 Rice	2 Rice	2 Rice	2 Rice
3 Neill	3 Nelson	3 Nelson	3 Nelson	3 Nelson
4 Hunter	4 Nicholson	4 Neill	4 Neill	4 Neill
5 Nelson	5 Hunter	5 Hunter	5 Hunter	5 Hunter
6 Hegan	6 O'Kane	6 Clements	6 Clements (Craig)	6 Clements
7 Clements	7 McMordie	7 Hamilton (O'Neill)	7 Hegan	7 Hegan
8 Nicholson	8 Hamilton (O'Neill)	8 McMordie	8 McMordie (McIlroy)	8 McMordie
9 O'Kane	9 Neill	9 Morgan	9 Dougan	9 Dougan
10 Dougan	10 Dougan (Cassidy)	10 McIlroy	10 Irvine W.	10 Irvine W.
11 Best	11 Clements	11 Best	11 Jackson	11 Jackson
Moscow 22 Sept: 0–1	Belfast 13 Oct: 1–1 *Nicholson*	Hull 16 Feb: 1–1 *Morgan*	Hampden 20 May: 0–2	Wembley 23 May: 1–0 *Neill*

1972 Wales	1972 Bulgaria	1973 Cyprus	1973 Portugal	1973 Cyprus
1 Jennings	1 Jennings	1 Jennings	1 Jennings	1 McFaul
2 Rice	2 Rice	2 Rice	2 O'Kane	2 O'Kane
3 Nelson	3 Nelson	3 Neill	3 Nelson	3 Hunter (Coyle)
4 Neill	4 Hunter	4 Hunter	4 Neill	4 Neill
5 Hunter	5 Neill	5 Craig	5 Hunter	5 Craig
6 Clements	6 Clements	6 Hegan	6 Clements	6 Hamilton (Lutton)
7 Hegan	7 Hamilton (Morgan)	7 Clements	7 Hamilton	7 Jackson
8 McMordie	8 Hegan	8 Hamilton	8 Coyle	8 Clements
9 Dougan (O'Neill)	9 McMordie	9 Dickson	9 Morgan	9 Morgan
10 Irvine W.	10 Dougan	10 Dougan	10 Dickson	10 O'Neill
11 Jackson	11 Best	11 Nelson	11 O'Neill	11 Anderson
Wrexham 27 May: 0–0	Sofia 18 Oct: 0–3	Nicosia 14 Feb: 0–1	Coventry 28 Mar: 1–1 *O'Neill*	London 8 May: 3–0 *Morgan, Anderson 2*

1973 England	1973 Scotland	1973 Wales	1973 Bulgaria	1973 Portugal
1 Jennings	1 Jennings	1 Jennings	1 McFaul	1 Jennings
2 Rice	2 Rice	2 Rice	2 Rice	2 Rice
3 Craig	3 Craig	3 Craig	3 Craig	3 Craig
4 Neill	4 Neill	4 Neill	4 O'Kane	4 Lutton
5 Hunter	5 Hunter	5 Hunter	5 Hunter	5 O'Kane
6 Clements	6 Clements	6 Clements	6 Clements	6 Clements
7 Hamilton	7 Hamilton	7 Hamilton (Lutton)	7 Hamilton	7 Jackson (Coyle)
8 Jackson	8 Jackson	8 Jackson	8 Jackson (Coyle)	8 O'Neill
9 Morgan	9 Morgan	9 Morgan	9 Morgan	9 Morgan
10 O'Neill	10 O'Neill	10 Anderson	10 Anderson	10 Anderson
11 Anderson	11 Anderson (Lutton)	11 Anderson (Coyle)	11 O'Neill (Cassidy)	11 Best
Everton 12 May: 1–2 *Clements* (pen)	Glasgow 16 May: 2–1 *O'Neill, Anderson*	Everton 19 May: 1–0 *Hamilton*	Hillsborough 26 Sept: 0–0	Lisbon 14 Nov: 1–1 *O'Kane*

1974 Scotland	1974 England	1974 Wales	1974 Norway	1974 Sweden
1 Jennings	1 Jennings	1 Jennings	1 Jennings	1 Jennings
2 Rice	2 Rice	2 Rice	2 Rice	2 O'Kane
3 Nelson	3 Nelson (Jackson)	3 Dowd	3 Craig (Dowd)	3 Nelson (Blair)
4 O'Kane	4 O'Kane	4 O'Kane	4 O'Kane	4 Dowd
5 Hunter	5 Hunter	5 Hunter	5 Hunter	5 Hunter
6 Clements	6 Clements	6 Clements	6 Clements	6 Nicholl C.
7 Hamilton (Jackson)	7 Hamilton (O'Neill)	7 Hamilton (Jackson)	7 Hamilton	7 Jackson
8 Cassidy	8 Cassidy	8 Cassidy	8 Cassidy	8 O'Neill
9 Morgan	9 Morgan	9 McIlroy	9 Finney	9 Morgan
10 McIlroy	10 McIlroy	10 McGrath	10 McIlroy	10 McIlroy
11 McGrath	11 McGrath	11 O'Neill	11 McGrath (Jackson)	11 Hamilton
Hampden 11 May: 1–0 *Cassidy*	Wembley 15 May: 0–1	Wrexham 18 May: 0–1	Oslo 4 Sept: 1–2 *Finney*	Solna 30 Oct: 2–0 *O'Neill, Nicholl*

1975 Yugoslavia	1975 England	1975 Scotland	1975 Wales	1975 Sweden
1 Jennings	1 Jennings	1 Jennings	1 Jennings	1 Jennings
2 Rice	2 Rice	2 Rice	2 Scott	2 Rice
3 Nelson	3 O'Kane	3 O'Kane	3 Rice	3 Nelson
4 Nicholl C.	4 Nicholl C.	4 Nicholl C.	4 Nicholl C.	4 Clements
5 Hunter	5 Hunter	5 Hunter (Blair)	5 Hunter	5 Hunter
6 Clements	6 Clements	6 Clements	6 Clements	6 Nicholl C.
7 Hamilton	7 Hamilton (Finney)	7 Finney	7 Blair	7 Blair
8 O'Neill	8 O'Neill	8 O'Neill (Anderson)	8 Jackson	8 Hamilton (Morgan)
9 Spence	9 Spence	9 Spence	9 Spence	9 Spence
10 McIlroy	10 McIlroy	10 McIlroy	10 McIlroy	10 McIlroy
11 Jackson	11 Jackson	11 Jackson	11 Finney	11 Jackson
Belfast	Belfast	Hampden	Belfast	Belfast
16 March: 1–0	17 May: 0–0	20 May: 0–3	23 May: 1–0	3 Sept: 1–2
Hamilton			*Finney*	*Hunter*

1975 Norway	1975 Yugoslavia	1976 Israel	1976 Scotland	1976 England
1 Jennings	1 Jennings	1 Jennings (Platt)	1 Jennings	1 Jennings
2 Rice	2 Rice	2 Scott	2 Scott	2 Rice
3 Nelson	3 Scott	3 Nicholl J.	3 Nicholl C.	3 Nelson (Scott)
4 Nicholl C.	4 Nicholl C.	4 Hunter	4 Hunter	4 Clements
5 Hunter	5 Hunter	5 Rice	5 Rice	5 Hunter
6 Jackson	6 Clements	6 Blair	6 Hamilton B.	6 Nicholl C.
7 Hamilton	7 Hamilton	7 Nelson	7 Cassidy	7 Hamilton B.
8 McIlroy	8 McIlroy	8 Hamilton	8 Sharkey (McCreery)	8 Cassidy
9 Morgan (Cochrane)	9 Morgan	9 Anderson (McGrath)	9 McIlroy	9 McCreery
10 Jamison	10 Jackson (O'Neill)	10 Spence	10 Morgan (Spence)	10 Spence
11 Finney	11 Finney	11 Finney	11 Finney	11 McIlroy
Belfast	Belgrade	Tel Aviv	Hampden	Wembley
29 Oct: 3–0	19 Nov: 0–1	24 Mar: 1–1	8 May: 0–3	11 May: 0–4
Morgan, McIlroy, Hamilton		*Lev o.g.*		

1976 Wales	1976 Netherlands	1976 Belgium	1977 W. Germany	1977 England
1 Jennings	1 Jennings	1 Jennings	1 Jennings	1 Jennings
2 Scott	2 Nicholl J.	2 Nicholl J.	2 Rice	2 Nicholl J.
3 Rice	3 Jackson	3 Rice (Nelson)	3 Nelson	3 Rice
4 Nicholl C.	4 Rice	4 Jackson	4 Jackson	4 Jackson
5 Hunter	5 Hunter	5 Hunter	5 Hunter	5 Hunter
6 Clements	6 Hamilton B.	6 Hamilton B.	6 McCreery (Cassidy)	6 Hamilton B.
7 Hamilton B.	7 Best	7 Best	7 Hamilton B.	7 McGrath
8 McIlroy	8 McIlroy	8 McIlroy	8 Best	8 McIlroy
9 Spence (Morgan)	9 McGrath (Spence)	9 McGrath	9 Armstrong (Spence)	9 Armstrong (O'Neill)
10 Cassidy (Nicholl J.)	10 McCreery	10 McCreery	10 McGrath	10 McCreery
11 McCreery	11 Anderson	11 Anderson	11 Anderson	11 Anderson (Spence)
Swansea	Rotterdam	Liège	Cologne	Belfast
14 May: 0–1	13 Oct: 2–2	10 Nov: 0–2	27 April: 0–5	28 May: 1–2
	McGrath, Spence			*McGrath*

1977 Scotland	1977 Wales	1977 Iceland	1977 Iceland	1977 Netherlands
1 Jennings	1 Jennings	1 Jennings	1 Jennings	1 Jennings
2 Nicholl J.	2 Nicholl J.	2 Rice	2 Rice	2 Rice
3 Rice	3 Nelson	3 Nelson	3 Nicholl J.	3 Nelson
4 Jackson	4 Nicholl C.	4 Nicholl J.	4 Nelson	4 Nicholl J.
5 Hunter	5 Hunter	5 Hunter	5 Hunter	5 Hunter
6 Hamilton B.	6 Hamilton B.	6 Hamilton B.	6 McCreery	6 O'Neill
7 McGrath	7 McGrath	7 McGrath	7 McGrath	7 McIlroy
8 McIlroy	8 McIlroy	8 McIlroy	8 Best	8 Best
9 O'Neill (Spence)	9 Jackson	9 Jackson (Spence)	9 McIlroy	9 McCreery
10 McCreery	10 McCreery (Armstrong)	10 McCreery	10 O'Neill	10 McGrath
11 Anderson	11 Anderson (Spence)	11 Anderson (Armstrong)	11 Anderson	11 Anderson
Hampden	Belfast	Reykjavik	Belfast	Belfast
1 June: 0–2	3 June: 1–1 Nelson	11 June: 0–1	21 Sept: 2–0 McGrath, McIlroy	12 Oct: 0–1

1977 Belgium	1978 Scotland	1978 England	1978 Wales	1978 Rep. of Ireland
1 Jennings	1 Platt	1 Platt	1 Platt	1 Jennings
2 Rice	2 Hamilton B.	2 Hamilton B.	2 Hamilton B.	2 Rice
3 Nelson	3 Scott	3 Scott	3 Scott (Connell)	3 Nelson
4 Nicholl J.	4 Nicholl C.	4 Nicholl C.	4 Nicholl C.	4 Nicholl C.
5 Hunter (Nicholl C.)	5 Nicholl J.	5 Nicholl J.	5 Nicholl J.	5 Hunter (Hamilton B.)
6 McIlroy	6 McIlroy	6 McIlroy	6 O'Neill	6 Nicholl J.
7 McGrath	7 McCreery	7 McCreery	7 McCreery	7 O'Neill
8 McCreery	8 O'Neill	8 O'Neill	8 McIlroy	8 McCreery
9 Armstrong	9 Anderson (Hamilton W.)	9 Anderson	9 Anderson (Cochrane)	9 Armstrong
10 Stewart	10 Armstrong	10 Armstrong	10 Armstrong	10 McIlroy
11 Anderson	11 McGrath (Cochrane)	11 McGrath (Cochrane)	11 McGrath	11 Spence (Cochrane)
Belfast	Hampden	Wembley	Wrexham	Dublin
16 Nov: 3–0 Armstrong 2, McGrath	13 May: 1–1 O'Neill	16 May: 0–1	19 May: 0–1	20 Sept: 0–0

1978 Denmark	1978 Bulgaria	1979 England	1979 Bulgaria	1979 England
1 Jennings	1 Jennings	1 Jennings	1 Jennings	1 Jennings
2 Rice	2 Hamilton B.	2 Rice	2 Hamilton B.	2 Rice
3 Nelson	3 Nelson	3 Nelson	3 Nelson	3 Nelson
4 Nicholl J.	4 Nicholl C.	4 Nicholl C.	4 Nicholl C. (Moreland)	4 Nicholl C.
5 Hunter	5 Nicholl J.	5 Nicholl J.	5 Nicholl J.	5 Nicholl J.
6 McCreery	6 McCreery	6 McCreery	6 McCreery	6 Moreland (McGrath)
7 O'Neill	7 O'Neill	7 O'Neill	7 O'Neill	7 Hamilton B.
8 McIlroy	8 McIlroy (Moreland)	8 McIlroy	8 McIlroy	8 McIlroy
9 Armstrong	9 Armstrong	9 Armstrong	9 Armstrong	9 Armstrong
10 Morgan (Spence)	10 Caskey	10 Caskey (Spence)	10 Caskey (Spence)	10 Caskey
11 Cochrane (Anderson)	11 Cochrane (McGrath)	11 Cochrane (McGrath)	11 Cochrane	11 Cochrane (Spence)
Belfast	Sofia	Wembley	Belfast	Belfast
25 Oct: 2–1 Spence, Anderson	29 Nov: 2–0 Armstrong, Caskey	7 Feb: 0–4	2 May: 2–0 Nicholl C., Armstrong	19 May: 0–2

1979 Scotland	1979 Wales	1979 Denmark	1979 England	1979 Rep. of Ireland
1 Jennings	1 Jennings	1 Jennings	1 Jennings	1 Jennings
2 Rice	2 Rice	2 Rice	2 Rice	2 Nicholl J.
3 Nelson	3 Nelson	3 Nelson	3 Nelson	3 Nelson
4 Nicholl J.	4 Nicholl C.	4 Nicholl J.	4 Nicholl J.	4 Nicholl C.
5 Hunter	5 Hunter	5 Hunter	5 Hunter (Rafferty)	5 Hunter
6 Moreland	6 Nicholl J.	6 McCreery	6 McCreery	6 McCreery
7 Hamilton B.	7 McCreery	7 O'Neill	7 Cassidy	7 O'Neill M. (Cassidy)
8 McIlroy (Scott)	8 McIlroy	8 McIlroy	8 McIlroy	8 McIlroy
9 Armstrong	9 Armstrong	9 Armstrong	9 Armstrong	9 Armstrong
10 Sloan	10 Spence (Sloan)	10 Spence	10 Finney (Caskey)	10 Spence
11 Spence	11 Hamilton B.	11 Hamilton B.	11 Moreland	11 Moreland
Hampden	Belfast	Copenhagen	Belfast	Belfast
22 May: 0–1	25 May: 1–1 *Spence*	6 June: 0–4	17 Oct: 1–5 *Moreland (pen)*	21 Nov: 1–0 *Armstrong*

1980 Israel	1980 Scotland	1980 England	1980 Wales	1980 Australia
1 Jennings	1 Platt	1 Platt	1 Platt	1 Platt
2 Nicholl J.	2 Nicholl J.	2 Nicholl J.	2 Nicholl J.	2 Nicholl J.
3 Nelson	3 Donaghy	3 Donaghy	3 Donaghy	3 Nicholl C.
4 Nicholl C.	4 Nicholl C.	4 Nicholl C.	4 Nicholl C.	4 O'Neill J.
5 O'Neill J.	5 O'Neill J.	5 O'Neill J.	5 O'Neill J.	5 McClelland
6 O'Neill M.	6 Cassidy (McCreery)	6 Cassidy (McCreery)	6 Cassidy (McCreery)	6 Cassidy (McCreery)
7 McIlroy	7 McIlroy	7 McIlroy	7 McIlroy	7 Brotherston
8 Cassidy	8 Hamilton W. (McClelland)	8 Hamilton W. (Cochrane)	8 Hamilton W. (Cochrane)	8 Hamilton W.
9 Armstrong	9 Armstrong	9 Armstrong	9 Armstrong	9 Armstrong
10 Finney (Spence)	10 Finney	10 Finney	10 Finney	10 Finney (Hamilton B.)
11 Cochrane	11 Brotherston	11 Brotherston	11 Brotherston	11 O'Neill M.
Tel Aviv	Belfast	Wembley	Cardiff	Sydney
26 Mar: 0–0	16 May: 1–0 *Hamilton*	20 May: 1–1 *Cochrane*	23 May: 1–0 *Brotherston*	11 June: 2–1 *Nicholl C., O'Neill M.*

1980 Australia	1980 Australia	1980 Sweden	1980 Portugal	1981 Scotland
1 Platt	1 Platt	1 Platt	1 Platt	1 Jennings
2 Nicholl J.	2 Nicholl J.	2 Nicholl J.	2 Nicholl J.	2 Nicholl J.
3 Nicholl C.	3 Nicholl C.	3 Donaghy	3 Donaghy	3 Nelson
4 O'Neill J.	4 O'Neill J.	4 Cassidy (McCreery)	4 Cassidy (McCreery)	4 McClelland
5 McClelland	5 McClelland	5 Nicholl C.	5 Nicholl C.	5 Nicholl C.
6 Cassidy	6 Cassidy (Hamilton B.)	6 McClelland	6 O'Neill J.	6 O'Neill J.
7 Brotherston	7 Cochrane	7 Brotherston	7 Brotherston	7 Cochrane
8 McCreery (Cochrane)	8 Hamilton W. (McCurdy)	8 O'Neill M.	8 O'Neill M.	8 McCreery
9 Armstrong	9 Armstrong	9 Hamilton (Cochrane)	9 Hamilton (Cochrane)	9 Hamilton (Spence)
10 Finney	10 O'Neill M.	10 Armstrong	10 Armstrong	10 Armstrong
11 O'Neill M.	11 Brotherston	11 McIlroy	11 McIlroy	11 McIlroy
Melbourne	Adelaide	Belfast	Lisbon	Glasgow
15 June: 1–1 *O'Neill M.*	18 June: 2–1 *Brotherston, McCurdy*	15 Oct: 3–0 *Brotherston, McIlroy, Nicholl J.*	19 Nov: 0–1	25 Mar: 1–1 *Hamilton*

1981 Portugal	1981 Scotland	1981 Sweden	1981 Scotland	1981 Israel
1 Jennings	1 Jennings	Jennings	1 Jennings	1 Jennings
2 Nicholl J.	2 Nicholl J.	2 Nicholl J. (McClelland)	2 Nicholl J.	2 Nicholl J.
3 Nelson	3 Nelson (Donaghy)	3 Nelson	3 Nicholl C.	3 Nicholl C.
4 McCreery	4 McClelland	4 McCreery	4 O'Neill J.	4 O'Neill J.
5 Nicholl C.	5 Nicholl C.	5 Nicholl C.	5 Donaghy	5 Donaghy
6 O'Neill J.	6 O'Neill J.	6 O'Neill J.	6 O'Neill M.	6 McCreery
7 Cochrane	7 Cochrane	7 Cochrane	7 McIlroy	7 Cassidy
8 O'Neill M.	8 O'Neill M.	8 O'Neill M.	8 McCreery	8 McIlroy
9 Hamilton	9 Armstrong	9 Hamilton (Spence)	9 Armstrong	9 Armstrong
10 Armstrong	10 McIlroy	10 Armstrong	10 Hamilton	10 Hamilton
11 McIlroy	11 Hamilton	11 McIlroy	11 Brotherston	11 Brotherston
Belfast	Glasgow	Stockholm	Belfast	Belfast
29 April: 1–0	19 May: 0–2	3 June: 0–1	14 Oct: 0–0	18 Nov: 1–0
Armstrong				*Armstrong*

1982 England	1982 France	1982 Scotland	1982 Wales	1982 Yugoslavia†
1 Jennings	1 Platt	1 Platt	1 Jennings (Platt)	1 Jennings
2 Nicholl J.	2 Nicholl J.	2 Donaghy	2 Nicholl J.	2 Nicholl J.
3 Nelson	3 O'Neill J.	3 Nelson	3 Donaghy	3 Nicholl C.
4 Donaghy	4 Nicholl C.	4 O'Neill J.	4 McClelland	4 McClelland
5 Nicholl C.	5 Donaghy	5 McClelland	5 Nicholl C.	5 Donaghy
6 O'Neill J.	6 McCreery (Caskey)	6 Cleary	6 Cleary (Campbell)	6 McIlroy
7 Brotherston (Cochrane)	7 O'Neill M.	7 Brotherston	7 Brotherston	7 O'Neill M.
8 O'Neill M. (McCreery)	8 McIlroy (Spence)	8 O'Neill M.	8 Healy	8 McCreery
9 Armstrong	9 Brotherston	9 Campbell	9 Armstrong	9 Armstrong
10 McIlroy	10 Armstrong	10 Armstrong	10 McIlroy	10 Hamilton
11 Hamilton	11 Cochrane (Stewart)	11 Healy	11 Hamilton	11 Whiteside
Wembley	Paris	Belfast	Wrexham	Zaragoza
23 Feb: 0–4	24 Mar: 0–4	28 April: 1–1	27 May: 0–3	17 June: 0–0
		McIlroy		

1982 Honduras	1982 Spain	1982 Austria†	1982 France†	1982 Austria
1 Jennings	1 Jennings	1 Jennings	1 Jennings	1 Platt
2 Nicholl J.	2 Nicholl J.	2 Nicholl J.	2 Nicholl J.	2 Nicholl J.
3 Donaghy	3 Donaghy	3 Donaghy	3 Donaghy	3 Nicholl C.
4 Nicholl C.	4 Nicholl C.	4 McCreery	4 O'Neill J.	4 McClelland
5 McClelland	5 McClelland	5 Nicholl C.	5 McClelland	5 Donaghy
6 McCreery	6 McCreery	6 O'Neill M.	6 McCreery	6 O'Neill M. (Healy)
7 O'Neill M.	7 O'Neill M. (Healy)	7 Armstrong	7 O'Neill M.	7 McCreery
8 McIlroy	8 McIlroy	8 McIlroy (Cassidy)	8 McIlroy (Brotherston)	8 McIlroy
9 Armstrong	9 Armstrong	9 Hamilton	9 Armstrong	9 Whiteside (Brotherston)
10 Hamilton	10 Hamilton	10 McClelland	10 Hamilton	10 Armstrong
11 Whiteside	11 Whiteside (Brotherston)	11 Whiteside (Nelson)	11 Stewart (Healy)	11 Hamilton
Zaragoza	Valencia	Madrid	Madrid	Vienna
21 June: 1–1	25 June: 1–0	1 July: 2–2	4 July: 1–4	13 Oct: 0–2
Armstrong	*Armstrong*	*Hamilton (2)*	*Armstrong*	

1982 W. Germany	1982 Albania	1983 Turkey	1983 Albania	1983 Scotland
1 Platt	1 Platt	1 Platt	1 Jennings	1 Jennings
2 Nicholl	2 Donaghy	2 Nicholl J.	2 Nicholl J.	2 Nicholl J.
3 Donaghy	3 Nicholl J.	3 Donaghy	3 McClelland	3 Donaghy
4 O'Neill J.	4 O'Neill J.	4 O'Neill J.	4 O'Neill J.	4 O'Neill J. (Nicholl C.)
5 McClelland	5 McClelland	5 McClelland	5 Donaghy	5 McClelland
6 O'Neill M.	6 O'Neill M.	6 O'Neill M.	6 O'Neill M.	6 O'Neill M.
7 Brotherston	7 Brotherston	7 Brotherston	7 McIlroy	7 Mullan
8 McIlroy	8 McIlroy	8 McIlroy	8 Brotherston (Mullan)	8 McIlroy
9 Whiteside	9 Whiteside	9 Whiteside	9 Hamilton	9 Armstrong
10 Hamilton	10 Hamilton	10 Amstrong	10 Armstrong	10 Hamilton (Brotherston)
11 Stewart	11 Stewart	11 Stewart	11 Stewart	11 Stewart
Belfast	Tirana	Belfast	Belfast	Glasgow
17 Nov: 1–0	15 Dec: 0–0	20 Mar: 2–1	27 Apr: 1–0	24 May: 0–0
Stewart		*O'Neill M.,* *McClelland*	*Stewart*	

1983 England	1983 Wales	1983 Austria	1983 Turkey	1983 W. Germany
1 Jennings	1 Jennings	1 Jennings	1 Jennings	1 Jennings
2 Nicholl J.	2 Nicholl J.	2 Ramsey	2 Nicholl J.	2 Nicholl J.
3 Donaghy	3 Donaghy	3 Nicholl C.	3 Donaghy	3 McElhinney
4 McClelland	4 McClelland	4 McClelland	4 Nicholl C.	4 McClelland
5 Nicholl C.	5 Nicholl C.	5 Donaghy	5 McClelland	5 Donaghy
6 O'Neill M.	6 McIlroy	6 O'Neill M.	6 O'Neill M.	6 Ramsey
7 Mullan (Brotherston)	7 Brotherston	7 McIlroy	7 Brotherston (Cleary)	7 O'Neill M.
8 McIlroy	8 Mullan	8 Stewart	8 McIlroy	8 Armstrong
9 Armstrong	9 Armstrong	9 Hamilton	9 Hamilton (McCreery)	9 Whiteside
10 Hamilton	10 Hamilton	10 Armstrong	10 Whiteside	10 Hamilton
11 Stewart	11 Stewart (Cleary)	11 Whiteside	11 Stewart	11 Stewart
Belfast	Belfast	Belfast	Ankara	Hamburg
28 May: 0–0	31 May: 0–1	21 Sept: 3–1	12 Oct: 0–1	16 Nov: 1–0
		Hamilton, Whiteside, *O'Neill M.*		*Whiteside*

1983 Scotland	1984 England	1984 Wales	1984 Finland	1984 Romania
1 Jennings	1 Platt	1 Jennings (Platt)	1 Jennings	1 Jennings
2 Nicholl J.	2 Nicholl J.	2 Donaghy	2 Nicholl J.	2 Nicholl J.
3 Donaghy	3 McClelland	3 Worthington	3 McClelland	3 McClelland
4 McClelland	4 McElhinney	4 McClelland	4 McElhinney	4 McElhinney
5 McElhinney	5 Donaghy	5 McElhinney	5 Donaghy	5 Donaghy
6 Ramsey	6 Armstrong	6 O'Neill M.	6 O'Neill M.	6 Armstrong
7 Cochrane (O'Neill J.)	7 O'Neill M.	7 McIlroy	7 McIlroy (Worthington)	7 O'Neill M.
8 McIlroy	8 Hamilton	8 Armstrong	8 Armstrong (Cochrane)	8 McCreery
9 Hamilton	9 Whiteside	9 Whiteside	9 Hamilton	9 Stewart
10 Whiteside	10 McIlroy	10 Hamilton	10 Whiteside	10 Hamilton
11 Stewart	11 Stewart	11 Stewart	11 Stewart	11 Whiteside
Glasgow	Wembley	Swansea	Pori	Belfast
13 Dec: 2–0	4 April: 0–1	22 May: 1–1	27 May: 0–1	12 Sept: 3–2
Whiteside, McIlroy		*Armstrong*		*Iorgulescu (o.g.)* *Whiteside, O'Neill M.*

1984 Israel	1984 Finland	1985 England	1985 Spain	1985 Turkey
1 Dunlop	1 Jennings	1 Jennings	1 Jennings	1 Jennings
2 Ramsey	2 Nicholl	2 Nicholl	2 Nicholl	2 Nicholl
3 O'Neill J.	3 O'Neill J.	3 McClelland	3 Donaghy	3 McClelland
4 McClelland	4 McClelland	4 O'Neill J.	4 McClelland	4 O'Neill
5 Worthington	5 Donaghy	5 Donaghy	5 O'Neill J.	5 Donaghy
6 Doherty	6 O'Neill M.	6 McIlroy	6 Ramsey	6 McIlroy
7 Cleary	7 McIlroy	7 Ramsey	7 Quinn	7 Ramsey
8 Penney	8 Armstrong	8 Armstrong	8 Stewart	8 Brotherston
9 Quinn	9 Quinn	9 Stewart	9 Armstrong (McCreery)	9 Whiteside
10 Whiteside (McGaughey)	10 Whiteside	10 Quinn	10 Hamilton	10 Quinn
11 Stewart (Brotherston)	11 Stewart	11 Whiteside	11 Whiteside (Worthington)	11 Stewart

Belfast	Belfast	Belfast	Palma de Mallorca	Belfast
16 Oct: 3–0	14 Nov: 2–1	27 Feb: 0–1	27 Mar: 0–0	1 May: 2–0
Whiteside, Quinn, Doherty	*O'Neill J., Armstrong*			*Whiteside 2*

1985 Turkey	1985 Romania	1985 England	1986 France	1986 Denmark
1 Jennings	1 Jennings	1 Jennings	1 Jennings	1 Jennings
2 Nicholl	2 Nicholl	2 Nicholl	2 Nicholl J.	2 Donaghy
3 Donaghy	3 Donaghy	3 O'Neill J.	3 McDonald	3 O'Neill J.
4 O'Neill J.	4 O'Neill J.	4 McDonald	4 O'Neill J.	4 McDonald
5 McClelland	5 McDonald	5 Donaghy	5 Donaghy	5 Worthington
6 Penney	6 McCreery	6 McIllroy	6 Whiteside	6 McIlroy
7 McIllroy (McCreery)	7 Penney (Armstrong)	7 McCreery	7 McIlroy (McClelland)	7 McCreery (Armstrong)
8 Ramsey	8 McIlroy	8 Whiteside	8 McCreery	8 Whiteside
9 Worthington	9 Quinn	9 Penney (Armstrong)	9 Quinn (Armstrong)	9 Penney
10 Armstrong	10 Whiteside	10 Quinn	10 Clarke	10 Clarke (Quinn)
11 Quinn	11 Stewart (Worthington)	11 Stewart (Worthington)	11 Penney (Caughey)	11 Stewart (Caughey)

Izmir	Bucharest	Wembley	Paris	Belfast
11 Sept: 0–0	16 Oct: 1–0	13 Nov: 0–0	26 Feb: 0–0	26 Mar: 1–1
	Quinn			*McDonald*

1986 Morocco
1 Jennings (Platt)
2 Ramsey
3 Donaghy
4 O'Neill J.
5 McDonald
6 McNally
7 Penney (Quinn)
8 McIllroy
9 Clarke
10 Whiteside (Campbell)
11 Stewart (Hamilton)

Belfast
23 April: 2–1
Clarke, Quinn

BINGHAM'S PLAYING RECORD
GLENTORAN: March 1949–October 1950

Billy Bingham made his league debut for Glentoran against Ballymena United on 12 March 1949. Until his signing for Sunderland
the following October he made about 30 appearances, scoring 15
goals. However, this is not an accurate figure because full fixtures
from that period are not available from the Irish League.

		Apps.	Gls	Cup Apps.	Gls	Int. Apps.	Gls
SUNDERLAND	Dec 1950–July 1958	206	45	21	2	33	4
LUTON TOWN	July 1958–Oct 1960	87	27	10	6	7	3
EVERTON	Oct 1960–Aug 1963	86	25	10	3	13	2
PORT VALE	Aug 1963 April 1964	40	6	2	1	3	1

Bingham made a total of 56 appearances for Northern Ireland
and scored 10 goals. He also won four Schoolboy caps and nine
Youth caps.

BINGHAM IN GREECE

30.9.71	Thessalonika	MEXICO	0—1
17.11.71	Athens	BULGARIA	2—2
1.12.71	Athens	ENGLAND	0—2
16.2.72	Athens	HOLLAND	0—5
4.3.72	Athens	ITALY	2—1
22.3.72	Athens	CYPRUS	2—0
12.4.72	Thessalonika	SPAIN	0—0
7.5.72	Ethiopia	ETHIOPIA	0—0
2.9.72	Athens	FRANCE	1—5
19.11.72	Belgrade	YUGOSLAVIA	0—1
17.1.73	Athens	SPAIN	2—3
31.1.73	Athens	BULGARIA	2—2
21.2.73	Malaga	SPAIN	1—3

BIBLIOGRAPHY

APPLETON, ARTHUR, *Hotbed of Soccer: The Story of Football in the North-East*, Rupert Hart-Davies

BINGHAM, BILLY, *Soccer with the Stars*, Stanley Paul, 1962

BRODIE, MALCOLM, *Linfield: 100 Years*, Linfield Football and Athletic Club, 1985

CARR, J. L., *How Steeple Sinderby Wanderers Won the FA Cup*, Grafton, 1985

English Football Association: Yearly Handbooks and Minutes

FORD, TREVOR, *I Lead the Attack*, Stanley Paul

HUGMAN, BARRY, *Rothman's Football League Players' Records, 1946–81*, Queen Anne Press

INGLIS, SIMON, *Soccer in the Dock*, Collins Willow, 1986

JENNINGS, PAT, with DRURY, REG, *Pat Jennings*, Collins Willow

ROBERTS, JOHN, *Everton*, Granada

ROLLINS, WILLIAMS and DUNK, *Rothman's Football Yearbooks*, Queen Anne Press

SHACKLETON, LEN, *Clown Prince of Soccer*, Nicholas Kaye

SOAR, PHIL, *The Hamlyn A–Z of British Football Records*, Hamlyn, 1985

TWAIN, MARK, *A Connecticut Yankee in King Arthur's Court*, Penguin

SOURCES

Belfast Telegraph; Ireland's *Saturday Night*; *Sunderland Echo*; *Sunderland Football Pink*; *Mansfield Chronicle Advertiser*; *Plymouth Sunday Independent*; *Liverpool Daily Post*; *Liverpool Echo*; *Sunday Mirror*; *Daily Mirror*; *Daily Telegraph*; *Sunday Telegraph*; *Sunday Tribune* (Dublin); *Irish Times*; *Irish News*; *Belfast Newsletter*; *Northern Whig*; *Sunday News* (Belfast); *News of the World*; *Daily Express*; *Sunday Express*; the *Standard* (London); *Sunday People*; *Observer*; *The Times* (London); *The Sunday Times*; *World Soccer*; *Soccer Magazine* (Ireland); *Reveille*; *Sun*; *Evening News* (London); *Guardian*; *Magill* (Dublin); *Luton News*; and: Belfast Central Library; Trinity College (Dublin) Library; Linen Hall Library, Belfast; Public Records Office, Belfast; Daily Telegraph Library; Daily Mirror Library; Guardian Library; Sunderland Library; Liverpool Central Library; English Football Association minutes.